D1180042

INNER TUBE

a novel by

HOB BROUN

Alfred A. Knopf

New York   1985

THIS IS A BORZOI BOOK
PUBLISHED BY ALFRED A. KNOPF, INC.

Copyright © 1985 by Hob Broun
All rights reserved under International and
Pan-American Copyright Conventions.
Published in the United States by Alfred A. Knopf, Inc.,
New York, and simultaneously in Canada
by Random House of Canada Limited, Toronto.
Distributed by Random House, Inc., New York.

Library of Congress Cataloging in Publication Data
Broun, Hob.
Inner Tube.
I. Title.
PS3552.R6824I56   1985   813'54   85-40227
ISBN 0-394-54201-0

Manufactured in the United States of America
First Edition

IN MEMORY
OF
QUINCAS BORBA

"TO THE VICTOR, THE POTATOES!"

INNER TUBE

You're not going to like this, but some years ago, in the family room of the house where I grew up in Lake Success, New York, my mother cancelled an unrelenting life by plunging her head through the twenty-six-inch screen of a Motorola color television.

Sadly, she was alone at the time, this being a suicidal method surely designed for an audience, she a woman who had played Broadway opposite David Wayne, had for several seasons been something of an attraction at the summer playhouses of Cape Cod. But we were all gone that night—my father at a political banquet, my sister in the dark solitude of northern woods, me on the job, vigilant in the newsroom of a major network—and I guess she just couldn't wait. Still, that someone so corroded by the defeat of her acting career should play to an empty house—this really fit.

Perhaps she satisfied herself by anticipating the impact our hideous discovery would have. But a neighbor got there first, a retired petrochemicals executive dropping by to return a belt sander. Official vehicles had gathered by the time I got home, and the mopping up was nearly over. I did not see her face charred by implosion, haloed with bright drainage from jugular and carotid.

I saw my father in his tuxedo, a fifth of vodka in one hand, talking to the room as though it were empty.

"I didn't know," he said many times. And then: "We were talking about a trip to Venice."

A man in a black raincoat, some functionary, took his arm. "Sir, you just can't predict these things like the weather."

My father snarled, turned, broke that vodka bottle over the man's head, and there was a fresh confusion of blood all over. I remember thinking: Not a bad move, Gordo. Not bad at all.

Her note, though explicit, made nothing clear. In green ink on monogrammed paper centered perfectly on the mantelpiece, it went like this:

Darlings—
Must go, must go. It's (I'm) all so ugly. Can't we please be rid of it. Nothing more, nothing less. Darlings.

Right there by the note was a bottle of sleeping pills. Did this mean she'd meant to go out sweet and calm? That the dive through the picture tube had been a mad impulse? So the others concluded, but I knew better. I recognized her lumbering irony; I understood that the pills, with a mother's infuriating thoroughness, had been left for the consoling sedation of her survivors.

But nothing could have quelled the noise of the next few days: surmises, recriminations, regrets, all the worthless usual. I tried to stay out of it. I felt miserable, all right, but it wasn't a matter of pride. My stance was she knew what she was doing. She had so many reasons to leave the world, enough to fill a Chinese menu, what difference did it make which one she'd finally chosen?

I was curious about something else, though. Chances are you'll like this even less, but I really had to know. The coroner's office had placed the time of my mother's death between 8 and 9 p.m. Hauling out the busted set, I'd noticed it was tuned to channel four. I snouted through old newspapers in the garage, traced the information down.

Minutes before her death, my mother was watching a Bob Hope Special.

It had been a brusque and stormy spring.

I watch, my attention paid like a war tax. I float obediently on waves that travel at the speed of light. Electromagnetic tides. A boiling mass of ocean miniaturized, tightened in a square. Color-coded, like the iodopsin-secreting cone cells of the human retina, 900,000 phosphor dots twitch and fluoresce on the aluminized screen. And I watch, under siege. Electron guns, red, blue, and green, fire information particles, their inexhaustible ammunition, at 167 million miles an hour. Weaponry controls and commands. So I watch.

But when I place my hand against the screen, feel its warmth, the static charge is a caress, a whisper that outlines my fingers with the tenderness of a perfect lover. Is this part of the menace, or the reason for it? Is it jealousy? That every living image is a rival? I lay my cheek now on the glass behind which guns are camouflaged, and listen to the gentle inside hiss. Vigilance, a song of the guts. Red gun. Blue gun. Green gun. Light sieves through the patterned bullet holes, each nine one-hundredths of an inch across, and cloaks my face like a woman's breath pushed slowly through clenched teeth.

Like all the others, I have prescribed patterns of work. Alert at my viewing station, I review an old Hope broadcast, Bob entertaining the troops at Da Nang or somewhere, all these kids hunkered down around the stage with their lawnmower haircuts and bared teeth. Boys will be boys is the order of the day. Hope fingers the shaft of his three wood and promises flesh:

Majorettes of the Big Sky Conference, like that. I switch to single-frame advance, dissecting the famous Hope sneer, observing each interval as he looks into the wings. I feel the tension of assassination film, of Hope turning toward the pop sounds.

Every animal society requires means of recognition: gestures, signs, insignia. The ant, which sees little and hears less, distinguishes the scent uniforms worn by others with the olfactory organs located in its antennae. Each ant nest, in turn, has its definitive aroma. Separate a colony into two groups, reunite them three months later, and they will go to war, unable to bear each other's smell.

The recirculated air here at the facility smells like cold styrene. My personal fume is an amalgam of nicotine, drycleaning fluid, and the shrimp salad I had for lunch. Also, spring-clipped to my shirt is a magstrip security badge with my photo in the upper lefthand corner.

So here I am, eighty-five feet underground, all tipped in with my keyboard and my liquid crystal displays. The hard contours and absence of reverberation can dull reflexes. People take vitamin D tablets and make uneasy jokes about "the bunker mentality." Nature sounds are piped into the lounge areas—birdsong, gentle rain, like that. And every thirty minutes a white strip moves across the bottom of my screen, reminding me to stop and rest my optic muscles.

I suppose what this is is a part of the new service economy. We serve the overdeveloped appetites; we chop, form, cook, and garnish the databurgers that they're all so hungry for. Record, observe, analyze. Amour-propre, the love that cannot speak its name. One of the things I like best about this place is I don't know who I'm working for.

The phone makes its bleating noise and I pick up. Delvino, one of the suit people with an up-there office he can see out of.

"How goes it?"

"Round and round."

"Reeling under the workload? If it's too much, I wish you'd let me know."

In his wallet Delvino carries a picture of General Sarnoff, that visionary of the steppes, that great broadcaster, a fisher of men casting wide his net.

"You take things too seriously," Delvino says. "That's my sense."

Then he tells me the Agronomists' Working Group of Ontario has telexed a request for some 4-H Club show off a station in Des Moines. *Farm, Home & Garden.* He throws a few numbers at me and I ask why he's wasting my time when he should be talking to someone in Dubbing. Office banter, a war of small moves.

"I don't know, I'm just loose. Such a day out there."

He must be looking at the wide lawn maintained by water piped from an underground reservoir forty miles away.

Got to rest more than my optics. I move down the corridor, past the cells of other workers, and into the elevator. Very peaceful. I pump myself up and down in the tube for a while, finally step off at Demographics and Profile. The walls are Caribbean blue with a continuous white stripe at eye level. The halls slant diagonally toward a hub, the hermetic domain of the mainframe computer. Empty halls, not a cyberneticist in sight. But I am close enough to hear the whirring tape drives, cooling fans, the nasality of printers printing. My superstitions are prodded: bad medicine in this place. Backtracking, I pass a door that was closed before, is open now. Two men with paper boutonnieres confer on a black Naugahyde couch.

"Remember that thing last year, those Alsatian separatists who blew up the daycare center?"

"Sure, sure."

"So I just heard ABC is planning to do it as a Movie of the Week."

I am back at my station in a darkness decorated by red indicator lights and soft glowing control buttons. I am once more in front of the guns, but mounting an assault of my own. In violent concentration, the synapses of my brain are flamethrowers. I fire neuron after neuron—chemical warfare, all-out bombardment. But these war machines are sealed away, one inside a console, one inside a skull; and now, between the two containers, waves begin to pass—magnetic waves, sine waves, alpha waves—that tangle and intertwine like the slippery arms and legs of lovers in a horizontal hold.

I feel buffered down here, safe. I feel as comfortably obsolete as the vacuum tube or the scanning raster. Have you ever visited a place, an old hotel, let's say, and felt yourself spliced into some powerful continuity? Like there's something just at your back but you can't turn fast enough to catch it? That's how it is for me, burrowed away with stacks and stacks of old TV shows. I am transformed in communion with the past. Like to see some fucking ant try that.

The town where I'm staying has just lost its post office to federal austerity. This is fine with the postmistress, who can now keep a better watch on her barroom, Boot Hill, where she suspects her nephew has been fudging the receipts. There is a gas station and convenience store, a gun shop, a Rosicrucian optometrist who works out of his home. And there's the Golconda Motel & Cafe, where I occupy unit #6. I am the only permanent resident, permanence being a relative thing out here. After my second month, Opatowski offered me my choice of paintings. I went from room to room and finally chose one called, according to a label on the back, "Fishing Village Morn."

"I understand," he said. "You need some water to look at."

Opatowski is fond of me, and not just as a steady source of revenue. There is a regional affinity. Opatowski was an electrician in Pottstown, Pa., before migrating. He laments the absence of pizza and the presence of crummy sports coverage in the papers, but he loves the weather. His wife, though suffering from lung disease, has taken up fossil-hunting.

"The woman has a need to know," Opatowski says admiringly.

Telephones are unreliable, the water is briny. No one asks me what I do. It's easy to be as small as the Golconda's comforts in this slim town, where in no time I have learned the common faces, brown and dug with squint lines from the sun. They teach me to be plain, to expect only what has already happened. I've sat in the cafe on Sunday afternoon with every table full and the only sounds coming from fork and plate and cup. I've been wrapped in anecdote like a mile-long bandage by amateur historians. Distinctions as dry as the air. Last week there was a fistfight at the gas station. The women were friends; each had witnessed at the wedding of the other. They fought over a pack of cigarettes and people stopped their cars to watch until someone crossed over from Boot Hill to pull the friends apart. Everything is easy here.

I pay one hundred thirty dollars a week for my room with a view: red rock dust, weary cottonwoods, a couple of rotten molar buttes. The bed is firm and the water pressure is good. I have lived in half a hundred rooms like this, but this is the first to be personalized. There are photos all around, production stills from shows like *My Friend Irma* and *Johnny Staccato* and *Broadway Open House*. I have the driving gloves my sister sent last Christmas tacked to the back of the door, my library in fruit crates beside the bed, a crucifix that glows in the dark.

Last night I went out back by the propane tanks and slid into one of the unreliable lawn chairs Opatowski puts out. The air had an unusual flavor to it, something like water from a corroded, mossy pipe. I shifted in the chair, tilted, drank warm beers. Past blotches of shadow—things half-repaired, empty boxes along the fence—the ground went out gray and flat, moving away from me like a conveyor belt. As absently as you might list baseball players, I thought up sexual extremities to pass the time.

"Night like this, I can barely keep my eyes open."

Opatowski took a chair. I waited for the plastic webbing to tear under him.

"First customer in two days and I have to run him off. He's got Siamese cats he won't leave in the car."

"Why be such a tough guy?"

"No animals means no animals. Hairs in the rug, little black turds. How's Heidi going to like that?"

"She's seen worse."

Then I changed the subject by handing Opatowski one of his own beers.

"Jesus," he said. "Take them, okay, but take them out of the cooler."

He wasn't kidding. A few minutes' silent sipping and he was fast asleep, dreaming maybe about capacitators or icy streets. I went by the office to lock up and turn off the neon. Early to bed, that was easy too.

I poured raisin bran into my magpie feeder—a plastic ashtray nailed to the outside sill—showered, and, burning every light, lay on the bed to dry. Home again. All the rooms I'd been in, like a hermit crab assuming empty shells. Home again and again. I'd paced in paper shower shoes, stared into empty medicine cabinets, at cigarette burns on a tabletop. And never have I failed to find what there is to find. Possibility. The imminence of leaving.

For children arrived since Hiroshima, television has provided first contact with the past, our first sense of a world larger than this one. In safe rooms, on the hard, sure glass of a light box, we observed ghosts without fear. Hitler, Dracula, Maid Marian, Red Ryder—all floated by us on the same low clouds. We found artifacts for the taking, jumbled and abundant, expendable as toys—chariots, fighter planes, crossbows, gold dust, igloos, plumes and spurs and buckskin, black glass floors and silk hats and white telephones, chivalry, palmistry, roulette, hanging—and from this disorder we let the past compose itself. Looking backward while staring straight ahead, we were not confused, as by the trim, sequential packages to come. History didn't need cunning or disguise; it strolled right on in. Adults adored the shape of indoctrination. "No TV on school nights," they would say.

I experienced third grade in a building of beige ceramic brick. We pledged allegiance ("one nation, invisible") under a portrait of Lincoln—or was it Henry Fonda? In November, we cut out paper pumpkins and heard all about the Pilgrims. Devout and intrepid men. Men with buckles on their hats.

"I know," flapping my arm, bursting with facts from *Witches of Salem*, which had bobbed up in the wake of Saturday cartoons. "I know something about the Pilgrims. They set fire to each other."

I was sent home with a note to my parents.

"Smart remarks don't win friends," Gordo said with his underlining tic, a short, sharp sniff.

"But it's true what I said."

"No allowance for two weeks."

Not until much later did I learn that the Pilgrims fed lobster to their pigs, bathed rarely, and then with their clothes on.

We had three televisions in our house: the family-room Motorola with wood cabinet and gold speaker cloth, a smaller console in my parents' room, and a tiny black-and-white portable in the kitchen—breakfast invariably meant *The Today Show,* crunching toast, "foaming cleanser," grumbling about the Berlin Wall. No mere furniture, beyond any appliance, they had secrecy, these three. They seemed alive to me even when dark, vigilant behind blank gray faces, reaching into unimaginable distances, and sometimes I'd be scared of them in silent night, just for an instant, till I could say don't be a baby. Obsolete qualms, so far have we moved in so short a time, incurious now, blending into our machines and tapping the power. The third-grader here, solemn in his programmable sensory helmet, plays 3-D Nova Wars with an invisible opponent, little-boy blips hopping from relay station to relay station, droplets in the data stream. And back there, thoughts of secrecy. Obsolete gestures from the past, as I once interpreted old film shot at twenty-eight frames per second and played back at standard twenty-four, custard pies flying, everyone hurried, a worried-stiff style of movement abandoned in our age of comfort. Obsolete even as memory itself, the mass attention span shortened into near-disappearance, here and gone, a blip.

Carla would have been ten that fall. She was tense for her age, grim, an assemblage of bone rods threatening to snap. Dark things appealed to her, and she never wanted to watch what I wanted to. After a documentary on the Great Depression, she took to wearing a stained jumper and a sweater gone out at the elbows. She picked at her dinners, preferring white bread and soda pop, and afterward sat in the driveway gazing up into the sky. Arriving at school barefoot, she told a teacher her family was too poor to buy shoes.

Mother restrained Gordo in favor of reason. She said it wasn't at all fair to those who suffered through the Depression to make a game of it. And what about all the families who'd seen it all through? Carla's grandfather hadn't stopped treating patients just because they paid with popovers and baskets of eggs. Mother had new dresses whenever she needed them and went right on with her flute lessons. Out came the brown family photographs, but Carla slapped them away.

"Liar," she yelled. "I know what I saw."

But did we know what we saw, in the sense of recognizing a thing previously met? Were we innocent as farm animals and in danger of being misherded? Was there any use in lecturing Carla about "facts"?

For children arrived since Hiroshima, the lines have been fine. Nothing but clarity would do, while contradictions dropped all around like leaflets urging surrender. Nostalgia was forced on us. We learned not to learn by example.

Dictum: In our world, nothing would ever be simple. The very best methods were required, each of us a little project separated one from another by fine lines. Everything in the technique.

"When you wish upon a star . . ." And they said for us all to sing together.

We learned from the evidence: It was all a job. We had to imagine furiously, find room inside those lines. Even that was a job, to be somewhere else. And scary sometimes, like you might not come back around. But the clarity was there. We knew what we saw.

Sometimes, without recognition of how or when, I will find that a tiny cactus spine has worked its way into my hand. I clench my teeth and feel sand grinding on my molars. I live in the desert now, but it is in no way novel. Here is the same quiet geometry of the suburb I come from; only the scale is different. Climate, topography—these things are interchangeable as wallpaper. I recognize the stunned atmosphere of this place, its heavy padding of silence, its isolation.

Lake Success. The name itself suggests a real-estate swindle, some collection of placards and surveyor's stakes at the edge of an alkali pit. In truth, we were only minutes from the city limits. Airline pilots lived there, and pharmaceutical researchers, and even a member of the state legislature. The streets were bright, lined with cars, and humid winds blew in from Little Neck Bay. But just the same, Lake Success was a ghost town waiting to happen. And waiting still.

I choose a typical Friday evening of twenty-five years ago: My sister and I are supine before the television in our flannel pj's, a bowl of cheese twists between us. A smell of cologne clings to the white shag carpet and the mighty thrumming of the furnace sends a buzz up through the floor to our bellies, recently packed with peas and lamb chops and spumoni. After the usual finagling with the sitter, we have been permitted to seal ourselves into the parental bedroom and watch their set. They are dining with friends at the country club, Mom in a brand-new dress. The thin, striped box and gray tissue are still on the bed behind us. I throw a cheese twist in the air, catch it in my month, and Carla giggles. The cartoon show is over and Carla gets up to change the channel. There are no arguments; we have canvassed *TV Guide* during dinner and agreed on what to watch.

Here, then, in all its triviality, is the lush life aspired to in those years. So it went in a thousand other suburban fast-nesses across the land—the lamb chops, the new dress, the freshly bathed children safely encapsulated.

We were really at no great remove from the L.A. sound-stages where the households of Ozzie Nelson and Donna Stone and Beaver Cleaver carried on their bloodlessly engi-neered relations. There we were in achingly white Cape Cod Colonials, each with tidy hedge and lawn, and inside the same vast Formica surfaces that Harriet polished so tirelessly, the same wide staircases down which Wally and Dave and Ricky scrambled on their way to baseball practice, the same spacious dens where Ward Cleaver tamped his pipe over actuarial tables. Surely my own family was as deserving of renown as these others.

I suggested this once to my mother, that we ought to have our own show. "You're prettier than Donna Reed," I said.

"And a hell of a lot better actress," she said, and drifted outside to sweat and pull weeds.

What we wish to believe is this: that all those shows were worse than ridiculous, that they presented idealized, dan-gerously illusory figures, and that our inability to live up to them brought on guilt and disappointment. (How eager we were some years back to accept the specious rumor that Jerry Mathers—the actor who portrayed Beaver Cleaver—had died a mud-sucking grunt in Vietnam.) But this is fatuous, self-flattery at its cheapest.

No need to look elsewhere for disappointment. That prede-termined Maple Street existence was very much our own, in all the canned events through which we moved like chess pieces, in the good cheer we displayed so methodically, in the very drabness of our squabbles over report cards, dating etiquette, crunched fenders.

What, if anything, can be concluded from all this? That I can no longer make distinctions, cannot see the differences between desert and suburb, video village and hometown? That I am a purveyor of counterfeit analogies? Very well, then, shove all aside for realism. Clear the decks for truth, and I will fill in the rest of that Friday night twenty-five years ago.

The movie we have chosen is a bore: too much dialogue and not enough of the giant clams. Carla tinkers restlessly with tubes and jars on Mom's cosmetics tray. I remind her that we aren't supposed to touch anything in the room. Carla is two years older and says so what to that. She sprays herself with an atomizer, smears her lips red. She opens a drawer, ties a scarf around her neck, and dangles off the end of the bed, waving her tongue like a lizard. All right, this is more interesting than the movie. We bounce on the heavy mattress awhile, then she paints me too. We rub mouths, wet and slick, tasting of soap, until the oily red is spread over our cheeks. There's even a streak on the coverlet and that means trouble. So I pretend to be mad, wrestle past her kicking legs so I'm on top, tickling her stomach till Carla begs me to stop or she'll wet herself, so I do.

And hours later the folks come home, drunk and bellowing. Mom bungles into my room and frightens me with her poking and her broken-glass voice. I curl against the wall to escape her reeking breath. Afterwards I hear thuds from their room and Dad being sick.

And all night I have strange pressured dreams. I wake up sore and hot with a thickness in my head.

And what began that night has been with me, to one degree or another, ever since: an unquashable sexual desire for my sister.

There. Happy now? While Jim Anderson does time for embezzlement, his Princess gives head behind the bowling alley to pay for her habit. Donna Stone, well, she's pretty dim these days behind the Woolworth's lunch counter, not a lot to say since that drunk driver took out her whole family Christmas Eve. And Beaver? Everybody knows about the Beav; he's torn and stinking under a betel palm as Charlie strips him of boots and wristwatch.

Realism, it may be seen, has no more to do with reality than anything else.

I was eight years old when I first saw my mother on the stage. Gordo drove us into the city for the Saturday matinee. We stopped for fried clams en route and Carla was sick all over herself the minute we rejoined traffic.

Gordo punched the gas pedal. "I'm not taking you in that condition," he said.

Carla kicked and sobbed while being led into Aunt Rita's Lexington Avenue apartment building, but I wasn't the least sorry she was being left out. The experience would be exclusively mine. And I wouldn't have to share the intermission candy that had been promised.

I remember the sense of event, the rustle of overcoats and the aromas of perfume and cigarettes, far better than the name of the play or even what it was about. A comedy, yes, one of those set in Westport or Bala-Cynwyd: tennis rackets and cocktail glasses, a long white sofa with tasseled cushions, and my amazement at the living laugh-track surrounding me in darkness that reached undiluted to an impossibly high ceiling dotted with gilt extrusions. My plush seat cradled me like an

outsized hand, and the program's coated paper curled and
went sticky in my small one.

You can see my attention was not where it belonged, and so
could my father, artist of laws. His hand fell threateningly on
my knee; he hissed. So I fixed my eyes in the prescribed direction, took in the furniture and the cellophane fire that shed
no light, passed quickly over yapping faces. I could follow
words individually, but completely missed their point. Too, the
voice tones were like none I'd ever heard. Considerably later, I
learned of projection from the diaphragm and reaching those
red EXIT bulbs at the back of the theater; but at that moment
all dialogue felt alien in my ear. I lowered my gaze to the rows
of heads in front of us, studying varieties of hair.

Gordo's elbow was sharp as my mother entered through
French windows at the back of the set. Disillusion took but an
instant. She had a white sweater tied round her neck by the
sleeves—a style frequently affected at home—and a bundle of
fat white blooms across one arm, as if she'd come in from clip-
ping the peonies that marked the edges of our property.
Where was the transformation? I knew what "playacting"
meant, like any third-grader, and this wasn't it. I felt like crying when she opened her mouth to speak and out came the
teasing snob accent she used to cajole my sister and me into
drab chores, or to dinners where we had to keep quiet.

This display of her ordinary self before strangers was inde-
cent. She was exposed, without even the small tricks of glamour a little boy could recognize. I noticed that Gordo didn't
laugh with the rest. His posture was stiff and defiant, chin jutting. Was he reading the same indecency that I did?

The curtain couldn't fall soon enough for me. With alarming suddenness, the slight pressure in my bladder had grown
into a torment. I shut my eyes against it, afraid to move. Then
I heard my mother trilling from the stage: "How do I get out of
here?"

The lights came up at last and I zigzagged my way to the
men's, praying the hot dribble inside my leg wouldn't turn
into something more. I didn't want to end up at Aunt Rita's
too. Finding an empty stall, draining myself, I thought for a

mad instant of hiding there until the theater was empty and explorable, but knew I'd be found. My father, I was sure, could order up a special police squad whenever he wanted. Nothing to do, then, but thread through the forest of people and find him. At least there'd be chocolate waiting.

His suede shoes made him easy to locate; they matched the carpeting. He wanted opinions from me. I mumbled around my Hershey bar. This was no time for lenience, though, and he prompted me so fiercely I could barely keep up. A Saturday matinee, indeed. What had been offered as a rare treat turned out to be one more privilege earned through adherence to ceremony.

As the second act got under way, I was a determined little gut-squeezer. It would take plenty to make me fall for their pretending. I would follow Gordo's lead, wedging myself in place like a one-man totem pole, taking it all in and giving nothing back. Coolly, I would tell Carla later on how I'd indulged the grownups. But all this went like dust before an angel's sneeze when my mother reappeared.

She floated in a strapless satin gown, hair a braided crown that revealed the pale column of her neck. Bright as her eyes, long earrings left glitter trails with every movement of her head. She looked like herself, but had become someone else. Her laughter was slow and low and filled the distance like an echo of itself. Edging forward, edging forward, I finally conked myself against a metal seatback and felt my eyes brim over with the vulgar distraction of pain. Band music spun on a phonograph and my mother danced with a younger woman back and forth across the artificial living room. I had never seen her move with such reckless grace.

Just as it had begun, with the suddenness of a detonation, this vivid interlude was finished. Lights blinked off, then on again, and the parade of dolls resumed. It was a mystery to me that such an abandoning didn't empty the place. But the laughers laughed, the snoozers snoozed, and I watched while not watching, in the manner of someone who leafs all the way through a newspaper without picking up any news.

After a while my teeth began to hurt from the effort of not

seeing and the press of discomposure. I longed to peel back time, to rub out those few glory-radiating minutes of satin gown and low laugh, to save my mother. Because what could she do from her place of elevation but slip, trip, and fall into grayness? Into the sad kitchen where we knew her as reluctant wife and nervous mother who stared into the freezer, rummaged in drawers, talked to herself, was constantly looking over her shoulder: Where was it? Had it been there at all?

After she died, I saw how huge her own longings must have been. It was only on the altar of the raised proscenium that power drew near. She inhaled it through open pores; she swelled with it and rose like a balloon. But there came inevitably a closing line and a final light cue, and the inescapable return to the place where she flaked dried gravy off oven mitts, bandaged knuckles scraped against the cheese grater. What had to be learned was that, over the long run, short respites only deepened the agony. How do I get out of here? You find a place of warm, dark peace where the lights never dim and there is always another page of script: the inside of a television.

The next thing I noticed was the curtain call—all of them up there holding hands, grinning with what seemed to be embarrassment. And why not? My mother looked right at us and gave a small wave. I looked at the ceiling. Out in the street Gordo bought some flowers and put them in my hand.

He unsmiled. "Give these to her when she comes out," he said.

We waited in a greasy alley. Dusk sneaked in and it was cold. Gordo turned up the collars of both our coats. He stamped and blew steam like an impatient horse. Then the star of the family arrived in a miasma of cold cream, and the two of them launched into a furious argument over Carla.

"Christ almighty!" She was still reaching for those EXIT lights. "You call Rita's right now and get her down here in a cab."

A dramatic rescue; an on-her-own ride through Central

Park as night fell. Carla, however, didn't appear glad to see any of us, even when fussed over (her dress had been through Rita's washer and dryer) and given the bouquet.

"That's all right," said the star of the family. "There's another show tonight and you'll have a seat in the front row."

Then she led the way to a restaurant with peppermint-stripe decor and an electric train that circuited the counter delivering orders. Carla and I threw petals at each other while the grownups sulked.

"Mom danced with a lady," I reported, taking my pizza-burger from a little B & O flatcar.

"Liar." Carla kicked me softly.

"You'll see."

"I don't know about this acting." Carla addressed herself to no one in particular. "We get sent to bed for it."

Note: Phoned main library in the city for data search. The play was called *Three on a Mattress*. It ran seventeen performances.

I was a small, dutiful boy who was never asked to clean up his room. My grades were steady, my deportment good. "Evasive" was a word I heard often. My mother, concerned that I was old before my time, sent me to a psychologist, who fed me sour-balls and asked repeatedly how I felt about Negroes. A homeroom teacher, óne Ted Buttonweiser, wrote my parents, speculating if my lack of extracurricular participation might not mask some deeper problem.

What must, from the outside, have seemed like timidity was inside the caution that proceeds from mistrust. To put a not very fine point on it, I had my doubts about close contact with other people. Still do.

I arrived at my sophomore year of high school with the single flamboyance of hair combed in a downward swoop over the brows à la Merseybeat stars Gerry and the Pacemakers. By now I was worried too. Without metamorphosis, and soon, I might be doomed to a life in which I bored even myself. But, of course, nothing is ever as hard as we make it. It took only one chance afternoon of quaint illegality, cruising the empty streets of a housing development with an unlicensed driver and a Baggie of airplane glue, to show me how little was required and how superfluous my caution had been. It was very much a case of instant possession. When I woke up and smelled the coffee, I moved to Brazil.

In pursuit of the dissolute, we had energy as never before. We were a cadre with secret codes and unbreachable unity; we were shaking things into a new arrangement, like glass bits in a kaleidoscope. I passed my sixteenth birthday at a gallop, wanting to leave myself behind. I saw the most pampered minds of my generation wild-eyed in the wake of petty vandalisms and inert upon leather furniture, their ennui as transparent as gelatin capsules yet to be filled.

All in all, it was pretty routine.

My mother, who took no interest in details, encouraged my new moves.

"Go on, explore," she'd say, slipping me a twenty.

Explore. Expand. See the world.

Carla, who had been sent to Puerto Rico in April for an abortion, gathered us after dinner one night to view her slides: pretty nurses smiling under coconut palms that flanked the clinic entrance, piles of fruit in the *mercado central,* a porpoise washed up on the hotel beach.

"When did you have time to take pictures?" asked Gordo with ominous calm.

"Was I going to miss an opportunity like that? I just loaded up on Kotex and hit the streets."

My mother welcomed it all. Prevented now, by herself, from achieving the safety of the stage, she relied on us for dramatic settings. And, obliging her, we expected her indulgence in return.

The day I was expelled from school for a supposed role in the pollution of the faculty lounge coffee urn with tranquilizers, my mother came to fetch me, wearing gumboots and a silver fox jacket. What fine technique as we drove home, such delicate shadings in tone. So skillfully did she modulate between fury and self-reproach that I began to suspect her of rehearsing on the way over. It was a nerve-jangling performance. Makeup striped with tears as we reached the driveway, my mother pressed her forehead to the steering wheel and whispered, "Can you get any more of those pills?"

Gordo, with no appreciation of the exploratory spirit, threatened me with a military school in Maine, which he'd found advertised at the rear of the Sunday *Times Magazine*. But my mother prevailed on him to relent, saying she couldn't bear my being so far from home. Eventually, he contacted a friend on the board of supervisors and got me reinstated. I wrote an essay on mutual trust for the school paper.

My girlfriend Sabra wrote me a ballad in which she compared her heart to a hydroelectric dam. She fluttered her kohl-rimmed eyes and blocked my approach with her guitar. Sabra was equivocal.

"I've been in real trouble ever since I got the idea that my father scratching my back had something to do with sex," she'd once told me in her lovely contralto.

Her father was a tall, recessive man who did reconstructive surgery. He did not like me and I don't think he liked his daughters much, either. Their house always seemed half empty, like they were getting ready to move.

In Sabra I could recognize that same caution which I, for the time, had turned upside down. But instead of drawing me to her in recognition and empathy, this irritated me.

"Are you sleeping with her?" my mother asked.

I told the truth.

"That's all right," she said gently. "You don't have to."

A good friend of mine whose career plan filled several note-books was stabbed during a concert at the Nassau Coliseum. My mother, citing the necessity of renewal, went to live with an old college friend in the city, came home again, moved to a hotel, was hospitalized for exhaustion. My sister, who'd become involved with a Senegalese exchange student, was beaten and gassed at a demonstration in front of the UN.

Spring came on like waltz music at the scene of an accident, and Sabra and I stopped seeing each other. I considered alternatives: a life of crime, never coming out of my room.

"If I had it to do over again," my father said in an unusual reflective moment, "I'd be the finest goddamn fishing guide in Nova Scotia."

I looked hard for omens, but nothing seemed helpful. Then, for reasons never to be clear, Sabra's older sister took an interest in me. In just a few short months I learned all sorts of things. Like how intimidating it can be to get what you want.

And the necessity for caution.

I improvised a tour for a delegation from the Uruguayan embassy. I spoke for over an hour to a woman whose son was the pilot of a hijacked airliner. I smoked hashish in Walter Cronkite's chair.

When it became clear that my unanimous rejection from college was due in no small part to incendiary statements I had put down on the applications, my parents were furious. But after a few smoldering months, during which I was effectively quarantined, they were prepared to accept, if not forgive, this act of sabotage.

"It's you who'll have to live with it," my mother would say. She had the inured piety about decisions of someone who never made any.

Gordo, who would happily have spilled blood on his way to Dartmouth Law, was more attuned to specifics. He towed me into his study and uncorked a bottle of liqueur that neither of us liked.

"If you really want to take the low road, that's up to you. Failure can be comfortable—I understand that, and I wouldn't deny you. Hell, let's all be comfortable. With the money I save on your tuition I can buy a sailboat. But where does all this leave you vis-à-vis the draft board, my friend?"

I shrugged and gazed into the purplish depths of my snifter. The old cross-examiner, he had me in a box.

"The truth is, a lot of parents, maybe most, would be inclined to let you pay for your arrogance. The boy wants to swim against the tide, so be it, they say. But we're not liable if he drowns. Your mother and I aren't ready to be so blasé. We don't want to lose any more of you than we already have, and we cannot have you over in some swamp ducking mortar fire or up in Toronto ducking the FBI."

I smiled encouragingly.

"All right, it can be taken care of. Not much point in shoveling as much shit as I do if I can't get a thing fixed every once in a while. So I can make some calls and I can get you a deferment. Takes me twenty minutes. But you have to pay your way here, my friend. You have to take whatever job I get you and stick with it and make a contribution."

CBS had its news operation in a one-time milk factory on Eleventh Avenue. The halls were extremely narrow, like the walkways in a submarine. People were forever flattening themselves. They called us desk assistants and took our fingerprints, but we were really copy boys. A hundred and ten a week, shirt and tie required, and all the pencils we could sneak out of the building. I worked turnaround shift on the TV side, midnight to eight. Four a.m. was the real dead spot and that's when I'd slide next door with Ron, the gay telex operator from Palm Beach, and toke up on the Evening News set.

It was a large blue room, but not that large. File cabinets, a blackboard, a few glassed-in cubicles, the big desk with the wall map behind, and off to the right the bank of wire-copy machines it was part of my job to look after. (The only time they were ever turned off was during the actual show, when a background tape was substituted; the real clack-clacking would have drowned out every word.) At that hour the place was sure to be deserted, and other than that we didn't give it much thought. But sometimes, sitting in that great delphic throne and hoodooing my brain, a peculiar sensation would steal over me. Looking into the dead eye of the camera, I would imagine millions of American hearthsides visible only from where I perched, that I could somehow reach through the eye and deposit in those deeply slumbering places all the secrets kept off the air. What I sent to them instead were lungfuls of smoke.

One night a network correspondent called in from Bonn. He was mournful and drunk and wanted to talk to anyone. They'd thrown him out of the hotel bar. His girlfriend had dumped him for a Hungarian diplomat. He had a gun in his room and was thinking seriously about using it.

I said, "Shall I tell them to cancel your satellite time for tomorrow?"

"Kid, listen to me, kid. I've lost it. Pride, control, whatever it is. Totally lost it. I'm nothing but a foul ball out here."

I told him to hold on while I got a cigarette. When I came back someone else was on the line and they were speaking German. I hung up.

But the man was on air the following night with his transatlantic feed, standing in front of the Bundestag solid as a pilaster, steam wisping out of his nostrils, eyes steady and hard. A real old-time reporter's face, on which a smile was a deformity.

The calls became a semi-regular thing, even after his transfer to Prague ("Best beer in the world, kid"). He was usually tanked, but not always, and we'd talk about whatever was bothering him that particular night: his colitis, his ex-wife in Cincinnati and the kids who never wrote, the articles *Atlantic Monthly* kept rejecting. It amazed me how anxious he was for my good opinion.

"How was the piece Tuesday? Did you see it?"

"Well, the fur hat. I don't know."

"So I looked ridiculous? Like a cat fell asleep on my head?"

"More or less. But the piece itself was fine. Really."

"Really?"

He wasn't the only one easily wounded in those days, so I told a lot of lies. I was young and I wanted to please.

It was in general a time for euphemism, of a withdrawal from fact as from an open grave. There was great outcry over negativism in the news. The populace was battered by candor and innovation and they were tired. They had no interest in narrowing the credibility gap. They did not wish to be notified on the black-bordered cover of a national magazine that God was dead. They didn't want their dinners spoiled by the nightly recitation of body counts, by images of angry milling dissenters in the street. Be gentle, they begged. Tell about the self-made millionaires, and kids who don't take drugs.

Network executives exchanged worried memos, then came out into the open rumbling about professional integrity and the free flow of information, their neatly barbered heads held high. The public's right to know was sacrosanct and they would defend it to the very last rating point. Few were owning up, but the heart of the matter was the power to decide what was Important. The old milk factory as colonial fort.

Like the time I was waiting on the corner for the crosstown bus, overheard these two studs from the documentary division:

"What I said was, 'You want me to recut the interview to

make it sound that way, I can do it, but take my name off the credits.' "

"Did he freak out?"

"Nah, just gave me the line about this is bigger than both of us and locked himself in his office."

"Running scared."

"So who isn't?"

The weight of Policy bore down on all and sundry, making their movements wobbly, creasing their foreheads. Instead of "How about lunch?" people would say, "Let's have a dialogue." They clustered like blowflies at the edges of the newsroom to discuss detachment and accountability. Voices were sometimes choked, sometimes grave. They compared measurements of cultural drift and electorate mood. They gestured with their hands and said things like "Morality cannot be legislated" and "Well, sometimes, guys, we can get a little insular." Early one morning, not twenty feet from my desk, two reporters interviewed each other for a Sunday think piece.

On one point wide agreement was reached: that the decade was of pivotal significance—that through turbulence and upheaval we were living a kind of instant history. How quaint that now seems, the earnest belief that all the noise amounted to something more.

Myself, I took to chalking slogans on the Cronkite blackboard:

THE TRUTH SHALL SET YOU FREE

FOLLOW PACKAGE DIRECTIONS CAREFULLY AND
DO NOT EXCEED THE RECOMMENDED DOSE

But slogans, you know, are the easiest things. The best I could do was share a little bourbon in paper cups with the uptown women who came to clean the offices at night. In one way or another, we were all fools.

Consider the hedgehog, whose stiff, spiny hairs discourage attack. Often, before eating a toad, it chews the amphibian's poison gland, lathering itself with toxic froth and augmenting its defenses. An efficient mechanism for an efficient mammal nicely placed in its niche.

Consider the overevolved creature whose most dangerous enemies come from within. Imagine the first useless panic, the first nightmare, the first crushing turn of anomie. Ten thousand generations later, all we can do is palliate. Misery abhors a vacuum and history is a list of sedatives; from animism to humanism to Haldol.

We choose our own methods for treating grief and fear. Superstitions and pharmaceuticals have their cost, and confession is too cheap. Brutality is circular and flight inevitably leaks. But there is a folk remedy as simple as the hedgehog, something more valuable in the institutional dayroom, the widower's autumnal parlor, than any drug or counselor's bromide. It is television.

I had a friend in New York named Chris Bruno. His father, a hotel man, kept trying to give him large sums and he kept refusing. Not that Chris had an overdrawn sense of his own integrity; only that the entailments of wealth didn't interest him. He did airbrush paintings of office equipment and kitchen appliances. He wanted to be a lounge lizard, bitter and languid, but he was too excitable and no lounge would hold him. How close were we? Chris is the only man I've ever wanted to sleep with.

It was a long time ago. He called me on Christmas Eve from his parents' apartment across town. He was just back from camping in Trinidad and very excited about music he'd heard there, fruit bats and clownfish he'd seen. We talked a long time, promised to meet the next day and eat oysters.

Just about one hour later Chris went sailing off his snowy balcony thirteen stories onto Fifth Avenue.

Wham.

A tragic suicide, his family announced. The guilty lamentation seemed so important to them that I withheld the more terrible truth: Woozy with goose and cognac, Chris had gone out to plot the stars over Central Park and, simply, slipped.

When his sister called me in the morning, I thought at first it was a joke. But the quaver in her voice turned harsh and she cursed my stupidity. I threw the phone into the wall. And then I sat for a long time on my bed waiting for something to come out or come up, for some physical sensation, but it was as though I were inside a test tunnel with everything unnaturally still. I went in the next room, turned on the television, lay naked in front of it. There was an electronic living-room show, a man in pinstripes being interviewed about group therapy. I thought how thin Chris looked in pinstripes, then stopped thinking at all.

For days, stuporous and inured, I lived there on that floor. The flickering blue screen was the only light in the room when night came down, and it was like lying at the bottom of a lake with people calling down to me, faces blurred and words indistinct. Now and then I closed my eyes to rest them, but never really slept. I absorbed loose time while stimuli bypassed my brain. Ashtrays overflowed, fur grew in the empty food cans, and the drone of noise and light went into me like an intravenous drip.

At the same time that I began to distinguish intervals in programming, I began to recognize, if not to comprehend, my pain. I wept at a hockey game, at a Petula Clark variety special.

I slept dreamlessly, holding to me like some stuffed fuzzy toy a great armful of hissing air. On waking, my skin seemed unfamiliar, a stolen envelope. Not quite dawn and the sky was a test pattern. I groped in muffled ignorance and found, horribly, the nub. Chris died.

I showered, put clothes on, watched warships crisscross a billowing flag for the sign-on anthem, then a tornado of identical cartoon mice engulfing Farmer Gray. Regaining volition now, I could pick and choose my channels. I knew right where I was and I didn't care. Chris died, but here was Bill Cullen to numb me.

It was January by the time I went outside. The streets were iced and I sprawled forward inside two blocks. No hurry to get up, now it was safe, safe to picture everything—Chris still smiling as he toppled, gracefully taut in his fast dive, landing, no bounce, with a sound like planks clapping, the bright blood, the taxis pulsing yellow at the corner.

I limped to a steamy restaurant and ate two portions of shredded beef with oyster sauce. "A poor workman always finds fault with his tools," my fortune cookie said irrelevantly. I phoned Chris's sister from a booth. She said come on over, there's plenty to drink. The TV was on when I got there. It was on loud.

Richard Conte said: "Ease off, buster. I've had about all I can take."

We drank rum highballs and glanced at each other.

Lisa said: "He had nothing to be angry about. Not one fucking thing."

I said: "He wasn't angry."

We stopped talking once the bottle was empty. We slept in one bed, touching, but fully dressed. I woke energized, without a hangover, and thinking widely: This could be easy. I could leave my whole sorry life behind like a pile of bloody clothes. Lisa was still asleep when I went out, and the TV was still on.

It was on loud.

I came to San Francisco with a clear calling, with an insatiable appetite for squalor. I'd torn up my privileges like losing exacta tickets. I despised my soft youth, and wanted to get rid of it as fast as I could. What could be easier? Snug as a bug.

I took a job in a porno shop and soaked up the desolations of my customers. I gorged myself on simplicity. Black latex capes and ball gags, all-wet full-color spreads, gobbling nymphos, teens in bondage, lesbian nurses. When Mr. Bob came by to pick up the receipts, I'd go for a fast meal at a Chinese cafe where the waitress had a harelip and the fried rice gleamed with fat. Then it was back until closing time, aligning vibrators in the display case and listening for murders on the all-news radio. Oh, I was a man for all seasons in there, like something growing on the wall. I wore the same brown corduroys for weeks at a time; they got so shiny that when I stood under the colored bulbs at the back of the shop, it was like a rainbow up and down my thighs.

I slept in my clothes and had breakfast in bed, canned bonito and chocolate milk. I'd smoke slowly, picking dead skin from my scalp and watching my ashes soak into the fish oil at the bottom of the empty can. Then, assuming I hadn't gone back to sleep, I'd be out prowling the neighborhood like some spawn of the freight yards—raking shoppers with my menacing eyes, spinning out heinous imaginings of the grimy little playground girls—until it was time for work. My off-days were spent in a bar where I was sure not to encounter any chess players or political theorists. The Forest Club was where beaten, cirrhotic honkies brought their pension checks and helpless repetitions. It smelled like old washcloth and the cigar box was always out, inviting contributions for one of the boys who'd landed in the VA—or worse. There was a notice in the john: DON'T THROW BUTTS IN THE URINALS—IT MAKES THEM SOGGY & HARD TO LITE.

Turpitude without hardly trying. I felt proud. But, unavoidably, I would recognize myself in the next instant, burrowed deeply into the muck at the bottom of Lake Success and still trapped. Would I ever get free of this Halloween posing? Would I stay sixteen the rest of my life?

I'd conditioned myself, following the squalor trail like a set of dancing-school footprints. But if I didn't find some new moves, it would be too late for everything—or so I thought. Everything seemed portentous that season, even the new "kneeling" buses that the city introduced.

On my birthday I walked twenty-two miles and made copious notes on everything I saw. Rewind, begin again. I bought two new pairs of pants, sprinted through books of crossword puzzles, switched to a new brand of cigarette, planted geraniums in a windowbox, rode the ferry to Angel Island and hunted starfish on the beach. I vacated the Forest Club for chummy cafes where I was sure to come up against members of my own subspecies, beings in flight from manifest destiny and Danish flatware. But I stayed on at the porno shop because, honestly, I liked the work.

In time, I was deeply submerged in a comfortably uncomfortable love affair. I still felt soft, but not as youthful, so things were looking up. Andrea gave me the energy she wasn't using. I went to parties without having to be coaxed. Like the one over in the East Bay where I met a truly wise man.

This was the routine: glasses on the floor, serapes on the wall, our host in a rubber Nixon mask, blue overhead bulbs, and a two-headed ax on the coffee table. Yosenabe came over to explain that the woman who'd brought him kept staring at me because she thought I might be one of the men involved in the theft of her Samoyed. He had a gray crew cut and wore steel-rim Tojo glasses right out of a WWII cartoon. I admired his nerve. When I said I came from New York, he revealed his shoulder holster, the plastic gun that shot green and red candy BB's.

Yosenabe was an art restorer, an expert on Japanese swords. Once he had made wildlife dioramas for the Museum of Natural History, but New York was not so good. He made too much money and the cold weather made him think too hard.

"This city nice and boring," he said. "Full of Japs."

It was several days later that I found an empty cigarette pack in my jacket, and Yosenabe's business card tucked in behind the cellophane. Through the blunting residue of the recent drunk, I could call back the apprehension that Yosenabe might let me in on a few jokes.

His studio was on the second floor of a wooden firetrap downwind from a mayonnaise factory. I went up the outside stairs and found Yosenabe chipping cotton practice balls with a nine iron. The place was crammed, a treasury, and I mentioned how very close to a porcelain vase he was coming on his backswing.

"No worries. This a repair shop."

We had green tea and pretzel sticks. But Yosenabe was in a hurry, packing for a trip to Yosemite. Proudly, he displayed the shoes he was taking, brand-new sneakers with diamond-shaped holes cut in the canvas. It was late autumn, the midst of the rainy season.

"You'll get soaked if you wear those," I said.

Yosenabe smiled indulgently. "Holes are for water to run out."

The logic hit me like an injection. Here, finally, was someone who understood the modus operandi of the world. I bowed.

Was this a turning point?

Well, here are the facts: Two months later I was in Los An- · geles eating fresh fruit all day long and teaching myself to dive. Before the year was out I married an anthropologist who was the greatest fuck of my life. We weren't very happy together and came apart in the end like burrs from a blanket.

Holes are for water to run out. Absolutely.

My ex-wife calls from L.A. She's a great one for staying in touch. Also, she has trouble getting to sleep sometimes, and it scares her.

"Just lying here in bed thinking about you."

"Alone?"

"Yeah. Me and the night and the music. I don't have a thing on."

Violet gives good phone.

I remember the way she'd talk to herself with an English accent in the mornings. I remember her smell of cosmetics and fear.

I was new to Southern California and I fell in love with Violet's driving. We'd go zipping through the canyons in her green sports job with the top down and the radio wailing, eucalyptus always in the air. Violet would tromp and slide and dig through that gearbox like a mole in a tunnel. She didn't struggle with modesty, could do without conversation. She shot a bullet through my heart.

It happened after a daylight banzai move along Mulholland Drive. Violet dodged a bottled-water truck by no more than a foot, Curtis Mayfield pouring from the speakers. My eyes watered and I knew I was right there at zero, had found what I was looking for: cathexis. She parked on some baked plateau below a water tank, beer empties and diapers strewn around, all the indicants of a *True Detective* scene-of-the-crime. She stared out over the hazy San Fernando tracts, her breathing steady as breakers. And she glistened.

"Let's drive to Vegas and get married," I said.

"Right now?"

"By tomorrow I won't want to."

Violet was embarrassed to be there in corduroy pants, but the minister told her not to worry. We had pink champagne at the chapel and a woman from Samoa took Polaroids.

That night at the motel I woke up feeling chilled. I said to myself: You're married to an anthropology professor and she's allergic to shellfish. Violet reached over to me and her palms were hot and smooth. She whispered in my ear.

"Right now?" I said.

The honeymoon didn't come until six months later, by which time I had my own car and Violet had renewed her prescription for antidepressants. She wanted to go to New Mexico to study Hopi sheep culturists, so we decided to call it a honeymoon and close the file on that. It was late July and we drank a lot of beer, got headaches. While Violet toured the pueblos with a Hopi activist in a rollbar Jeep, I watched *Wheel of Fortune* and *Break the Bank*. Actually, knowing how much she wanted to, I was touched she didn't fuck him. I watched *Password* and *General Hospital* and *Championship Bowling*. She went all over the valley gathering oral histories with a tape recorder. Some of the old people wanted money, some were too drunk or crazy to remember even last year, last month. At night I would go all over Violet's body looking for sheep ticks. After about ten days, we went back to L.A.

The money on both sides of Violet's family comes from long citrus holdings. But when I think about being married to Violet, I think of tangerines. I think of her slender toes, pink as grapefruit.

"I'm on something new," Violet is saying. "Not a tricyclic."

My mouth is dry and I'm drinking cold instant coffee. "Does it help?"

"Who knows? It's the ritual of the thing, mostly."

"Sure. Along with the artificial flavorings."

"Another thing is I have this paper with a publication review committee and I probably should have heard from them last week. So it's tense. And I know one of the women on the committee, a cunt. She likes to scuttle careers."

"What's the article?"

"Don't be polite. . . . Textiles, it's about textiles."

Stacked by the phone are some of the books Violet has sent. The one on top is called *Poetry by Aphasics* (Chain Mail Press, Rochester, Minn.). Her munificent intellect, her pitiable turns of phrase. "I'm afraid I'll destroy you," she'd often said.

"Tense," I say.

"Exactly so. I cook these fancy dishes and then pour them down the disposal. I lie in the empty bathtub with my clothes on."

"You call up your ex-husband and get cute."

"But today I took off and went to the beach," she says, changing the subject without changing the subject. "I got there early, around ten, so I caught all the high sun. The heat and the glare made me dopey. I passed out on the towel and when I woke up my shoes were gone. There's the purse with my money and credit cards, there's the watch I took off so it shouldn't leave a white line around my wrist, and some lunatic steals my shoes."

"No getting away from it." This is a sad fact about her.

"Thought there'd be blisters from walking across the parking lot barefoot. But I feel just lovely since I got home. There was a little brandy left in the bottle and I had that, wrote some letters."

"Any of them to me?"

"I send you books. I don't send you letters."

"Yeah, why is that?" Do you begin to see how violently Violet she is?

"Well, you know, we all have our avoidances. I've started letters to you; it's not that it doesn't occur to me."

I know it's wrong, but I go: "You don't like writing because it leaves evidence."

"Dammit, dammit. Don't spoil it."

I recognize that voice. "I'm sorry. You want to tell me about the beach?"

"No . . . no, it was afterwards. At night this flush came on me from so much sun, like a fever almost. And my head has been ringing slightly, not unpleasant at all. There are new sheets on the bed and it's like I can pick out every thread against my skin. See, my skin is so dried out, when I touch my shoulders or my legs it's coming off like little flakes of cellophane. But here's a bottle of baby oil. Don't you think I should rub some on?"

Like the sweet chromatic horns in a Joe Tex song. Violet gives the best phone in town.

The sky is turquoise and cloudless. I take Heidi out to White Tank Hot Springs for the day. There's a little park there, sawbuck tables and cement barbecues, so we bring beer and a big steak from Opatowski's kitchen. Heidi puts on clear nail polish as we drive and tells me a story about losing her kid at Sears, having to pick her up at the sheriff's office.

"They questioned me for an hour, like I wasn't a fit mother."

We go past dark cinder hills the texture of macaroons and then the road begins to climb through piñon and juniper. The river runs in slow thin twists beside us and the car fills up with the smell of toluene.

Parked in the shade, we open a couple of beers. Not many

cars here, so it shouldn't be a mob scene. Heidi's wearing a green leotard to take the waters in.

"Like a xylophone," she says proudly, strumming her ribs. The thing I like most about her is the feel of knotted bones.

She goes ahead of me down the path, carrying her strange necessities—magazines, aspirin, jumprope. Her legs are stalks that move smoothly but without give in landing and the musculature of her back surges like a horde of caterpillars on a wall. I begin to pick up voices and at the edge of the gravel, spoor: yellow foil packaging for a roll of film.

Heidi picks up speed. "Come on, potato pants."

Ground water gathers heat from deep volcanic crust; it percolates down to the hot zone, then rises back up by convection. And that's about the size of it. Only a few thousand years from start to finish.

Heidi gets out of her clothes like they were on fire. She does a handstand, a cartwheel, and some of the puckered seniors applaud. We inch down into a natural caldron, lean on one another. Silvery gumball bubbles break the surface of the water and steam disappears in the sunlight. My head tilts back on its own and behind clamped lids it is flat, blank, orange.

A finger touches me. "A perfect day," Heidi says. "We're together on a perfect day." Then, a minute or two later, "You smell bad eggs?"

I take her by the chin and turn her, point out the string of mudpots behind us where health addicts dangle themselves in faintly sulfurous ooze.

"Natural gas." I whisper it.

"Yes, professor."

My finger curls around hers and we tug gently. Lately she wants more and more from me, I know. Her cautions are falling away. She calls me from her house during dinner, slides her arms around me in the street where her in-laws could be passing. Although the fantasies she harbors are never mentioned, I'm afraid of what they are. I open my eyes.

Fleetingly I consider explaining myself, warning Heidi not to begin undoing the tangle of husband and kid, but I see it's impossible, part of the problem. A sort of language barrier: We can only talk of immediacies.

Her husband's name is Wade. He works as an attendant at Cherry Ames Memorial Hospital. In a few more months he will be upgraded, allowed to administer injections.

"This sure is different," Heidi says, splashing herself. "I never take baths, only showers. Don't suppose I've been in a bath since I was maybe ten years old and still playing with boats."

Her daughter's name is Tasha. She spends a lot of time with the neighbor, a widow with failing eyesight. In another year or so she will start first grade and socialization.

I think it's the predictability that's so difficult to face. Hard to detect much volition out there. Still, we gather by the water hole thirsty for something, wary of predators.

The picnic area: matched poodles, a man in lederhosen who can't keep his pipe lit. Heidi jumps rope deftly, clicking her tongue in rhythm. I make a fire, rub mustard into the meat, toss it on the grill. We squat in the grass to eat, one penknife between us, bread slices mushy with juice and fat. Heidi sucks her fingers after every mouthful. I watch her jutting teeth with wonder. More solid bone. Against all this geology she looks immovably elegant. I almost want to take back my thoughts and say, Let's murder your husband.

Down by the trash barrels there's a hunched old ratnose with rubber-tire sandals and his white hair in a ponytail. He's a harvester, picking out cans and stuffing them into a burlap sack. All business, he comes over to ask if he can have our beer empties. Aluminum scrap's bringing a nice price right now, he says, but you've got to know the right people. Heidi, with her automatic solicitude, says, Why don't you sit down and empty one yourself?

There exist certain individuals who are born historians, detail men, nickname givers. They exude a kind of mental formalin in which unlikely remains are preserved. Adapted to such habitats as bus depots and cafeterias, they learn to move quickly and take advantage of the slightest opening. This E. L.

Dobbs, age ninety-three, needs only a minute or two to surround us with rambling vines of talk.

Do we know that this place, here where we sit, belonged to winemakers in Prohibition times? Beautiful vineyards all around and Judge Naylor had claim to the first pressings. You made your own way then or shriveled up. Wild days and up along those crags hundreds and hundreds of eagles, with nests five feet deep. So many birds they took all the fish out of the river and a posse went out to mop them up. Eagle feathers in the hatband of every dude after that. Sure, sell feathers or snakeskins or quail eggs hardboiled. Through the windows when the train came through. You did what you had to, whatever it was.

"Now me, I had to quit pharmacy school when the diphtheria took my daddy off. And what could I do but jump up and take a job nobody wanted. About that time we had a woman killer, dropped her babies down a well. Tiny little thing and pretty as a saint, but the jury said do her. Had a hangman didn't know his business and when the trap fell her head ripped right off her body. Helluva thing. I knew some anatomy and I said, Let me handle it. Fifteen years I was known up and down as the gentle hangman, and not one of my people experienced the slightest pain. Had a rope hand-woven out of soft bark fibers, kept her wrapped in special papers inside a moistureproof box. Hell, I did them all. Dr. Blount, Bill Tate, the Black Mesa Butcher, Joaquin Ramirez, and that anarchist . . . What was it? Greuber, yeah, and still singing when I put the hood over him. Tell you what, though. The job showed me something. Gave me the key to things early on."

He stops, waiting to be prompted, but we look blank. I'm wondering what song the anarchist was singing.

"The whole thing is this: to go out of this world as late as possible."

"That's it?" Heidi says, like someone's just taken her last dollar with a pair of loaded dice.

"Strive to survive and fight for every last day you can. That's all there is, dearie."

"This shit I don't need." Heidi gets up and heads for the car. She's genuinely pissed.

No more than a mile since we passed a speed trap, but there's her foot pressing down on mine and the gas pedal is to the floor.

"Lighten up, sugar. We've got plenty of time."

"You always say that."

"Meaning what?"

"Well, it's all so easy for you, isn't it?"

She has a taste for absolute terms—always, all, never—and I have neither the desire nor the arrogance to try and interest her in subtleties.

"Sleepwalking through life, that's me."

"You asshole, and you're proud of it."

I start to touch her face and she plasters herself against the door. "There are things that matter, you know. It's not all just a dance." Her arms are folded tight, her lips stretched thin.

I don't understand this friction, do you? A perfect day. She said so herself.

Romance is for most of us like a career; we pursue it solemnly, unscrupulously, and meet its usual disappointments with ill grace. In the course of things I have slept with seventeen different women and the lies I told them were ones I myself

believed. Complacence, inconsistency, self-defense—I am a
thoroughly ordinary man. But think of this: The cruelest thing
we can do to one another is to have expectations.

Just now I am having an affair with the maid at my motel.
Heidi is straitened, but a woman who breathes freely no matter what. She has hard eyes and a ninety-six pound whippet
body. Her face is a battlefield—long nose, prominent teeth,
and the acne scars that shame her, that she tries to disguise
with Max Factor foundation, which cakes up like silt in the
pits. There is ambivalence in her, but no confusion. Families
are the affliction of her life. The family she came from, the one
she helped to start. Heidi needs to be alone. I want to help
her.

She was fourteen in Zanesville, Ohio, when her mother died
like this: Working part-time at a luncheonette, she was badly
burned by the deep-fat fryer. A friend volunteered to drive her
to a hospital but the manager said for insurance purposes she
should go in an ambulance. The ambulance hit a patch of ice,
flew into a lake, and all aboard were drowned. Heidi answered
the phone and it was a state trooper calling.

A couple of months later she moved west with her sisters
and her father, the mine inspector. She went to high school in
five different states and married the first man who thought to
ask her.

I had been at the Golconda less than two weeks. It was a
Saturday morning and a girl let herself into my room with a
key. I was naked in bed, smoking and watching the set: cartoons with no sound. Like a lush-worker on New Year's Eve,
wasting no time, she started right in on me.

"You got any complaints about the room, mister, I'd like to
hear them."

The best I could do was "No," and spread out the sheet a
little.

"Okay then. Maybe you're from Canada or somewhere, but
we got a deal out here where you leave a little something for
the girl who does up your room. I been waiting on you, figure
maybe you're one of those end-of-the-week, hide-it-under-the-

pillow types. But nothing. Not gratuity one do I see from you. Maybe you think I don't mind bending over to wipe scum off the toilet rim or pick toenails off the carpet. But it's some shabby work moving through strangers' crap every day. They pay me like an Indian and never once . . ."

She waved it all away, turned to one side. "Oh God," pressing fingertips against her hairline, "you must think I'm a total idiot acting like this."

"No. You're right. It's me. I have a way of missing out on obvious details. My jacket. It's rolled up behind that chair. Go ahead in the pocket and take whatever you think's fair."

"You're serious?"

"So they tell me."

She drew a bill from my pocket with two fingers, then looked over at me plucking hairs above my sternum. She had a laugh like a tropical bird, a trill I could watch moving up her throat.

Lifting her eyes to the ceiling, "Mama, this ain't how it looks."

"Not at all. I had a lovely time. What's your name, anyhow?"

"Linda," she said, leaving no doubt it was a lie.

"Linda. That's Spanish, isn't it?"

She went out the door, then curled her head back around. "Something else you could do for me is quit throwing your dental floss in the sink."

Monday morning I was ready for her. I'd called in to the facility, reported car trouble, and when she showed around ten I had candles burning and a bottle of Solano County champagne iced down in the sink. Leaning up against her utility cart with bangs awry, she had a sullen white-trash look of too many years' macaroni and soup beans.

"What the hell are you up to?" she said.

And I wondered myself. But once I'd coaxed her inside I sensed as before her scrawny heat, and desire rose in me like nausea. I popped the cork.

She looked suspiciously into her glass. "If this is about the other day . . . Listen, I was under some pressure, driving all around for a place to let it out, and you got elected, that's all."

"*Salud,*" I said.

"What I mean is don't take me at face value, okay?" Then she grimaced, tossed her head in a way that told me she had realized a possible reference to her homely features.

"Sit back and relax," I suggested.

She turned from me to look out the window at the cars.

"Linda," I said, "I'm not worried about values at all. Now why don't you sit down here and watch while I take care of the room."

I grabbed fresh linen off the cart and started stripping the bed.

"You must be drunk already." She reached for the bottle, willing to catch up with me.

I wiped the ashtrays, emptied the wastebaskets, laid in fresh soap and towels. I made merry with brushes and spray bottles, touched up with aerosol disinfectant.

"Very nice." She was rolling soft candle wax in her fingers. "Is there a point I'm not getting?"

"Now we're on equal ground," I said, having no idea what I meant.

We sat watching television for an hour or so, and then I left for work.

You were, I suppose, expecting a seduction. As there was no disappointment on my part, let there be none on yours. I cannot change the facts: Lust no more obviates the need for skepticism than it cures banality.

Heidi was compliant in her thoughtless way, positioning herself amid the furniture like a showroom mannequin. Compliant but inapproachable. Something forced me back from my impulses to put on a tape of Erroll Garner playing "Penthouse Serenade," to slide my hand along her spine and look for her heartbeat in the wrong place; some nameless instinct did this. But all I can be sure of is what I don't know.

On Tuesday I got her name and number from Opatowski,

who volunteered that he'd only hired her because she looked so underfed.

Her husband picked up the phone, instantly truculent.

"Mrs. Romar, please," I said in my own voice.

"Yeah, who wants her?"

I pretended to be from a national recipe contest, first prize a trip to Tokyo and ten thousand cash. He put her on.

"Hi, it's room six. Did I get you at a bad time?"

She agreed. She agreed to everything. We would meet at a neutral site after midnight and take it from there. I purposely arrived fifteen minutes early, but she was already waiting.

"I've never done anything like this before," she said.

"Me too."

The stars were like pinpricks. We went behind some rocks, laid a blanket on the ground, and fucked like prairie dogs.

About sixty times a second. That's how fast the hummingbirds beat their wings as they hovered at the bottle of red sugar water that hung outside our bedroom window. Violet brightened on mornings they'd arrive, taking it as an omen of sweetness for the rest of the day. At night, like the birds, she would lapse into a state of torpor. It wasn't the casuistries of the Soc-Anthro industry getting her down, but me. This was during my early wanderlust, after the first thirteen weeks of marriage had played.

Violet was altogether charmed by the idea of "keeping" me, and for a span so was I. It's not easy to denounce pampering no matter how kenneled up you start to feel. So I donned the Chinese silk pajamas, shaved more often than was necessary, tried different fruit combinations in the juicer (her parents' hesitant wedding gift), and when toward evening I grew punchy, I would sometimes read aloud to myself of infant mortality patterns in Southern Asia or of Uzbek shamanism from the scholarly journals my wife stacked like furtive beaver mags in her closet. A day would perish by a kind of melting process. Never fully awake, I found it the most natural thing to slither into bed whenever Violet came in. Dinner was brought to me on a tray.

Still, it was a purely expository interlude, like the tumbling calendar leaves of an old movie. A vague fragrance of bed linen followed me everywhere and I started to cut myself up while shaving. Violet crayoned in my silences with the records she brought home by the armload; guaguancos and sambas, gamlans and cane flutes. Soon my nastiness was uncontainable.

"No," I shouted, "I don't want you to run me a fucking bath!"

Poor confounded Violet. I was worse than one of her students. It was a larger sample that was missing. I needed to hear someone else's thoughts and opinions.

I had a friend who lived in Tuna Canyon, as yet a lightly populated zone. His place was up high near an air force radar tracking station and you could step out on his deck to look over dark sky and water and say, "It's a tuna moon-a tonight." The sun was direct all day long, could make things pretty stifling in the greenhouse; you misted yourself along with the plants. My friend's business was illegal horticulture. Opium poppies, psilocybe mushrooms, Hawaiian wood rose, like that. He also brokered smuggled tropicals (even orchid collectors have their intrigues), and serviced an impressively wide market for bootleg roses. That's right. Next time you buy one of those boxed hybrids, look at the little medallion it wears: ASEXUAL

REPRODUCTION OF THIS PATENTED PLANT WITHOUT LICENSE IS
PROHIBITED.

So I was up there one day singing my usual blues as I
watched Marsh feed seedlings with an eyedropper.

"Frankly," he said, "I don't get all this static you're putting
out. She's a bloody gem."

"But, Marsh, I live like an invalid."

"Exactly. That's what paradise is all about in this town.
Those Bel Air grandees spend all kinds of money and effort to
achieve that state of utter helplessness. So get with the program, son, join the party."

Okay, paradise meant having your own nutritional counselor and a Central American refugee to pumice your bunions.
This was not an insight I could use.

"I daydream about auto accidents." Taking a defensive sip
from my rum collins. "I call up dentists and make imaginary
appointments."

"You should stop fighting your own normalcy, that's my
opinion."

"It's consumerism. Nothing but appearances."

Finally Marsh told me to cheer up or shut up, I was disturbing the plants. I decided to do both.

But three days later Violet's car was stolen from her campus
parking space and we were plunged into a time of internal
exile. Huddled in the apartment like a couple of Soviet dissi-
dents, we developed a conversation of codes after wearying
each other with previously covert intimacies. Traditional
doubts, the plucking of questions—they belonged in this
space. But a sense of artificiality was best for both of us. It was
simpler to play hand after hand of five hundred rummy. We
were such lazy people.

"The only things you can fix are machines," Violet said
after another immaterial call to the police.

I adored her sloppy exasperation, the rabbity twitching of
muscle pads along her jaw as she ground her molars. I did not
like to think about how much she'd invested in me.

"My darling," I hummed.

"I mean it," she said.

The timer dinged for the cheese pudding she had in the oven, and then I said something about what was one more missing Fiat, they were busy keeping the streets safe for plutocracy. Violet sometimes worried that I was in love with my own mouth. She stood up with such sadness in her loose arms and . . . well, certain things do not wish to be described.

Violet garnished our plates with sprigs of cilantro and carrot coins and I dealt another hand. That night we went for a walk, held hands, saw a huge man playing on his lawn with a turtle. He called it by name. Fritz. We held hands and looked at the stars (but only out of the corners of our eyes) and we wished for something. We were always wishing for something.

When I first came to L.A. I didn't know anyone. It was summer, dead center. I sunned on bus stop benches. I looked at women browsing in drugstores. Burritos three times a day. Hunting for toilets. Mumbling into the wind. I wanted a job at the zoo. A Mexican in gumboots was hosing out the lemur cages and he laughed when I asked about it.

"You got to take a test," he sad, and wrote his initials on the back wall with spray.

Violet, at this same time, was involved with someone ten years younger. Fragile. A troubled homelife. He was a lifeguard at a condominium tower in Marina Del Rey.

"I sort've liked it when he tied me up," Violet told me. "An enthusiastic kid. Such bright black eyes. It felt like a camping trip or something. He'd want to show me every knot."

Other men stressed her, but she always felt cool inside with him. Violet, sober by profession, don't forget, distrusts flash and style (translation: anyone else's), and he was so impervious, so very much without either, even wearing turquoise glasses and glistening with cocoa butter in his high white chair.

So imagine, please, her grim contorted Violet-like sense of shock when, on a weekend she was visiting her parents, he let himself in with the key she'd given him and slashed all her clothes, cut careful triangular holes in the crotch of all her panties.

She moved to the Valley, leaving no forwarding address.

It took some time to adjust to the ephemeral ambience, to find an empty socket in the fast-buck, dollhouse economy. But not that long. I had a two-room efficiency with fifties Sputnik furnishings, and thirty-two hours a week at a sporting goods warehouse. I was doing all right. With my off-time I did as little as possible: listened to the all-news station on the radio, began to keep a scrupulously trite diary. Rain arrived with the fall. I asked myself, Is this the way that Arthur Bremer felt?

Violet was in therapy at this point, compiling pills. She says now that the whole thing was an indulgence, like splurging at the dress shop, but I don't know. At least she had a woman doctor. The doctor had a degree from the Sorbonne and a boundless faith in chemicals. Violet had such severe depression that she lost eighteen pounds and sensation in the ends of her fingers.

"The terrible thing," she says now, "was that I'd look at myself in the mirror and say, 'You've never been more beautiful.' "

Her mother came to live with her for a week, went home in tears. Violet stopped filling the prescriptions. After a while she could type again. The thing that brought her out of it was buying that car. The pine-green little scooper that slid us down Mulholland Drive.

Marsh and I talked security systems and watched the sun come up across from his deck. Marsh knew a guy who installed lawn sensors. He'd installed them for a French movie director who moved out two weeks later. Dobermans were more popular than ever. And someone had just opened a gun shop on West Wilshire, filigreed shotguns with pump action.

"I've got the flyboys right over here," Marsh said. "My security comes free of charge."

There was a sick beige light over the oil drum half we'd roasted a neighbor's goat (strictly legit, a gift) on. A long night in the hills burning eucalyptus wood. I considered eventual billboards: HOW MUCH SECURITY CAN YOU AFFORD?

"Just a little coffee and then that's it." My hands were shaking.

He went into his endlessly forming smile, leaning toward the water. "It's full of submarines," Marsh said.

Around eight-thirty I stopped at a doughnut shop to call the wife. Out all night with the car, still suffering from performance anxiety, and by no means just the one kind. A honey-I-fucked-up-again job.

She said, "I'll cancel my classes. We'll go to the beach."

The last fringe of afternoon has disappeared. With curtains drawn back, light in #6 is part blue, part gray. The radio says we should have unseasonably cool temperatures through tomorrow.

"Really, I have to leave."

I slide up and kiss her eyes. "That's what you said half an hour ago."

"I can't keep claiming I had engine trouble." Her jutting teeth clamp on her underlip.

"Ten minutes, ten more minutes, and I'll dress you myself."

"Shit." She reaches across me for the cigarettes. "I want to sleep beside you. We've never really done that."

The phone goes off and we look at each other. If Heidi's husband calls looking for her, Opatowski usually lets us know. She's already got her panties on by the time I pick up.

But it's Violet.

"Hi, sweetie. Going my way?"

I shake my head at Heidi, pat her half of the bed. "It's been a while."

"I know. Hectic out here. We had mudslides two weeks ago. You probably heard."

"The place is all right?"

"More or less. A couple of new trees in the backyard, but the rest of it missed me somehow. Anyway, I'm sitting here listening to those Dinah Washington records and it made me think about you."

Heidi looks inquiringly at me from the foot of the bed. Her arms hang like pale siphons.

"I always hated the arrangements. All those violins."

Heidi mouths: *I'm going.* I pull her down next to me.

"But so romantic." And there's that Violet laugh, like water over cool rocks. "I always see a penthouse with the moon shining in."

"Who is it?" Heidi whispers.

"Actually, this isn't the best time for—"

"You're put out with me, my long silence. Is that it?"

Heidi blows smoke in my eyes, flicks my nipple.

"I'm a little pressed right now, that's all I meant."

"Hurry, hurry. All right, good for you. I'll give you the hard news and let you get on with whatever it is."

"Don't sulk. Please."

"I'm not. Just shifting gears. I thought you might like to know a friend of mine has offered me a job in Virginia. He's team leader on a dig starting up next month in Surrey. Seventeenth-century village, underwritten by the Ford Foundation, I can be their physical anthropologist if I want."

"Real auspicious, Violet. Have you decided?"

"Violet?" Heidi's tipped off now, pokes me hard. "Who's Violet?"

"I can get a six-month leave of absence and . . . Is there someone with you?"

"In fact, yes."

"You must be in bed. My God, where else could you be in a motel room?"

"Look, Violet . . ."

"Don't tell me you're embarrassed. You were incapable when I knew you."

I'm wondering about this "friend" of hers. Probably an ursine type, pipe and corduroys, always under control, collects Elizabethan limericks. But not above exacting a favor in return for one of his own. I don't like him.

Violet is tracing the mandatory ambivalences, teasing herself, while Heidi tugs on the phone cord.

I say: "Go ahead, talk to her."

Heidi freezes up once she's got the receiver. I can make out Violet's voice, flat and clipped like a taxi dispatcher, but no words.

"I didn't know," Heidi says finally. She marches to the bathroom. Wham goes the door.

"What the hell did you say to her?"

"I can't imagine. It was all perfectly neutral, factual. Is she upset?"

I sense Violet's lecture-hall personality emerging. Maybe I can still head it off. "So you're soaking up some Dinah, huh?" And I sing the last verse of "That Old Feeling."

"I'll miss you, Violet. Over there in Virginia with your relic brushes."

"No need. They have telephones there."

"But the geography is different, the mileage. You won't be nearby anymore. Means nothing in practical terms, but that feeling, I don't know, it always seemed important."

Violet breathing into the mouthpiece is like a light rain on fallen leaves.

"You're awfully sweet," she says. "I should come and see you on my way across. I think I will. But go on now, you have to take care of your friend."

Click.

I have neglected to tell you how beautiful Violet is. She knows it, too. No wonder her students kept calling at all hours. There is no excess in her face, no one element that dominates. Everything about her is smooth and light. Touching her skin had the delicacy of floating. And I remember her walking away from me one afternoon along a row of Lombardy poplars; she was tall and streamlined, like the trees, and her fox-red hair coiled around her head in the wind. "You don't need me, you need an entourage," I said. She kept on, but her stride shortened.

I open the bathroom door and Heidi's hands come up over her breasts. Indignation has dissolved the casual laxity of fifteen minutes ago. Her mouth is tight and her lungs are pumping hard. On the edge of speech, she changes her mind and shoulders past me. Silently, and so vehemently I'm worried they'll tear, she gets into her clothes.

"Heidi. We've been divorced for over three years."

"And you still talk to her that way. 'Ooo, Violet, it's been such a long time.' " Her imitation is fruity, singsong.

"Am I obliged to hang up on her?"

Heidi curses the zipper on her dress, turns her back to me. "I don't really care what you say or how. Forget that part. What hurts is you made her a secret."

"Not like that, not like I was purposely keeping anything from you." She jerks away from my hand as if it's electrified. "So I was married for a while. That doesn't amount to shit right now, right here."

Heidi gains momentum as she untangles her hair, smears blusher on her pitted cheeks. "Right here. It's like a coded message when I'm with you. We never talk. You never tell me things."

"What is it you'd like to know?"

"Miss the point, go ahead." She pops the *p* and a mist of saliva settles on my chin. "This thing or that thing, it's not the facts I'm after. An even chance is all. You're supposed to be so smart and I have to lead you by the nose. What does it come down to when people make secrets? What do you suppose it means when two lovers . . . We are supposed to be lovers, *verdad*? Or am I in the dark on that too? I'm not a pickup, goddammit."

I know it's a mistake, the contrition I give her. I know I should protect her from expectations. But I'm not a complete prick. Heidi's entitled to some comfort. On any reasonable scale of operation, this comes under the heading of being polite.

I hold her, rock her. I promise not to hide things anymore.

Running my hand up the back of her dress, I come upon a dot of crusted secretion, hers or mine. She says all I have to do is trust her like a friend, and I say okay. We're standing by the window, saturated by the yellowish light of the Golconda sign. WEEKLY & MONTHLY RATES. A trailer truck rolls past, air brakes snuffling. Dishes clank in the cafe and the jukebox comes on; someone's pushed the buttons for a ranchero.

At last, Heidi peels herself away. "I've got to get out of here."

"I know."

Her skin is cool, she's smiling, and her eyes aren't the least bit moist. "Get some sleep. You'll need it." She hurries toward her car, then turns back, rotating one finger against her skull. "Thank God."

"Thank God what?" I'm standing in the doorway holding a towel closed around my waist.

"Thank God my casserole only needs to be heated."

Wake up this morning with pizzicato *Lunchtime Movie* music running in my head. It won't stop. Implanted violins follow me in and out of the shower. I Q-tip my ears extra hard, but the plinking doesn't leave with the wax. Turn on the radio to drown it out and a baritone reads to me:

"Puerto Rican terrorist Concepcion Buendia said today that he spared the life of Treasury Secretary Richard Goodyear when Secret Service agents made their dawn raid to rescue the kidnapped official because he couldn't bring himself to hate him.

" 'I had all the time I needed to shoot,' Buendia told investigators. 'But I could not succeed in seeing him as an enemy, only a man who was sleeping.' "

I think that once or twice watching a woman sleep, overcome by her stillness, I have wept. Not something I am particularly proud of, but there it is. Every tub on its own bottom. Every lonely beast in its own separate bed.

No time for coffee, have to get moving right away. This *Lunchtime Movie* room is like something pressing on my throat. I'll drive with all the windows open and the speedometer pinned. A couple aspirin for my stiff neck and then I wrestle clothes on over my wet skin. Boots in case I feel like hiking, a hat to shade my eyes. On the way out, I check one of my experimental stations. Day 10 for the mold garden, if I haven't flubbed my count, and a good crop of cottony mycelium growing on the little wedge of papaya; thousands of light-gray spores so it resembles mouse fur. In the other mayo jar, beginning liquefaction of a freestone cherry indicates the presence of larval maggots. Some things are running smoothly and right. The speechless things.

Mrs. O. is folded into the cement bench by the office, waiting for a cab. Her feet dangle in the air. She looks ready to turn to powder inside, and seeing her just now, for some reason I imagine small birds spit-roasted over an open fire. I pick her lumpy red handbag up out of the petunia bed.

"Took no notice when I put it down," she says. "Been fasting and I'm just a bit lightheaded."

"Fasting?"

"Fruit juice four times a day. I needed to move out all the starch that was clogging me up."

Mrs. O. is planning to spend the afternoon at her breath alchemy workshop with Master Han. Self-healing, she explains, is the only kind that works, but at the same time you need to be guided.

"Master Han believes in reeducating the brain by tracing how a person moved in infancy from prone to standing up. He tries to discover gaps in your movements supported by the endocrine system. Glands can reflect mind states, you know."

"You want to save the cab money, I'll ride you over."

She grins and runs her knuckles up my arm. "You're a good New York boy, anyone can see that. Generous. No, you go ahead your way. I like to talk to Mr. Suarez on the trip and I brought him kugel."

One of the lumps in her bag, cold starch. So I leave her there by the petunias with the sun sparking yellow on her stainless steel cane.

I head west out of town, a squirrel's jawbone swinging from my rearview mirror on black thread. I picked it from desiccate remains near a convenience grocery, just a few feet beyond the asphalt apron in a snarl of sticks and paper. Kneeling there, smelling the exhaust of cars left running for the quick-stop shop, I tugged at the small worn teeth and they came away in my fingers. I head west toward itching thirst and the air force test range. The matinee violins are still with me, but the tempo has slowed.

The topography of space operas. Except for what my three thousand pounds of Detroit steel displaces, the air is motionless. But something in it seems to bend the light, angle it into my face so that even behind my defenses of tinted glass, visor, and hat I must squint. As I go straight and hard down the blacktop I pass a million invisible roads of lizard, millipede, coral snake, tarantula, giant hairy scorpion. Scattered plants are spiked or spined or even venomous. No escape from this landscape, its inaudible ferocity.

Now begins the barbed fencing, the fat red lettering of NO CIVILIAN ACCESS. Bleak buzzard acres you could prospect for spent casings and pilots' bones, where the shallow soup holes are poisoned with radon and sulfur. Far off, below the rusty red foothills, I sight a line of sheds. Hard glare on metallic roofs, and tan smudges that must be plywood nailed over doors and windows. Haunted barracks, maybe a nerve gas depot now, heavy drums all sealed away. Another mile of fencing, AUTHORIZED PERSONNEL ONLY, a corroded and de-tired Jeep— human earmarks more ominous than forlorn. And some- where it can't be seen, so Opatowski says, they've built a rep- lica of Saudi oilfields for paratroop maneuvers, and a dum- my target range of silos.

I pull over to consult my map. Nothing ahead, for thirty miles at least, until a place called Holy Smoke. But not the tin- iest blister in the black line that represents the road, only the name floating above it. A cartographer's prank? Holy Smoke. I'd rather try for it than turn around.

A good twenty minutes without billboard or marker before I find a turnoff. A crude wooden sign says: THIS IS NOT A ROAD. That's good enough for me. I head up the gravel track, steer- ing wheel wobbling in my hands. It takes very little time to es- tablish the bona fides of that sign, the conscientious citizen who scrawled it. Dry gulches intersect the nonroad, logs and cobbles in them I have to clear away. Revving and swaying, revving again, I lunge across. The pungent aroma of scorched hardware reaches me. Now the washouts are rougher and the stones sharper. I stop to check the undercarriage for wounds. Nothing yet. Then I remember my spare is low on air, also bald. A cooler head would prevail, but that's something else I didn't bring.

Starting upward now into jumbled hills, I ignore what the dashboard gauges tell me. My tongue is a spoiled oyster, sour and thick. And too weary to tell me what a fool I am. On these steeper grades the rear wheels hesitate and spin, but I make the crest; then down, which is just as bad or worse, slewing into chuckholes, sledding over loose rock when the brakes lock up.

In what passes for a valley here, a barely sloping trench be- tween low sills of rock, I stop for something to chew: juniper needles. A trifle dizzy, but it's easier to focus from this small wedge of shade. Those dark lumps, yes, it's there just a few hundred yards down the line (like all good explorers, I had to find it by mistake). Holy Smoke . . . or something. Not the trim oasis I'd let myself imagine. No oil company logo rising on metal stilts, no hope of iced pop. I think I hear the wail of a dog, lovesick or dying. Maybe just a streak of wind in the remnants of a useless place.

Leaving the machine to recuperate, I step out for dereliction with a cautious stalking pace. Apprehension fades the closer I get. A street full of sage balls and dead wood, two rows of tilted buildings, no more than lumber teepees, some of them. I announce myself by drumming on a mangle washer halfway buried in sand. No answer. A ghost town even the ghosts have left. Like all good explorers, I've been betrayed by my map. And by my zeal to move forward. I remember a character man on *Gunsmoke* pulling his whiskers and drawling, "This country is hell on a Christian." I remember the story of a boy scout who survived Death Valley by drinking his own urine. But long as I'm here I might as well poke around. The amateur enthuses in the implacable face of error. I ease my head through windows fringed with cobweb, look over great floorboard holes in which biting things are lurking in the cool. With a piece of glass I carve the date and my initials in a soft gray doorpost. Splintered furniture, buckshot patterns on old tin, are signs that more than weather has pulled this place apart. But not lately. The shotgun holes are rusted, the liquor bottles milky from the scouring of blown sand. In the last house on the left, a brick chimney all that's holding it up, I find under gummy fallen shingles a toy shovel and a 1952 issue of *Field & Stream*. Rats have chewed the pages up for nesting fodder and the rest comes apart in my hands. But I wonder what the people in this house so far from water thought as they read of salmon climbing a waterfall, walleye in the deep blue lakes of Michigan. Probably not much. Living on the edge of things this way, you give up the capacity to envision. The rest of the world gradually disappears behind layers of fuzzy curtain, while on your side there is nothing but the abuse of the sun and this fierce, racking ground that extends on and on to the ocean, wherever that might be. Day-to-day survival becomes a kind of madness. This comforts me as I

squat in the rubble with my hat sweat-pasted to my head, trying to keep myself from staring into the sun. The nothingness
comforts me. It is pristine.

A ruthless hiss that echoes. I look up. Above me five combat
jets in a **V** indite white lines across the sky like a trail of poisoned bait. Time to go. Definitely time to go. Back to my machine, to paving and noise and ice.

At least the violins are gone.

Culver Tubbs had eight professional fights and lost them all.
Now he's a happy, lumbering heavyweight in the Golconda
kitchen and a deacon of the Assembly of God church up the
road in Organpipe. His fire-and-brimstone pork chops jab at
my stomach, unpacified by the Jose Cuervo I've been pouring
over them. Opatowski and I are alone in his bar. He looks out
the one small, high window and shakes his neat head.

"The wide open West. How about it. Never missed a Saturday matinee when they had Hoot Gibson or Bronco Billy. It all
looked so good from a shitty little Pennsylvania mill town. I
said, 'Won't eat soot all my life. Gonna go where the skies are
not cloudy all day.' Only took me about fifty years to do it."

And only because they told his wife to go ahead and write up
her will. Opatowski didn't bother with questions. (All doctors
are liars, he says.) They sold everything but their clothes,
drove off for air that was light and warm, bought this place at a
sheriff's auction for cheap.

"The one good thing about her sickness is it scared us into being brave."

I've seen him with a rip chisel in his hand, chasing obstreperous drunks into the parking lot and growling like a badger. I've seen Mrs. O. heading out on a rock hunt with collecting bag and slender hammers, pushing along a green oxygen bottle on the rack her husband has specially customized for the rough terrain.

"Hard or easy, you have to keep on learning," Opatowski says. "What did I know before about portion control or scaled rentals? Zero. But out here, with that feeling of being pitted, man against the elements, you really want to apply yourself."

He sucks at crushed ice drizzled with bourbon, chips away at the pressed pulp of an Olympia coaster. There is comfort in this hard-lit space, both of us supposedly preoccupied, no apprehensiveness of the empty public room, but instead the happy tedium of a family dinette. His left hand, the one with four and a half fingers, lies on the friction-smooth black table as if it's died there. His small, neat head makes one of its slow angles, eyes wide without really taking anything in.

"Slow and steady wins the race," he says, as though the phrase, after long deliberation, has just now come to him. "One foot in front of the other."

My glass is empty, but I have a little salt anyway, replaying the night Opatowski came to my (his) room and confronted me over Heidi. The tracery around his eyeballs told me he'd had a few belts first, but he was steady as magnetic north.

"You just better know what you're doing." He sidestepped, blocking my view of the television. "She's probably more curious than someone her age has any business being, and maybe not so strong as she ought to be. But so far strong enough. That Wade she's got is a pretty good man, worked eight shifts a week when they were saving up for the baby. . . ."

I interrupted to say I had no ambition for home-wrecking, that my attention span was too short. This did not reassure.

"Fuck 'em and forget 'em, is that it?"

"Look, this is as much her idea as it is mine," I said, and it was close enough to the truth.

Opatowski grimaced with impatience. Two zebras nuzzled on the screen behind him.

"What if it is?" he said.

Not actually suspecting him, but irritated, I said, "Are you protective or just jealous?"

His voice was even, calm, potent. "I'm putting you on notice, that's all. An inkling, one false rumor that you haven't treated her right, and you're out on your ass without so much as a razor blade."

He folded his arms with the gravity of an Arapaho elder, and then, in another few seconds, had fallen puffing and pale into the other chair. Then he fell for several minutes into wheezing sleep, his legs thrown out stiff and straight like a little boy's in a pew. He woke up nostalgic, helping me shell and eat a sack of peanuts while describing his two years of ceaselessly headphoned Signal Corps service in Wales.

"Well, hey. That sweet old hound," Heidi said when I told her about the cautionary visit. "And I was even thinking he might can me when he found out."

She brought him a chess pie the following day.

Opatowski looks over lemon and lime wedges that are drying out in their Tupperware bowls. He nudges fanned-out cocktail napkins, cups his palm over the goblet of red stir straws.

"Might as well clear out," he says.

"But it's only quarter of eight."

"You want to wait for the nobody that's coming, it'll have to be by yourself." The neat head rolls resignedly backward. "I'm gong back to the apartment and listen to my Ezio Pinza records."

He reaches behind a trellis of plastic grapes and flicks a breaker switch that kills everything but the refrigeration. I follow him out into the thin blue chill. The stars are too bright, like bulbs around a makeup mirror.

"Vacancy, goddammit," he shouts at a passing Camaro.

Motor chuffing, lights beaming into featureless outback, a provisions truck has parked by the kitchen entrance. Tubbs, in an apron with Appaloosa markings of old grease, is helping the driver unload.

"Supposed to have been here a couple hours ago," Opatowski says without annoyance. "Got lost probably. It happens all the time."

I lend a hand while the slow-and-steady seigneur gives instructions that no one hears. Frozen blocks of hash browns, rime-coated cartons of breaded veal from a plant in Wyoming, enough to lay the footings for a small patio. Portion control?

"Got an uncle moved down from Wisconsin, carves duck decoys," chummy Tubbs is saying. "Not a lot of call for them around here."

"I'm a quail man myself." The driver has turquoise bracelets on each wrist, a trim vice-squad mustache. "Even though there's not much on 'em but the breast."

"I like something big enough to stuff. Then you wrap it in bacon and bake it nice and slow to keep the juices in."

"What part of Wisconsin?"

"Fond du Lac."

Opatowski grabs a bag of fish fingers and we walk back to his place. I can use the company as much as he can. We tip quietly through darkness to the living room with its sunburst carpet and mounted horse skull. Mrs. O. is asleep, Pinza's "Some Enchanted Evening" barely audible. Opatowski peers into the shoebox bedroom, recloses the door. We whisper, both of us, moving with the soft and wary foot placements of burglary. Parchment-colored light seems not to flow from the little gooseneck lamp but to escape. I take out my cigarettes, but Opatowski shakes his head. He slumps, the Jim Beam bottle braced on one knee, hand wrapped around the neck like it's some kind of control lever.

He says: "What I've got to do is get ready for when she won't be around at all."

I turned the clock away from me, wanting to sleep in. The air in #6 was heavy and my dreams were irritating, full of vouchers and memos. Sleep here and there, but no rest. Noise began to mount up—motors, voices. I lay awake with my eyes closed and imagined spies at the foot of the bed, roasting me with motionless eyes.

"Thirty-five hundred deaths per kiloton isn't even in the ballpark," Sonny insists.

Sunday brunch at the Golconda Cafe. Fried ham and French toast, a lake of syrup on my plate. Glucose opens the flaps of my metabolic carburetor and I'm all in a hurry with nowhere to go. From Sonny's silvery tape machine, between us on a chair of its own, come highlights of a Nuclear Survivability Conference.

"Don't worry about civilization," says a curiously accented voice. "Concentrate on staying alive to enjoy it."

I went out prowling for relics. A garrulous Mormon, one of those Old West hobbyists who sometimes pass through, had tipped me to a likely site and drawn a map on a Golconda napkin. I was moving along a shale track toward dark lava tongues emerging from the sand like mummified brontosaurs, paying more attention to the elementary ballpoint diagonals of the map than to what was right in front of me. It took a second or less for the offside tires to slip from the troughs, over the unbanked lip of shale, and dig themselves in. I was alarmingly tipped and stuck fast.

Opatowski told this one: Two years ago, in the next county, an old man had lost himself, blown his engine on a forgotten length of ranch road. Some pitiful, turtlish instinct made him stay inside his car and in a day or two he'd baked to death in his underwear. They found a note on the dashboard asking that someone inform his grandson, who ran an air charter service in Valdez, Alaska.

But I had a two-quart canteen and the sense to start moving, shirt knotted over my head. No sleepwalking, stay on the offensive mentally. I took up, in order, the following: ultraviolet rays so intense in Antarctica that the atmosphere is nearly germ-free; the scheme, continuously discussed, to squeeze petroleum from hidden terraces of Rocky Mountain shale; long-vanished swamps and three-story tree ferns turned now to coal; sulfates and alkali and the sweat that was burning my eyes. Be watchful too. Avoid confinement in a narrowing corridor of heat. But I didn't find any arrowheads or pot pieces along the way, no shapely bits of bone. I saw a hubcap half buried, a chuckwalla retreating into a crevice of porous yellow rock. My tongue contorted and my head was clanging, clanging hard. Mission bells, *campanas*, responded my obedient brain. What fun.

Following the curve of a dry wash, I heard a whang and watched sand spit over my feet.

"No sweat, amigo. Just holding my perimeter."

The man was jug-eared and thick through the chest. He wore camo fatigues and a black beret, held the AK-47, now aimed at the sky, against his cheek.

"That was a fucking bullet," I said pointlessly.

"You're fine. Gun control means being able to hit your target."

I spread my arms and threw up a smile just as wide, the way you'd handle a guard dog.

"Regular army?"

"I'm just a citizen," Sonny Boyers said. "Like you."

I looked flat fucked out, he thought. I should come back to camp, meet his family, share some lunch. Why disagree? He resembled, with his shiny black boots and oiled rifle, a break-neck mercenary, but moved with the diffidence of an art student, and I followed along. He fired into the air as we approached the camp, and an answering shot came.

Dawn Boyers was glaringly blonde, round-faced, heavy-breasted. A sly, burly couple they made, two escapees from a beer stein bas relief. She wore the same dappled fatigues, but a blue chiffon scarf girdled her solid neck and lumpy turquoise earrings hung like beetles from her ears. The two silent, unboyish boys stood on either side of her, grade-school sentries with recalcitrant eyes.

"One for all," and Sonny combined wink and smile without completing the motto.

How to fit in? Yucca stalks, erosion, hard perimeters, children in combat regalia. The only reassuring thing was their truck. It had wide tires, hydraulic suspension, and probably enough juice under the hood to pull my car free.

The boys started the fire with a bow drill and blackened hot dogs at the end of forked sticks. Lemonade was yellow powder shaken with water in a plastic jug. Portions were carefully equalized and Dawn said grace.

"Make blessed what we are about to consume. Help us in our struggles to reach strength, but guide us, too, in the path of your safekeeping. In Jesus' name. Amen."

The reverent commando family ate with eyes downcast, in silence, chewing warily as if alert for broken glass. How to fit in? I understood that I was among people quelled by belief, for whom irony was no base metal. They saw clearly. They moved along an unwavering white line. I had only to ask a stupid question or two and the precepts were delivered, all glossy and round, like nuggets from the transparent globe of a Kiwanis gumball machine.

Societal collapse was imminent through war, revolution, economic disintegration, natural catastrophe, whatever came first.

"I don't know when it's going to happen," Sonny admitted.

"Noah didn't know exactly when the flood would come. He just knew it would."

A family prepared could renew and rebuild. The boys had been taken from school so they could be properly taught in the home. All worked together toward the goal of a self-sufficient unit. Knowledge was the tool that couldn't be stolen: herbal first aid, knots and lashings, shelter construction, orientation by sun and stars, firearms training, tracking and reconnaissance.

"Survivalism is misunderstood," Dawn squeaked like a cork twisting in a bottle. "We aren't paranoid and we aren't bloodthirsty. We just want to live."

The boys plinked cans with their .22's. Sonny didn't mind pulling my car free, but first he wanted to show me how to draw water from cactus pulp and set deadfall traps for lizards.

"You might not be so lucky next time," he said. "To have somebody come along like I did."

Sunburn bloomed on my forehead. I thought of a family trip to the Adirondacks. My mother sprained her ankle sweeping out the cabin. My father went under some birches with Dubonnet and a canvas chair and read through the works of Charles Evans Hughes. Carla sat for hours by the lake, afraid to go in because of sharp rocks and leeches.

Velma, in the black acetate waitress outfit Opatowski asks her not to wear, freshens my coffee. She looks dubiously at Sonny and his tape machine.

"What we're talking about are plans for the conquest of this planet," he says. "While they're promoting this détente business with one hand, they're stockpiling warheads with the other."

"The Russians then?"

"Who's predicting? I just say study the evidence, the patterns. The inevitable . . . Okay, like a big curl of a wave coming in and it's casting a shadow on the beach. We're right now standing in that shadow."

"You want high, swift drama. Glorious climax. But I'd bet on something much slower, degenerative."

"What, you mean like cancer?"

This is like the time Sonny told me you could make an emergency radiation suit out of plastic trash bags and duct tape. He can be as literal as a chunk of laterite.

"Entropy. The second law of thermodynamics."

"Stick to the facts," Sonny says irritably. "Anyhow, time's coming when there won't be any laws."

Velma says, "You got music tapes for that thing?"

"There's some Johnny Paycheck out in the truck. Some Allman Brothers."

I say, "Sonny, it's real simple. People don't want to hear bad news."

Velma says, "Just put the damn music on."

I was ten years old when I saw Khrushchev on the Saw Mill River Parkway. My mother was driving me to camp, where I didn't want to be, when the pace of traffic slowed abruptly. I hoped for a flaming crack-up, something to turn us back. Cars pulling onto the grass verge, people aligning; we joined up. A woman in tennis whites told us who we were waiting for.

"How theatrical," my mother said, her ultimate accolade.

We all waited in cruel, quiet sun for the godless tubby who'd promised to bury us. A million happy families turned to landfill. The motorcade roared into view; we screamed, jumped, waved, and it was already gone. But I'd seen Khrushchev, a pale split-second smear inside the black car.

I see him now on my screen, horse teeth and rumpled suit,

stale piroshki easily imaginable on his breath. Quaint postures of 1959, the American National Exhibit in Moscow, the Great Kitchen Debate. Nixon, with his sturgeon eyes, talking up a Washday Whiteners Gap, an Electric Can Opener Gap, reminding the man who gaveled the UN with his shoe how many work-hours it takes the average Ivan to buy a pair of his own.

Or something. I'm running the clip without sound, fascinated by the Supreme Soviet face, that touching, hog-farmer gramps face all round and warty, the nose a prize root vegetable, the skull shiny as ice in a washbasin.

I remember my mother saying, "He could be such a star. Like Red Skelton."

I remember her mysterious tears when she left me at camp, the smell of perfume spilled in her handbag, the ideology of withdrawal that saw me through the summer.

"Coming?" Ellen atwitter with notepad and reading glasses.

"Nice hair. What'd you do?"

"Slept on it wet. Come on or we'll be late."

She's still new here, still worries about demerits. We chase up to the West Tunnel conference room, but nothing much is going on. Familiar faces browse over platters of sliced fruit. Familiar turns of phrase: "Another strategic fallback." "He's a razor blade in the waffle batter." "Pissing up my back, telling me it's rain." "More proof that galaxies are moving outward."

Ellen gazes in dismay at her black pumps, like broken glass on the rug amid all the bright nylon recreation shoes. She takes my hand in her cold one and flattens the edges of her mouth.

"I need to slow down."

A grimacing brunette slinks by with handouts and it's clear from the title page that we're in for a slow afternoon—The Framed Cognitive Model: A Metastrategy for Systems Performance. Ideology drifting, ubiquitous as soot.

We look for seats in the back, end up next to Foley.

"Behold the jewel in the lotus."

Foley, the ruined newsman, the idealist deformed by dreams of conspiracy, once a public relations man in Haiti, now sending alimony checks to a nurse in Oklahoma. He wants you to think he's older than he really is, wants you to ask what the hell he's doing here so he can say, "Well, it's better than writing for the airline magazines."

"Behold."

He shows Ellen the overhead autocam that records all meetings. She tries unsuccessfully to reflect mischief into his grave eyes.

A rustling as of choir robes. Mounting the lectern is our Section Director, the gray and immutable Dr. George Borrow. He semaphores his tufty eyebrows, smooths his text. The autocam beams down.

"Our Framed Cognitive Model is a self-refining road map for organizational development with applications that entail both enhancement and modification of core options usage. Shifting complexities must be charted and triaged, thereby clearing the path for a truly expansive . . ."

I scan appropriate, still faces around the room. Wrapped in attention. Foley conducts self-palmistry, staring down into open hands. Ellen writes the same sentence again and again on her notepad: *I will not exert my intelligence.* Her thick fingers surround the pen like tentacles, her thickness everywhere a sign of bravery. I admire her nihilism, its vitality. But here she is, like me a moving part, and neither one of us with the dangling logic of Foley at his tether end.

The hunger injected into this room is for purity and control. Abide and conquer, a pride of arrogance. Arguably, my desires are just as cold, areas of the heart selectively deadened as in a procedure to correct arrhythmia. I detail myself as the accommodator, the soft self watching its every motion, and Ellen shames me with her strength of dread. But aren't things more difficult for her? More sapping? I will not exert my intelligence.

It's late when I get back to #6 and I've had too much alcohol for what I find there: socks and underwear washed and hanging from the shower rod, roadside flowers by the bed, red lip imprints on the mirror where her note is taped.

Maybe the joke's on me, but decided to pretend today was Valentine's. Took a soak in your tub, pictured you on the other side of the door getting ready to take me out. So tonight on your new sheets you'll maybe dream of me?

I love you—
Heidi

I love you, that useless incantation; the thing she's never said before, not even while coming. And Heidi signed with two hearts to dot the *i*'s. So full of impulses, this unfair maid. ("You let me be aggressive," she says with gratitude.) Ambushing me unfairly at the edge of this unpleasantly thickened night. Shifting complexities. Right.

I avoid the bed, pulling from the swamp of books Diane Di Prima's *Revolutionary Letters,* full of words that sizzle, of defiance I wish I still could summon. Much as I need distance, distraction, the type bleeds away off the end of the page and I get up to pace the room, which, I suppose, in our mimicked domesticity, is as much Heidi's as it is mine. Striated, intricate as fingerprints, her careful kisses on the mirror form an ideology of their own. It hovers, a cloud, appealing for belief.

I unmake the bed she's made, settle onto new sheets the color of pistachio ice cream. I undress myself in darkness with her sharp, impatient hands. My eyes travel to Heidi motionless and white under the trellised roses of sheet music. I can dream of her if I can do no more.

Heidi's mother knew her parents from pictures. She was two when they dropped her off at Grandma's, said they were going to the races in Wheeling for a couple of days. The sole trace of them after that came six summers later from an uncle who thought he'd seen them boarding the Lake Erie ferry. So she grew up in the brick house across from the Lutheran church with a woman who was easy to fool and too old to care.

Heidi's mother never was pretty, but she knew how to be popular. She wore tight sweaters and high heels that made her toes blister. She taught herself to play bumper pool, and Patsy Cline songs on the guitar. In Zanesville in the 1950's you could make a name for yourself without giving it all up. Men stocked her grandma's freezer with game. They let her tell lies and drive their cars. One night she knocked someone down outside a roadhouse called Pogo's Hi-Life and kept going. When the cops came for the apprentice barber whose name was on the registration, he went quietly. That's how popular she was.

And, predictably, the first man she fell for, a teetotaler nearly twice her age at thirty-six, had her bedded and wedded in a matter of weeks. She called him Popeye because of his forearms, and he called her all sorts of things, but only in a whisper. They bought everything on time.

Heidi was supposed to have been a spring child, but came prematurely. A week's weight of ice took the lines down and the incubator she was in had to be powered by a backup generator. Finally they brought her home and were frightened; the baby didn't cry, would not even blink. Heidi's mother doted happily until speech came to steal her little pet and leave her feeling swindled. Heidi's father worked for a coal company. He went to look at mines in West Virginia and Kentucky, sometimes for a few weeks. Further swindle. There was much "us girls" talk around the house, but it didn't seem to help. The bits Heidi's mother read from the paper were about women abandoned or molested or beaten. She would curl up her mouth and nod, as if to say, "Your future. Get used to it."

Heidi wore T-shirts and high-tops, chopped her hair short with blunt scissors, burned caterpillars. Her father was bewildered, but saw this was his only chance. He bought a football and tossed it to her in the concrete alleyway that separated the garages from the kitchen doors. So skinny her hipbones were like little holsters, but she could throw three garages. And they'd see her mother coming through the dusk from work in her stiff aqua uniform, coming home just long enough to change out of it and then float off, never a word, toward the taverns.

Heidi wriggles, sighs, continuing to pull me down the damp aisle between her buttocks.

"I always remember that slow nod of hers when something bad would happen. Like she got some perverse enjoyment out of it. 'Another pound of flesh.' So was she wrong? Drowned in an ambulance, just barely thirty-two."

I breathe into the taut nape of her neck, sink further into the amorous mist amid which I have received this family history. Heidi sighs again, relaxes everything but her grip on me. I suppose the exposition, her release of it, is meant to represent some new increment between us.

"Once more, love. Let me."

"We came out of the high country," I begin. "Tall timber."

Squabble noises intrude, child whines and thunking car doors, a tourist family working out a history of their own. An out-of-state station wagon . . .

"I'm listening. Go on."

Hands that have scrubbed a hundred miles of bathroom tile, exactly right.

"My one grandfather owned a planing mill and the other one built boats. Rugged capital. Hymns. They both died in nursing homes, not remembering a thing. My dad went to England to study, except the war happened and he had to come back. They said astronomy, okay, you must be good at maps, put him in some underground Washington war room where he pushed little plastic battleships around like a croupier. He heard my mom singing on the radio and went AWOL to follow the band. . . . Hey. Watch your nails."

Heidi says to keep talking. Her face is hot and fever-dry when I touch it, her eyes trying to penetrate my viscera.

"They had a restaurant the New York newspapermen came to. There was a picture of my sixth birthday party in the *Daily News*. We lived in a duplex on top of the restaurant and there was a roof garden where my dad kept his telescopes. . . ."

A skinny trunk chafed expectantly numb but rumbling in its liquid roots, her fingers telescoping, digging sweetly there. I can't get out the words—my mother at the Village Vanguard, my sister with hemophilia. Heidi grunts encouragingly, circling my prostate, and curls above, an alarming little gymnast breaking compulsory form. I reach for Carla, bathed in teardrops of blood like a saint, and Heidi descends to catch my trembling shot against her stomach. A perfect ten.

Mist now a low canopy of fog, we roll apart. She takes one of my cigarettes and plays with it unlit. I still can't get any words out, my heart an oversized lump and my head slowing its spin, wobbling like a juggler's plate at the end of a stick. Heidi, who dislikes aftermaths, must immediately fill them, begins to talk about her daughter—Tasha on her tricycle, Tasha's first long-distance call. Aftermaths reassure me, and so, her hand stroking mine, her words drifting into fog, I go protectively to sleep.

I dream of Heidi serving me grape soda in a deserted luncheonette. Bandages thickening her hands are stained with an aqua bactericide that matches her dress. She lines glasses on the counter, refusing to talk. The glasses are slick and slippery, but I must empty every one. This is important.

I wake up alone, at night. I have coffee and aspirin for dinner, realizing it is time to satisfy a certain curiosity—if curiosity is really the word. And is lying the real word for the spinrack plot of astronomy and big bands which I gave her?

I climb back into my clothes without washing, into my car without misgiving. The night is moist and warm, a culture medium. I pass adobe remnants, angry dogs, a pancake house, a heavy-equipment yard. The road is empty under sodium lamps. I turn right into the housing tract that went up at the same time as Cherry Ames Hospital, park two houses down and walk back, forlornly toeing the patchy brown lawn as if it were my own.

Kitchen curtains are parted, the window set so low I need to bend my knees. A pretty child, hair tied back in a bow of purple yarn. She gnaws a carrot, looking coyly at her father, who leans against the checkered countertop, naked to the waist. His torso is well defined, still beaded here and there with bathwater. The child slides into his hip and he swings his arm thoughtlessly around her. Eyes lowered, he says something to his wife that is sheepish or apologetic.

It seems from this angle as if Heidi is looking right at me, her one hand stirring something in a crockpot while the other comes slowly up to rest on the naked chest. Her child moves the carrot up and down like a distressed airplane. Her husband plants a kiss on the air and bumps it to her with a motion of his chin. Heidi tastes, smiles, stirs.

In the closeness of the car I discover her smell on me, an aftermath that spirals inside like a worm. I drive slowly, fingers barely touching the wheel. I pass dental offices, a drive-thru bank, unmoving horses in a pen, lobes of rock, depthless shadow. The road is empty under dim, anonymous stars.

With my little electric stylus, I etch data codes on the emulsion side of leader tape. I am transferring kinescopes to half-inch cassettes using the latest digital equipment. Riffle through the punch cards, prepare Storage Clearance. Enhancement filters clean the wobble and grit out of the old pictures. Philco TV Playhouse #26-A w/spots & ID, and the ingenue's teeth are as even and white as tombstones in Arlington National Cemetery. Drudge work. Maintenance. I don't pretend this is craft, like some cellular operators down here who give themselves dignity the way a street creep hypes morphine.

As, in my mail slot today:

> The use of computers in archival management is the topic of a program entitled "Computer-Aided Archival Management," to be held from the 8th to the 11th of this month at the Institute for Advanced Archival Management in San Diego. The program will focus on the uses for computers in the management of archives. Anyone interested in attending should please . . .

"Is your headache as bad as mine?"

Ellen has stalked in from next door, her face the usual tense puzzle. She has on one of her dress-for-success outfits, wet horseshoes under the arms of the high-collared blouse.

I pull open a desk drawer, turn back to my scanning.

"Codeine?"

"Help yourself."

She gulps three capsules without water.

"Why don't you take the rest of the day off?"

Swollen with air, her cheeks gradually deflate. She counts her top teeth with her tongue.

"You think my head stops hurting at home?"

Ellen lives in the city in one of the company housing towers, the one called Coral Tree. She travels to and from on the company's electric buses. It isn't that she lacks a sense of humor, only that in her perverse tropism she turns inevitably toward what is blackest.

Once, with her morbidness tented over me, I gave Ellen a perfectly ripe papaya and said, "Hey, cheer up."

She said, "No, thanks," and handed it right back.

Things not explained I can sometimes obtain by osmosis; her movements through a city with 4.3 rapes reported daily, of mariachi bands at the airport and renowned sunsets, where a cylindrical glass hotel shimmers in hundred-degree heat and tar paper flaps on abandoned dream homes three years old. An ocean has been manufactured on flatland dotted with cactus—a semicircular reservoir there, a hydraulic mechanism that goes off like a cannon every forty seconds, crowds who come to ride the artificial surf on their fiberglassed boards. Only the sand beach is real. Ellen goes there to pick up women and I can see her cool, oblique approach, sunglasses retracted into tangled hair, smoke rings casually blown.

I was working late on a news assay. Some globalcorp planning a court case wanted a review of its coverage over the last five years and I'd been a dozen hours or more with the talking heads, dubbing pieces off for the transcript, footnoting as I went. The preliminary work had to be in by morning, but my eyes kept fluttering shut. Enough of tariff barriers and assembly line robotics. Even when I cut all dials to zero, patches of noise kept in-and-outing like radio signals on a stormy night. Fuck this company and that, I was going back to #6 and have some sleep.

But a smoky slant of light stopped me in the hall. It came from the slightly open door of the work cell next to mine, un-occupied for weeks since that Stanford boy poisoned himself with sopors. I stepped closer, peered in. She was small but heavy, and occupied the dark space decisively. A black-and-white scene of dismal resolution, as turbidly underlit as the tapes of a police undercover operation, played silently on the console in front of her. Restless movements, a covey of them, in no way diluted the calcium hardness of her attention. I edged even closer and aimed my beaten eyes.

A girl's room, scalloped curtains and stuffed animals, the girl sitting on a white canopy bed. She is wearing a loose cotton nightgown. Brushing her hair, she looks into the camera and smiles. Makeup tubes and pots scattered beside her on the bed. She pinches baby fat under her chin, files her nails, swabs her face with alcohol-soaked cotton, squirts white cream into a little round palm, upraised. She smiles again and lifts her nightgown. All the time she looks into the camera, thin mouth rapidly moving, though it is obvious that she's talking, perhaps singing, to herself; all the time that her sticky white fingers are rippling between hairless lips, sliding back and forth in her rectum.

I was certain, from the moment she entered the frame, that the low-slung woman in the baggy T-shirt was the same one wrapped in cigarette smoke, sitting with her back to me. On screen, the girl's narrow body disappeared under hers and narrow ankles crossed over her back.

"Touch me and I'll chew up your eyes," the decisively placed woman said to me without turning around.

I felt invasive, excited, afraid. I thought of something to say, but what came out was: "I work next door."

She stood and faced me then, cigarette straight and firm in the corner of a wanly smiling mouth. Her lids were heavy and her hands were down in her pockets as far as they would go, knuckles moving up and down like valves against the denim.

"You look like a real practiced point-shaver to me."

"Your secret's safe, don't worry."

"There's no secret. I don't like men."

"Me either."

"That's not how I mean it."

"Me either."

She turned away again, staring at images which I saw now as an abstract shadow play on her tilted face. "And I suppose"—she gave way a little, leaning her weight against the counter edge—"I suppose voyeurism comes with this job."

Anyway, I worry about her. Three codeine on an empty stomach, no telling what lines she may have crossed. I'm parked by the antenna field, waiting. The sun descends and wind hums across the guy wires. Buses cluster and I look for my friend at the back of the alphabetical loading line. Could she have passed out? Cracked her head on a sink or something? Then I see her drift around the corner. A security man has her arm, but he's only supporting her, guiding her along. She boards the last bus, takes a seat in the rear. Her head sags and the hive of tight black curls is squashed against the glass. I wait for the bus to pull out. It's almost dark. Ellen sleeps with mouth open, reading lights burning all around her.

"Oh, go on and look," my mother said, pulling me across her lap. "You've never seen the ocean from up here."

Visible through the TV-shaped plastic window was a green swatch dappled here and there with white.

"Can you see the ship? That tiny thing?"

"Mmm-hmm."

I returned to *A Study in Scarlet* and my hoarded packets of airline cashews. Across the aisle, my sister hissed her exasperation. She was teaching herself to knit. Like me, Carla viewed this Florida vacation as an ordeal, a decree in the guise of a gift. Very recently, in humiliation rather than triumph, she had donned her first brassiere.

We'd never met Mother's "dear Cordelia," widowed by a faulty outboard motor, or the twins we would be expected to make friends with. All we knew was that they lived in Vero Beach, had their own tennis court, and never ate meat.

"If this is such a neat trip, then why is Daddy staying home?"

Carla had an unerring instinct for the conversation-stopper.

All we knew was that Gordo had been sleeping at his office a lot and had come upstairs as we were packing to present us each, amid motions of great secrecy, with a salami.

"You'll need to keep your strength up."

Florida, my mother informed me as we taxied to the terminal gate, was unique in all America. All I knew was that the Dodgers held spring training in Vero Beach and that alligators were known to slip by night into backyard swimming pools.

Cordelia Bontempi was blind in one eye, which to an eleven-year-old was the most interesting thing about her. Tim and Dan, the twins, had bad teeth, white-blond hair, and all the latest toys. They were eight and consequently of no interest whatever. Eggplant fingers were dispensed as treats and the wooden wall around the swimming pool was too high for an alligator to climb.

"Ten whole days," Carla moaned that night. "I may just die."

She had come to my small room from hers across the hall and, unwilling to sit, paddled around the end of my bed in flannel pajamas she'd outgrown. Her fledgling cones had never been pointier.

"You know there's not a TV anywhere," I said incredulously. "Those two little saladheads aren't allowed."

"Oh, God." Carla gripped the sides of her head as if steel balls were clacking inside. "Why can't Momma ever have friends who are just regular?"

"Let's eat salami," I said.

I slept poorly that night, thinking of my sister's cones and how salami grease had made her mouth so shiny. I knew we couldn't be real friends anymore and it scared me.

"Why don't you show them your racing dive," my mother said, pulling me across the flagstones to where the twins were scraping paint off little metal trucks.

She wore a loose shirt patterned with red and yellow flowers. Well out away from her, like something that might claw or bite, she held a frosty glass.

"Don't be such a mope," she said impatiently.

In I dove, surfacing at the shallow end with a victorious grin though chlorine burned my eyes and I had water up my nose. The twins waved excitedly, my mother pressed frosty glass to face, and Carla, awkwardly hunched in a narrowing strip of shade, her new bathing suit out of sight behind a quilted robe and a copy of *Mademoiselle,* said, "Your watch, stupid."

Condensation had already started beneath the crystal of my little man's Timex.

This, along with Mother's fainting over lunch (zucchini fritters) an hour or two later, more or less set the tone for the rest of our tropical sojourn.

"Now I know why Daddy stayed home," Carla observed as we nibbled cold hot dogs outside the examining room where an intern was removing the treble hook that had lodged in Dan's cheek during the climactic minutes of our deep-sea fishing trip aboard the *Tina Marie III.*

"Maybe it'll leave a hole," I said, really far more interested in clear tears dripping from Cordelia's milky eye and onto my mother's sunburned neck.

"Great." Carla twisted her lips. "He can blow baked beans out the side of his face."

My sister's hormonal shift rendered her mordant and sharp rather than nervy and shy. This would hold true for some time to come, and, as now, would bring her grief. As now, over-hearing the remark, Mother came forward to swat Carla across the mouth, and not the behind, befitting her incipient woman-hood.

All of which left me the only dry-eyed passenger for the ride home.

So it wasn't much of a pleasure trip. A field trip, then? A re-search project? That "unique in all America" line had a dis-tinct textbook flavor. Wasn't Mother always pointing, naming trees and flowers? It seemed reasonable to suspect we'd been set up for one of those enriching experiences. Anyway, here came three days of uninterrupted rain, and what could we do but observe?

Steamy drizzle outside, puzzlingly overcast inside—the house was large enough to have its own weather. Long and heavy silences were forces to be overcome by the intrepid party. Of course, there were the usual trifles, things learned to be forgotten, like card tricks or the script to a Bozo the Clown record the twins refused to tire of. But there were more last-ing, more indistinct things as well: a flimsy feeling in the stag-ily cluttered rooms, the curiously intense behavior of the adults, conversing in pressured whispers behind half-closed doors. Most of all, there was stout, sighing, distant Cordelia with her childish braids and clumsy motion, the side-to-side uncertainty of someone on a pitching deck as here she came with more cocoa, another plate of pineapple rings. Small things required great effort from her. Sighing, she alluded to her exhausting responsibilities. What? There was a woman from the Virgin Islands to do her cleaning, a man in a pith hel-met who mowed and pruned and raked, even hosed down all the white statuary. Well, something was bullying her, threat-ening any minute to leave her in a clumsy heap on the ter-razzo floors. Was it grief? Five years—nearly half my life—had passed since the day Mr. Bontempi attempted to prime his Evinrude and fragmented into the sea.

Carla shrugged. "She drinks too much. So what?"

I went to my mother to confirm this observation, smelled

the gin in her grapefruit juice before I'd asked anything. Her face was slack, her eyes seemed very old, and it scared me. Not as much as my sister's developments, but enough. It was ten o'clock in the morning on the third day of rain.

By that evening the air had cleared, though a few drops still fell. I'd spent the afternoon in random observation, moving from room to room, a junior Sherlock, opening drawers and closets, reading things that were none of my business. Descending the stairs thoughtfully now, my head jammed with clues, I was confronted by a strange tableau: my mother snoring into the sofa, the twins inert among crayons, Carla, open-mouthed and held tightly in her own arms, fast asleep under an oil portrait of Mr. Bontempi, pensive in dark tweeds. Dire tactics! I suspected gas.

"The prodigal returns," Cordelia said, clumping toward me in her scarlet muumuu. "Seems we're the only ones left to enjoy the stars."

That was it. Cordelia had drugged the cocoa. But too late; she'd already grasped me ferociously by the hand, was tugging me onto the patio. We stood in the soft mist, on the wet bricks, and looked up. My hand grew numb in hers.

"Winking lights." She pulled me against her hip. "But don't let anyone tell you that your life is written out up there. That's rubbish, you hear?"

Yes yes, all right. Why was she shouting?

"My hand . . ."

"Misery may have your name on it, but you'll be the one to put it there. You and nobody else."

She let go of me to gesture bitterly at her looming home, and I took off. There wasn't any way of locking the door to my room, so I braced a chair under the doorknob as I'd seen people on television do. Sleep would have to wait. I stood at the window and looked out over statues glowing thinly in the dark.

Next day we visited a chimpanzee attraction down the coast, where someone let the air out of our tires. Cordelia, dutiful hostess, left her Fleetwood in the parking lot and took us home in a cab. This necessitated borrowing her gardener's car the following morning so she could take Dan in to have his stitches removed.

Not until our last full day did we make our first visit to the beach, a private beach, part of some club Cordelia belonged to. Waiters came with cork-lined trays when you got thirsty and the glasses, half-filled with ice, were drippy and slick. The members looked well-dressed in nothing but swimwear; they glistened and smelled of cocoa butter. My mother wore khaki pants and shirt, sunglasses, and a canvas hat that appeared to be melting—a redundant costume in the shade of a wide green umbrella, but, like the headache and the absorbing German novel, it went with her sulk. She dreaded returning to New York and was making no secret of it. With all this, though, as was so often the case, she gained a cool serenity. She was indifferent to the complaints of her children, as she should more often have been.

I think it was out of frustration at this that Carla put on lipstick, slipped off her robe, and placed herself, hands on narrow hips, at the edge of the water. Her suit was as red as the lipstick and her skin was as white as the clouds.

"What a picture," Cordelia said rather sadly.

"Hmmm?" My mother peered momentarily over the top of her book.

Carla pulled the barrettes from her hair, corkscrewed her toes in wet sand. The screaming of children and the screaming of gulls combined with canned music that drifted out of the snack bar. I didn't know what I felt as I watched her, but whatever it was called was pulling me tight.

The boy who spoke to her was slightly older and much taller. He had a deep scar on his leg and a Dodgers jacket which he kept zipping and unzipping.

"She's fine," my mother said when I reported that they'd walked off out of sight.

"A protective brother," Cordelia sighed. "I wish I'd had one."

What was with these two? They huddled in the shade, one staring at a book, the other at her bulbous freckled knees, both of them dully immune behind their plastic lenses to the shiny pleasure all around. I saw women sprawled in white chairs, women oiling themselves and being oiled, tugging at their bikini tops and laughing hard enough to spill their drinks, but my sister was nowhere among them. I remembered reading in her diary on my rainy Sherlock expedition.

"What bothers me most," she had written in her jagged cursive hand, "is that all this being afraid will keep on and get bigger."

When Carla got back, spraying sand as she pounced into our shade, she was wearing the Dodgers jacket. Her mother reached over without looking away from the heavy book and lightly stroked her face. Cordelia began to pack away the unused towels and tanning creams. I poked my sister in the stomach, looked hard at her. She just laughed and wiped the lipstick off on the cuff of her new jacket.

I had one more observation to make. It came later on that day, during a lull brought on by humidity and imminent departure, and like almost any observation, it was avoidable.

"Go see what your sister is up to."

I slowly climbed the stairs, my hand slippery on the banister. Silence was thick as the air and a strip of fading sunlight lay like a gangplank on the hallway floor. Carla wasn't in her room, but a smudge of red registered in the corner of my eye as I passed the entrance to the skylighted bedroom where our mother had been sleeping. Carla, in her bathing suit, took on poses before a cheval glass. She balanced on one leg like a ballerina, bent down like a shortstop. I began to applaud her but managed to brake my hands. She was peeling the suit down to her waist and, with a soft, investigatory expression, touching her little breasts.

"Leave her alone," my mother said, pulling me across the aisle of the plane and away from her daughter's knitting, which I had been attempting to pull apart. "What's gotten into you?"

"Nothing, Ma."

Into me for sure, pulling me tight. And horribly now, I had a pretty good idea of what it was called. I could have told her.

It was August and the girls were barefoot, awkward and uncertain in their shorts and sleeveless tops. I was ten years old and peering out at them from an upstairs window. Though a breeze stirred the curtains, which crackled pleasantly against my face, the room was stuffy and hot. I itched inside my clothes. Their laughter was sharp and their faces were pink with excitement. I wanted to barrage them with water bombs, but didn't.

The grownups were away for the day at a wedding. A paving contractor Gordo knew professionally was marrying his chauffeur's niece at a country club in Massapequa. Carla had been left in charge of the house. She called up her three best friends the moment the car cleared the driveway and said come on over. She then coldly and quietly informed me that if I was the least bit bratty or tried to embarrass her, she'd lock me up in the laundry room without so much as a comic book.

The secret rites of girls. They'd brought a phonograph out on the deck with extension cords and played the same record over and over. They danced expertly with each other, teased and stretched, tried on hairstyles. They yakked about dreamboat Dick Chamberlain, Dr. Kildare in his white bucks. And my sister yakked the loudest, tried hardest to make the others laugh, sprayed herself with root beer. She had grass stains on her knees and her eyes were big and wild.

How crushing was my disappointment. I thought: This is how she really is. The distant, placidly scornful Carla that I knew was nothing but a fake. All the cunning strengths I'd imagined her to have were lies. She probably couldn't even beat me up; I'd test her soon. Here I could see her true form: a gumdrop. An empty-headed blabbermouth.

The record began again. "Cupid, draw back your bow / And let your arrow go / Straight to my lover's heart for me." The aromas of bubble gum and hair spray reached me in my high window. I pretended I had x-ray vision and could see through their clothes.

It was January and the sidewalks had been salted. I was twenty-three years old and working part-time in a florist shop. Though I had friends who didn't mind paying for my drinks, I had lately been keeping to myself. I was fractious and horny. I wanted to break away from my circular thoughts, but could not.

The phone wouldn't stop ringing, so finally I picked it up and there was Carla on the other end. She was down from grad school, shacked up with a biology instructor at the Americana Hotel, and insistent that I have dinner with them that night. It had been six or seven months since I had seen her last and we'd ended that evening arguing bitterly over trivialities. But I was curious about the man she was with and very hungry, so I agreed to meet them at an Italian place in the west thirties.

"Don't be too hard on Ted," she urged. "He's jittery enough."

"Mr. Charm," I promised. "I'll ask him to tell me all about cell division."

Il Grifone was jammed. I pushed past the nurses and policemen who were three deep at the bar, skirted the chicken-wire-enclosed boccie court that thrust through the middle of the dining area, and found Carla and Ted at a back booth, already tucking into a platter of clams oreganata.

Carla was as beautiful as I had ever seen her, gleaming in silk and tweed, lips glossed, unequivocally in command. Naturally, this did nothing at all for my attitude toward Ted, who came up out of his seat to gladhand the younger brother. His eyes made importunate contact. His hair looked to be just now lengthening into Prince Valiant fashionability. He made me think of a turbine salesman who paints seascapes on the weekend.

"Anything you like," he said, handing me the wine list.

"We drove the whole way with a broken heater." Carla embraced herself momentarily. "I was all for grabbing a motel in Connecticut, but Ted convinced me to persevere and now I'm glad."

"Me also," I said. "I was thinking you'd scratched me off your list or something."

She pulled my head to her padded shoulder. "You bonehead. How could I do a thing like that?"

Carla released me. I pushed the hair out of my eyes. Ted righted the sugar bowl she'd upset.

"Since that's cleared up," he said, "let the revels begin."

The veal was somewhat dry, Carla rambled a bit about her doctoral research in Shaker architecture, and revelry was hardly the word. But it was jolly, by and large. Certainly Ted was not the stiff-necked drone my jealousy had cast him as, and the interest he showed me went beyond a weighed desire to cement his position with my sister. Carla, brazen with after-dinner brandies, sang the Canadian national anthem in a clear soprano that had the busboys applauding. Then, while Ted was off buying her cigarettes, she impaled me with intimacy, grasping my hand and pitching her words so low I was forced to lean close in order to make them out.

"It's Ted who's smitten, poor kid. I just wanted to get out of Boston for a few days. Not that I mind sleeping with him, but he gets so arduous over things. Makes me want to tromp on his feelings when he pushes them at me so much."

But I saw the way she nestled against him as they waited for a taxi, nodding raptly while he recited an anecdote about his travels in Surinam in pursuit of a noctilucent freshwater shrimp; and through condensation on the back window I watched her fingers lace around his neck as the taxi pulled away. Then I walked myself home, fifty-three miserable blocks.

The following night I returned from a card game thirty dollars poorer and found her straddling a suitcase in front of my door. She had a vivid bruise above one eye.

"Ted," she said, pointing to it.

As Carla summarized the incident, Ted had been unable to deliver on a promise of tickets to a sold-out musical, she'd made some remarks about boasts that couldn't be backed up, and, just that fast, he jumped his tracks. She appeared to be more repelled than angry or upset.

"He cried right afterwards. He said he'd never struck a woman in his life, but I've got him turned inside out, with all his nerves exposed. What nonsense."

"Good thing we're not Old World," I said. "Else I'd have to go looking for the bastard with a tire iron."

Carla said, "He wouldn't be hard to find." And then she asked would I mind unplugging my phone.

After that it was like we were kids again, only better. We watched terrible old movies on TV and ate peanut butter and red onion sandwiches. We told all the jokes we could think of and when Carla laughed I could look in and see every silver filling in her mouth. But it got later and we decelerated. Something had been settling on us all the while, like dust.

"Do you ever want to turn around and go backwards?"

I didn't quite know what she meant, but I said sure.

"Like you missed the turnoff somewhere and are getting more and more lost? It's that way for me about half the time. And Boston, the people around me all trying to be so hip and loose and ending up mostly just trying."

"Could be you're getting too old for school."

"Compared to what? Remember, I had two whole years to think about it and what did I do but go running on back. The institutional setting. And I haven't earned a single gripe, have I? So I'll get my degree and go to work for a museum or someplace where I can restrict myself to old things. Because I'll tell you, this new stuff is too goddamn flat for me."

I pictured her on a landing strip in the middle of Nebraska

with no trees anywhere around; and I could share the terror of a horizon that began at the edge of her shadow and never really stopped.

I said, "There's a Randolph Scott western on channel two." Where I wanted to give comfort, I could offer only distraction. And the bruise above her eye, now shading into a dismal range of purple-brown, was like a litmus gauge of her feelings.

"It's late and I really have to turn myself off," Carla said.

Persuading her to take the bedroom, I stretched out on the couch with a folded topcoat for a pillow. I didn't expect to sleep much anyway. I saw the strand of light under the bedroom door go out. I picked at dead skin on my lip and listened to the radiators knock. Herding my thoughts through the minefield of inadmissible love was no easier than it had ever been. I composed a fantasy of Carla and me living in a windmill. We had leaded windows and wooden utensils and a garden like a Brueghel painting. There were soft, forgiving contours as I dozed slowly off.

I came awake to the sound of running water. Carla emerged from the kitchen with a drinking glass and became in the blue cast of the streetlamp a character from a 1915 children's book. I pretended to sleep, my lids raised just enough to see. She had a man's white shirt on and her hair spilled over the collar in a way that made me dizzy. Pressing the glass against her swollen brow for a moment, she looked down at me with what I imagined to be tenderness. I would never know. She placed the glass on the floor next to me and went back to bed.

I did not sleep again until the sun was up, and briefly then. But Carla moved on in that time. Her note said she was taking an early train in order to catch a friend's on-campus dance recital. For breakfast I had a bowl of coffee ice cream. I dusted and mopped and rearranged the contents of the refrigerator. Finally I went in and sat on the bed. I noticed that it was snowing, had been for some time. There were pigeon footprints on the white sill. I would never know. Rolling onto my stomach, I inhaled what I could from the indented pillow.

The phone rang only minutes after I plugged it back in. It

was Ted. He sounded unhinged. He told me he'd been drinking all night, submerged in remorse and confusion.

"I don't understand what she does to me. It's unearthly. She's so steady. She's so impervious. How do I figure out what goes on inside her?"

I hung up on him. What he had to say I already knew.

This, somehow, is my fourth day off in a row and I feel listless, out of touch. Didn't I have more stamina when I was young? Wasn't it easier keeping the balls in the air? I head out for the Boyers place to say how's business, hoping something or other will chime.

They're in the garage, packing up orders—boot knives, freeze-dried stroganoff, like that. The slogan is stenciled on the wall: YOUR KEY TO SURVIVAL IS KNOWING WHAT THE DOOMED WILL NEVER LEARN. Last year Sonny went up to Denver for a three-week course in mail order merchandising.

"Where you been holed up?" he says.

Dawn turns her back, picks at a line of window putty.

"You know, the usual places."

She's wearing cracked mules and a coral housedress; her soft swaying bulk seems lethal. Sonny busies himself moistening strips of package tape on a gray sponge ball, and something strains against the seam of his mouth. It's awkward in here, thick with the poorly hidden anguish of a hospital waiting room. Always expecting bad news, these two. Maybe they've had some.

"So how're the boys?" I say clumsily.

Dawn sends a black look to her husband. "Off at Curry's on a sleepover."

Sonny, breathing hard, makes a wet weave of the tape.

"Clear them out to clear the air," she adds cryptically. Her tough, shiny hair is rumpled, like a doll's pulled from the bottom of a toy box. "Not like they done anything."

I notice the can of Mace fastened to Sonny's belt and I wonder about domestic strife with so much weaponry at hand. I study cobwebs, look at my watch.

"It's not any of their decision," Sonny says.

Dawn brushes past me. "Ain't anybody's."

Then, through gypsum board, we can hear her clanging and banging in the kitchen. The chalkboard is in there, the textbooks reinforced with masking tape, homemade stools where the boys sit to receive instruction from their mother—a little diorama of the pioneers.

Sonny drops onto a stack of sealed cartons; his lips contort. "They say if you give respect you're supposed to get it."

Things aren't chiming so much, but I'm curious, drawn in. Otherwise I'd make some sense, say, "Came at a bad time," and get moving. All these tools collected here, canteens and manuals, the hard details, convince me there's something to look for. I want to light a cigarette but I've left them in the car.

And now Sonny has on his bully pulpit face. He wants me to know that every American child will consume by the age of eighteen the energy equivalent of sixty thousand gallons of gasoline, that in a minute's time twenty-five babies are born for whom there are no protein resources.

"Dawn doesn't want to grow up." He shrugs. "I just don't get through to her."

"Why can't you meet in the middle?"

Smiling, Sonny confides that later in the week he is scheduled to enter Cherry Ames Hospital for a vasectomy.

"Dramatic," I say, but it isn't the word I want.

"I know, I know. My old man was alive, he'd say just chop

the damn thing off and be done with it. I come from five brothers and three sisters, fruitful. But that was then and this is now."

Suddenly I feel like a tired cop pressed by duty against the rancor of strangers. I really want that cigarette.

"And it's no more than what she wants for herself. She's got to grow up and face up."

He looks straight at me, his tight eyes asking me to take sides.

Trying to change the subject, I ask, "Still planning that extension off the back of the house?"

But for Sonny there is only one subject. "Crying for the space, God knows. All squeezed like we're in a toothpaste tube. Something to face up to is the plain and simple limits of where we're at. I'm not getting rich with this mess," slapping the cartons under him, hunching himself as if yoked, in traces. "Just to get us all through, all together. I'm no fucking swami."

The family man deflected by his family. He looks up, down, looks ahead, looks for an escape hatch. The only reassuring thing I can think of is it isn't me.

"Self-sufficient," I remind him. "You're keeping an edge."

He agrees reflexively and begins an aimless rummaging through the clutter of his family business. What the doomed will never learn. But it seems that Sonny, if only for the time being, has gone off the edge of his map. This comforts me; I feel less out of touch. And probably Sonny will regain his bearings in the clean, fresh, pastel symmetries of Cherry Ames, in the confidence of highly trained professionals and the irrevocable snip.

No daughters for Dawn. I see her sulking at the sink, molars clenched as she peels crust from a skillet. Her grudge will be immaculate and worth holding on to. Her back will be a broad wall in the bed, her face thick and curt in the long mornings.

I am expecting to be asked for dinner, and certain I will stay.

Son of a loan officer, debating team captain and cum laude grad, Tory essayist, figure man, braggart, moralist, fixer, my father goes through life with antennae fully extended, alert for the smallest threat and ever ready for battle. No grievance escapes notice, and no surly mechanic or slow-witted bank teller escapes imperial rebuke. He is a tireless author of letters to the editor, will hang on the phone an hour or more, waiting his turn to cross swords with a radio talk jockey.

Never, in any comradely way, have we been close, but at the time when such things still mattered, I did all I could to displease and disappoint him. We overlapped, then, as adversaries, like ink stains on an office blotter. His dictates and my flaunted heresies notched together, achieving an intimacy that we never could.

When Carla and I were still quite small, he began to organize us in dispute games, assigning pro and con roles on a current events topic or courtroom recreation. The winner was rewarded with a blue ribbon strip pinned on by the loser. Another learning experience was trying to mediate between him and our mother—in short, learning not to. Their harsh, spiraling set-tos were precious to them, the cream in their coffee, oddly but consistently comforting, and not to be intruded on. Later, having the eligible skills, Carla and I were allowed to come in and widen the war, sniping away at targets of opportunity until we, and usually mother too, were routed by Gordo.

His triumphant rages would immobilize the house. He'd bellow and stamp like some parodic Lear while we hid out in our rooms.

Carla pretends that he has softened in recent years, paled like his pearl-gray eyes. But I say once a bully, always a bully. She wrote me to describe his long afternoon walks, his enthusiasm for azaleas, the swaying of his liver-spotted hands over reference books as he composed another crossword puzzle.

"He's not as ashamed of retirement as I thought he'd be. True, they've kept him on some sort of oracular retainer. . . ."

No doubt. This is the man who finessed the Hotel Armonk case and quashed a governorship. Carla, gently wishful, veils the record of the past with her azaleas. But I remember the cruel mimic, the arm-twister, the scary drunk who grew more silent and impermeable as the level in the bottle fell, the unending smallness of this man who had his monogram faced in brick above the fireplace and once threw a close friend's toupee over a yacht railing in order to resolve a cribbage argument.

"I'm certain he's ready to reconcile," Carla went on. "If only you'll make the first move."

Dear, dimly available sister, it's already done. We are as reconciled as two sums in an accounting ledger.

I was living in L.A. the last time we spoke. Violet and I were separated but not yet divorced, and I was brimming over with aimless nostalgia. It was Easter Sunday and the Long Lines were overloaded with ritual calling.

"What's up, Dad? Are you dyeing eggs?"

"No."

"It's eighty degrees here and I can see palm trees from my window."

"Eggs, trees. I suppose you've got a couple of canaries with you."

The gaseous hush of vodka was in his voice.

"Just me, Dad. Me, myself, and I."

"Fine, fine. And what are you doing for money?"

"That's not why I called."

"All right then, surprise me."

I could see him looking at his watch, at his dull reflection in the black surface of the hall table.

"Actually, I was trying to remember which cheek your ski-pole scar is on. It's been that long."

"The Alps, my God. Now there's one sight I go right on seeing. Nothing on your horizon, is there? Movieland. All that stucco. Marquees and fruit juice stands instead of peaks."

"And not a crumb of snow."

"So then. You're still with that whatsername of yours?"

"Not right now."

He filled the space for judgmental militance with a slow question. "Shall I send a check?"

"That's not why I—"

"Yes, fair enough. You don't have to shout."

No, I really didn't have to. Finally.

"Your sister has invited me for holiday dinner," he went on blandly. "The wine will be corrosive and the lamb will be underdone. Some little barefoot friend of hers will ask me to dance."

"Give Carla my love."

We exchanged bad jokes, promised to send postcards, and that was it.

Definitive technique. Precise scrutiny. A conviction that nothing is missed. Certain group vanities are encouraged among the staff here, keeping foremost in mind that we register only as units in a system. A system, elementary in its perfection, to surround and contain a precise whole. And each movement within the system a refinement, a distillation. They want us comfortable in such beliefs, like mice in a warm winter burrow.

Do I contradict? I typify. Another nibbling mouse, a 2T five-year man sent down to this edit room dismal as a Bulgarian subway, on an errand that demonstrates the system's reach, the ability of its agents in the field to surround and contain. Their booty is now before me, racks and racks: the random tape inventory of a small independent station in west Texas, now, along with its owner, defunct. It had offered the sort of programming favored in trailer parks and residential hotels, old reruns and cut-rate movies, a world of black-and-white. It had offered a removal in time, an undoing of age and failure, something to still the guts. Cramped, retching feed clerks, the manicurists and windmill mechanics, muttering, smoking, sniffling, conjuring dust shapes from out of the furniture, were soothed by *Petticoat Junction* and *Mr. Ed.* In sepia Mexican melodramas, they found a past more favorable than their own. And now, under my hands, all would enter into the system, a minute flicker of refinement.

The tepid denouement of *Bachelor Father* unspools before me, a commercial extolling the spreadability of a peanut butter named for J. M. Barrie's androgyne. I reach for cold coffee and a fresh log sheet, am riven by a voice.

"Rich in emulsifiers," my mother says.

The last television appearance of her paltry career, a cosmetics spot. Immaculate, she moves dreamily at the edge of a formal garden.

"Treat yourself like royalty," my mother says.

On her pilgrimages into Manhattan, she usually had lunch with Sonia Brooks. They had both sung in the choir at Temple University, had both seen their young ambitions wither in the perpetual shade of a city too tall. Sonia would never get a seat on the stock exchange and my mother wasn't going to star in a prize-winning revival of *Anna Lucasta,* so they foraged for ethnic restaurants and obscure museums, drank in hotel bars and flirted hazardlessly with waiters.

Sonia's husband, a Scottish homosexual, ran an advertising agency named after himself. His client list included a hotel in the Poconos, a commuter airline, textile mills and medical supply houses, the tourist bureau of a blighted Caribbean island, and a brand-new product called Dewbeads.

"Made from goat placentas or something." Sonia tied a knot in her cocktail straw. "And this TV ad they're planning—I've seen the storyboard and all—it's perfect for you. Mature but handsome, a vision from the tennis court, like—"

"Too bad I don't work anymore," my mother said.

"Damn you." Sonia hissed like a sub-code steam line with drunken belligerence, her tipped Punt E Mes bleeding into the tablecloth. "Damn your reticence. Ian has an awful case of amoebic dysentery and he'll do anything I say. Do you want the thing or don't you?"

Rising at 4 a.m., breakfasting on vodka and grape juice, my mother was limousined to the location, an estate in Lyme, Connecticut, that had recently come under the aegis of the National Historic Trust.

The company man was distressed. "It's a fucking castle. It's intimidating," he said. "Okay, the look is nice, but we've got to move product."

"Exteriors only," said the director, a graduate of the Austrian State Film School. "No castle."

In the garden, union men in green jumpsuits sprayed blossoms with glycerin water while my mother circled a marble fountain and tried to remember her lines.

"You must be calm but underneath in flames," the director told her. "You await your lover here. You are wet between the legs in anticipation. In every movement of your body, we must read this sad history."

On the first take, she trembled so badly that the company man asked if she was on drugs. She took it too fast, too slow, missed marks. A light stand fell, a plane passed overhead. On the sixteenth take, she tripped on a flagstone and soiled her white dress.

"Better pull yourself together," the wardrobe lady cautioned. "They're really frantic out there."

My mother sobbed on a cot inside the little airless trailer. She considered making a break, heading off into the trees, but imagined them tracking her with dogs.

"Just pretend everyone else is like out on bail," said the wardrobe lady. "That's how I do it."

Outside, the sun was high, seemed to pulse. Unhappy with lighting conditions, the director worked himself into a tantrum, struck at a mike boom and ripped open his hand. The company man fled to phone New York.

"There was something about the sight of blood," she later told us. "It filled me with a sense of peace."

They wrapped on the twenty-first take and my mother passed out on the limo ride home, dreamed of Sonia selling shares in a Viennese blood bank.

The Dewbeads commercial aired for the first time on a network telecast of *Charade* with Audrey Hepburn, and we all circled the set to applaud.

"I've never seen you look so beautiful," Carla breathed, plucking her lip, smelling of bath talc.

"Convincing," judged Gordo, and filled his mouth with cashews.

I said: "Mom, this is what you need to get restarted."

"Mmm-hmm." She looked wistfully at the screen, where George Kennedy was swinging the shiny metal hook he had in place of a hand. "I even have new pictures to send out."

I no longer believe, as I did then, that she allowed herself any real expectations. And, in fact, nothing ever came of it, beyond a personal appearance at a shopping plaza in Valley Stream. Dewbeads, widely reported to cause skin rash, was eventually removed from the market by the Food and Drug Administration. Sonia Brooks went to live on a Moravian farm near Wilmington. The glossy eight-by-tens remained in a bedroom drawer, unsent.

I watch it over and over again. The tidy rows of zinnias and marigolds, boxwood and hemlock in topiary geometrics, sun glinting on the fountain's distant spray. In white, lovely as a stranger . . .

I am bound to her by chemical strands impossible to sever,

by an overwhelming, overriding instinct: avoidance of pain.
Damn our reticence. I've thought of her countless times in the
long years since her dive into the tube and never once missed
her, never once wanted to pull her back out. She is where she
belongs, and so am I. On opposite sides, each one, blinking
reflexively.

"Dewbeads," my mother says. "Because we deserve it."

Overtrimmed white houses with circular driveways. Lawns
clipped and edged, alike as burial plots. Two girls in pleated
skirts and kneesocks who rush excitedly toward an open convertible where lettermen slouch in wait.

The marine amoebae Formanifera exist inside calcite shells
and send out branched filaments in search of food. One million fibers make up the human optic nerve and mine are hard
at work, assembling this picture of an unlisted street, an in-
vented town.

That kind of day at the facility: imagining relationships that
aren't there, looking over my shoulder. Too much time underground and I suspect myself. Now here's Eduardo with the
mail cart and a smile that slides all over his face.

"Something personal."

He dangles the envelope and I see a jaggedly halved lipstick
heart on the flap. Violet, only Violet. A collector of the gestures
of romance.

"Going to read it out loud?"

"Not to you."

He tugs at his left ear, mangled by a highway patrol bullet. "You shouldn't be so stingy with Eduardo. Don't you know he's culturally deprived?"

The envelope is thick, addressed in the angular, pressured handwriting.

Darling—
This took courage to send, but I had some saved up, there being little call for it out here. The Virginia position I phoned about has evaporated . . . funding cuts as well as "personality differences." A juicy tale here, which you can only have in person. It's a round-trip ticket, as you can see. No traps. Last night I cried just from looking at a cake pan. I remember small things with you, and the smaller, the more trivial, the sharper the twinge. Please say you'll come. I'll bake unforgettable cakes.

Vee

Sharply pointed Vee, expert scene designer, quick-change artist, greatest fuck of my life. I never could keep up with your generous provocations, or the empty difficulties that came up just as fast. But when you had a grip on yourself, which, as I discovered, was just barely most of the time . . .

No traps, you say? Don't feed me that angel food. I can match you recall for recall: winding, with a tight focus anticipating the classroom, your German alarm clock sans numerals; that pertinent walk when you weren't really going anywhere, arms swinging close as if you were polishing yourself; exuberant eyes as your machine emerged from the car wash slick and glistening like a newborn; a low, two-syllable hum while I excavated by suction those rich salt deposits below the rim of your instep.

So on and on. Uninterrupted, uninterpreted. Letting images spill is the easy part, no distinctions made. But to look away, to say no when temptation is hard and sharp against your stomach like a spear, is connivance at its best. Anyway, something close to it.

There is no more call for courage where I am than where
you are, but the air is light and easily penetrated. I see things:
my narrowness, blundering capacity for harm, suspended appetite for the activities that make up a "life." Dear angular,
deeply clefted Vee, I am useless to you, a hard, rebuking vacancy like the silence after a thousand cake pans clatter.

Skirts and letter sweaters swirl in the flimsy-looking malt
shoppe, below the sign that says NO DANCING. Youthful high
spirits, Mr. Mayor. They're celebrating the big win over South
Central State. Lindyhopping fringe bit actors whose animat-
ing thoughts are of doing *Bus Stop* in an amphitheater, or an
unannounced, show-stopping Cohan medley at a benefit for
crippled children; who celebrate raw delusion with every
swirl.

So I look away, into the sure alignments of this airline
ticket. Depart. Arrive. Carrier assumes no responsibility for . . .

For ex-wives who, to be sure of anything, require regular
distress. And not enough the subterfuges of students or some
incident on the freeway. Violet needs the intimate, twisting
jabs of someone close. But her mother is too old and soft to
peck as she once did, her twist-expert sisters gone with their
ambitious husbands to Bahrain and Fort Worth, her usual
friends too feckless or too repressed. Why can't I comfort her?
Make the awful quiet go away? Because the speed and the
stamina are all gone. As James Brown used to croon, I'm tired
but I'm clean.

Here. I'm here, Violet, and that's all. I'm all packaged up
here, in my viewing booth, in my car, in an air-conditioned
unit that Heidi keeps straight for me. Yes, Violet, and it's so
easy to be with her in that cool, dark room. She's tense and
bony as a child. She's fitful and clammy and disorganized. And
when the mucus pours from between her legs, mouth around
her own frantic fingers, Heidi doesn't know who I am—or
care. Nothing asked or surrendered. Two creatures following
the dictates of their chromosomes.

That's right, sure. Smoke is just particulate matter in suspension. And the television picture is only a description of
light—light hitting a surface.

Mrs. O. must be feeling stronger. For the second Saturday in a row she's in among the flowerbeds with clippers and weeding claw. The sun is high and she wears a maroon-and-white baseball cap advertising electrolyte salts for livestock. Strap-on rubber pads protect her knees.

I'm here with my feet propped on the air conditioner, watching her through the window. A slow news day. My pet scorpion slumbers under pine bark, water drips from the showerhead, and all I see when I close my eyes is a plate of shredded lettuce floating in space. The old lady shames me. Come on, slick, get those corpuscles moving.

Into the heat, across the empty parking lot. I squat down slowly and dabble my fingers in the dirt, ask Mrs. O. if she could use some help.

"My biorhythms are very favorable today." She grins, a display of shoepeg teeth. "I like to get nice and dirty when I can."

"I could do the edging along here. I'm good at that."

"Sometimes, when I have to stay lying down, it's like forgetting who you are. . . . The size of him! Those worms mean good aeration, you know!"

The sun is like something prying at me, a sharp tool.

"Do you want your package now?"

"Now?"

"With the prettiest stamps all over. You'll see."

The stamps, from the American Reptile series, are avocado

green. Another book from Violet: *Tom Swift and His Photo Telephone*. A bold black box on the flyleaf in which the publisher promotes his whole line: "These spirited tales are impressed upon the memory and their reading is productive only of good."

Without explicit warning, Violet went to Mexico for a divorce. She took me out to dinner the next week, and, in the middle of a monologue on Toltec burial practices, handed over a teller's check for two thousand dollars.

"Your settlement," she said. "It would be more, but they rolled back my cost-of-living adjustment."

Eyes fixed on my mulligatawny soup, I said, "I'm a chiseler, Violet. I held out on you from the start."

"Relax, you earned it. Hazard pay."

I wasn't talking about money, and she knew that. But she was so prepared, so clipped in her attitude. I wanted to explain where the fault lines were, why I'd dodged away, what to avoid next time.

Violet pressed cool fingers over my mouth. "Send me a letter."

At eleven that night I boarded a Trailways Night Owl Express for Las Vegas. Crescent moon over the Shadow Mountains, high school lovers across the aisle. I smoked until my throat felt torn, surprised to discover so many regrets. At sunrise a wide woman with greasy blonde hair stepped into the toilet with a flight bag and came out dressed as a cowgirl.

Breakfast at the top of the Strip: silver dollar pancakes, keno numbers dropping out of the loudspeaker. The man on the seat next to me held a vibrating device to his throat in order to speak.

"Lost my wife," he said, sounding like a Martian. "Wouldn't mind 'cept she's got the car keys."

That seemed like my cue to get started. Nothing in the way, so run. I took my divorce money to the cage, came away bulging with chips, found an empty blackjack table where I could play multiple hands. Lorraine, the dealer, kept pulling four-

and five-card miracles and I was down six hundred before I could finish my first gratis cocktail. Nice.

I went up a brass escalator, into something called the Red Rooster Room, where dull-eyed union musicians played sleeve-garter jazz. I had some martinis and thought how grim industrialized pleasure could be. Right on schedule. I was lighting the filter ends of cigarettes and talking to myself, about to cross over into perilous nobody-seems-to-care territory. Blessed instinct led me back to the pack. I wobbled south past the Stardust and the Flamingo, where Bugsy Siegel started it all, from crap table to crap table, throwing away ten dollar chips on the field numbers, into and out of Romanesque bathrooms to confirm my hunted look in mirrors. Bells and bars and plums. I finally went broke, quarter by quarter, in a shiny corridor of slot machines, bellowing my relief until ejected by a black security guard.

Next thing, I was crouching by a fountain lit with blue lamps. Above me on fluted columns rose a huge sign announcing the week's headliners: SHIRLEY BASSEY and JACKIE GAYLE. I crouched and shivered and rubbed my red eyes. A car pulled up on its way to the street and the driver rolled his window down.

"It ain't deep enough to drown in."

I peered at his ruffled shirt, velvet bowtie hanging from the near half of its open collar like a festive little animal. I thought about our wedding chapel, Violet's and mine.

"Scene of the crime," I muttered.

"Take it to the pit boss, they'll usually come up with your bus fare home." He looked away from me to study his teeth in the side mirror, big wide teeth. "Okay, so get in, go ahead. I feel righteous tonight and you look harmless enough. Jesus, do you look harmless."

The name was Vic. He worked the lounge backed by a trio. Ballads and belt, special material written specially for him. He showed no curiosity about me, probably figuring he knew my story without having to listen to it. He drove carelessly, ignoring lights, to a mini-mall east of downtown and sent me to pick up his order from Joey's Jade Pagoda. Vic was in a hurry, still five sets to do.

"Drop you and the chow off with Addy, then I got to get in the wind."

Addy?

She was Vic's "baby" sister: pallid skin, heavy glasses, beer opener nose, and a quilted satin jacket that matched the spread on the enormous circular bed. She didn't want to shake hands with me for fear I might give her something.

"Bad kidneys, weak heart," Vic whispered as I began to unpack egg drop soup, steamed noodles, sweet-and-sour chicken wings.

Addy rolled her eyes and clucked impatiently for her dinner. I couldn't tell if the fumes made me ravenous or sick.

"Really, no fucking around," Vic said on his way out. "She keeps a gun under the pillow, and believe me, she'll use it."

It was past noon when I woke up on the floor near Addy's bed, face down in orange shag carpeting that smelled like baby powder. I heard television voices debating the international debt crisis, then Addy saying her toenails needed trimming.

I laid low with the Farbers for almost a month. It was one of those situations that seem to create themselves, a natural balancing out. Addy nourished herself with complaints and requests, I lost thought in the tasks, swam lap after lap in the pool, and Vic was free to disappear for days at a time.

I took Addy's temperature each morning, pretending it was other than normal. I squeezed grapefruit, administered cool cloths and tablets, massaged her spasmed muscles, read aloud to her from gothic novels. Addy liked to pout and sulk so I would coax her out of it.

"This just isn't worth it," she'd say, twisting into the pillows. "I shouldn't wake up anymore."

And why was I expending my compromised resources trying to persuade this willful, bone-white crank to take a walk in the sun? I suppose because that was the part in which I'd happened to be cast. Everything bright like the yellow grapefruit and the red marbleized countertops I sponged before and after each meal.

Vic came by to drop off grocery money. He looked fit and refreshed, tighter around the eyes. We stood on the little concrete condo balcony and watched a fat boy pour chemicals into the pool. It was dusk, warm and wistful.

"So how're you and Addy getting on? . . . Super, super." He ran his hands along the railing as if smoothing something out. "I guess you can see how much she needs someone. She can be hard to follow sometimes, but there's so damn much there."

The vehemence took me by surprise. He couldn't get out of there fast enough. But he was back at 3 a.m. with an Australian showgirl and a gram of coke. The freshness was gone from his face, his eyes droopy again. The girl was going to spend the weekend, he said. An old friend. She looked at me vaguely and cupped the crotch of her motorcycle pants.

On Saturday Addy threw a tantrum, sobbing and calling us all parasites, until a doctor arrived to give her a shot. Vic paid him in cash. A Panamanian knocked out a French Canadian in a televised welterweight bout. Addy slept. Vic and the girl emerged from the shower. Out on the balcony, they grilled salmon steaks and argued. Vic popped out to the liquor store. The girl came over to my sofa. She talked about convent school in Canberra while she masturbated me. Addy slept. Vic opened the Medoc and sang "Falling In Love With Love." I took four aspirin before curling up on the sofa.

Very early Sunday, the girl jostled me awake.

"This scene is too bloody sick," she said. "I think we should both get out of here."

There were warming sunspots on the backs of our heads as we headed west in her Trans Am. It was good to be moving again, even back the way I'd come. I started to talk some talk, feeling shrewd.

"Sister!" The girl clicked her tongue. "I can't believe you fell for that schtick. They've been married seventeen years."

Once, watching gulls wheel over the drilling rigs off Long Beach, I was told by a friend zealously colorless save for the ownership of an armadillo-skin guitar from Paraguay, a hawker of Spartacist magazines frequently shoved, occasionally decked, outside factory gates, that "All information is propaganda." As absorptive as any generalization, probably more useful than most. I have been put upon and overworked; my theoretics, in turn, have been overindulged, my brain peptides allowed to swash and roil, perhaps to overflow. My desk is littered with papers where blanks are to be filled and boxes checked while I blearily ponder such imponderables as: Connection between listening groups organized around radios in the street by market research pioneer J. Goebbels and coin-op TVs now ubiquitous in airports and bus depots across U.S.? I evoke my friends here now, the apparitional strumming of some coal miner's anthem on his armadillo guitar, and his warm bath of certainties. I hear him say: "Communications technology is a byproduct of empire, developing out of military/industrial operation. As simple as the acronyms. OSS. RCA. NASA. COMSAT."

Today, as I said, has been excessive, an overlapping of the tiresome and the inflammatory, a granular, unedited movie of unstable colors beginning with a two-car head-on barbecue half a mile from the facility entrance. Breakfast cereal arrived in my duodenum like bark chips. A lobby stooge who didn't look old enough to vote compelled me to pass through the metal detector. I received in the mail an academic paper titled "The Protestant Supernatural: *I Dream of Jeannie* and *My Favorite Martian*," and by phone a reprimand from a drone, who wouldn't give his name, for failing to undergo the biannually required medical exam.

And so to work, a mild trepidation, admittedly with some precedent, that I was going to pick up interference—portents not only unnecessary but undesirable—dropping over me like a mist net. Two of my work orders had been urgently annotated with red felt marker. I slipped these to the bottom of the stack and spent more time than I had to on an abstract of the early sixties quiz scandals. I reviewed, on microfilm, the news play (son of prominent literary historian weeps in disgrace), and scanned a few of the culprit programs, *Dotto*, *Twenty-One*, etc. ("Welcome our returning champion and art lover, Gunnery Mate Bill Gwynn!"). How quaint all the shock and indignation now seemed, these elementary manipulations drawing a hot bewilderment like that of children discovering their parents in bed. The day's first imponderable: Innocence lost or skepticism earned? Had the Apollo moonwalk actually been faked in a studio?

Chewing antacid mints, I moved on to a little project slugged SENSITIVE by the always chary Assignment staff. Evidently, a midwest interactive cable system—with, I assumed, a few pols in the background—wanted to move in the direction of the viewer-response political referendum. Your living room a voting booth! Should the administration continue its support for the Israeli occupation of Crete? Press now. Data enter. Suffrage by remote control seemed logical enough; all the wiring was in place. My task was to search out and analyze extant paradigm models, that is to say, see if anything similar had ever shown up on a TV show. A complex and detailed indexing system is in force here, but I didn't know if it was up to this feckless job. Shit or Shinola? Was there a difference? I put it off on a pliable Third Tier researcher and went to see Ellen with mixed, vagrant feelings.

I found her watching Tommy Sands sing "Teenage Crush" on *Kraft Theatre.*

"My dreamboat."

"Is this work?" I asked.

"What the fuck isn't?" she said balefully.

Then, as if her mouth had been formed around speech long before I came in, as if the speech had been long thought out, if not definitively composed, she began to describe a week of compulsive pickups, of kneeling on car seats, lost clothing, fear in public parks. Her voice was low, smooth, cold. She spoke with a balance of obfuscation and detail that made my stomach clench and my cock stiffen, dropped finally away into glaring silence. I canted my eyes away, occupied my hands with a cigarette, thinking: She moves far outside your gravity, in a path too clean and swift for you. Don't think it. Don't even think it.

Ellen resumed her speech. "And all for the stupidest reason. Because my father married again. His fourth." Pause. "A little thing from Dothan, Alabama. A platform diver." Long pause. "Shit, it's not that. Not that unsavory, secret Daddy love they paint on women with a stencil. I don't care who he fucks. But the gratitude, the catering—to me, I mean. God, all that sugar water. The reminders are enough to choke me."

"Reminders?"

"That he doesn't have the slightest idea who I am."

"So you have to go out and show him."

"No." She glared emphatically. "I have to deaden myself, pursue sensation until I reach insensibility. It isn't the volcano erupting. It's the lava after it's gone cold."

"I like a good aphorism."

Delvino just inside the door, shiny as a wax-sprayed supermarket apple. Predatory eyes. The roving reporter. He affected leather-trimmed suspenders and his normally invasive geniality inappropriate for any situation.

"Can I help you?" Ellen said without much noticing him.

"Probably to see me," I mumbled, starting out.

But Delvino came further in. "Good seeing both of you together. Chemistry is so very important. We've always felt that."

"Yeah. We were just volleying a few ideas back and forth."

"Exactly. This is a cooperative."

Ellen had measured him out by now and sat, short hands in wide lap, like a houseguest in an uncomfortable chair. Nowhere the small rote defiance I might have expected.

"I don't think you and I have been to the same parties," she said.

Delvino did not move or smile, a mandarin. "I wouldn't guess you care for parties."

The glass beads at her wrist clicked like a tapped phone line. "Birthday parties, political parties. Do you suppose it's because I'm too easily embarrassed? I like to walk downtown and pretend I'm from a foreign country."

Delvino nodded, still not smiling. But he moved now, across and around the Panelyte rectangle, face molded in aimlessness. He riffled papers, weighed things and turned them, traced surfaces; not in purposive inspection, it seemed, but with the restful, not restive curiosity of someone waiting for an appointment.

"No grid overlays?" he said at last.

"I can do them in my head," Ellen whispered.

"I'm the man for taking care of glitches. Anything else I should know about?"

I imagined Delvino taking an extension course in Interrogation taught by an ex-Miami cop, more recently Tenneco chief of security in Guayaquil, Ecuador. Delvino's contempt for the other students is so complete, so automatic, that he is unaware of it. He takes voluminous notes, does outside reading, gets an A.

"You're sure?" he was saying. "Resentments you might have been saving up?"

"I don't save them," Ellen said. "I spend them right away."

Delvino's laughter was something that came all in one burst. He cocked an appreciative index finger at her.

"Can we keep each other up to date? Can we do that?" He

swung round in the doorway, twinkling. "Have a good week-end, you two."

Ellen came up out of the chair and shoved me back. "You were a big help."

"What, I think he really likes you."

"Don't be an asshole."

Hoisting a jangly black shoulder bag, she curved her mouth in exasperation. "Some watchdog you are."

"That's rich. Since when am I in any position to . . . Where you going?"

"Home. Where the heart is."

"But the buses don't run till . . ."

"So I'll call a taxi," her voice fading down the hall. "I can afford it."

Today's dialogue all ominous and overcareful. And where was the heart? More propaganda. Rumbling, as of a distant waterfall. Was this work? I was supposed to lead myself to conclusions. All right: Ellen's father was craven. Her chair was still warm. And I had placed myself at such a remove it had made her angry. My theoretics again, my pulled punches. But after all, where really was the heart?

Back inside my own rectangle, which I should never have left, I found materials relevant to the SENSITIVE project. Impressive speed on the part of my 3T man. I looked over the précis codes and inserted the first tape.

"There is nothing wrong with your television set. We are controlling transmission. For the next hour we will control everything you see and hear and think. You are watching a drama that reaches from the inner mind to . . . The Outer Limits!"

This seemed antithetical to what those midwest telecrats were hoping to sell and I went no further. Why not confabulate a report? All propaganda is information. Would anyone care? Would anyone notice the intrusion of manifesto?

"From this image of a distrustful electorate it is possible to proceed almost syllogistically to a translation of the core values individuality, mobility, diversity as solipsism, instability, product differentiation."

Would anyone, and certainly I include myself, be able to look at a straight line and see the arc of an infinite circle?

So I sit here in the dwindling afternoon watching a Japanese cartoon about a cow that plays the banjo. I feel indistinct and confused. Distinctions blur and sure dimensions are made unrecognizably soft. I have an aphorism for Delvino: One must ignore the obvious and look for the pertinent. Quite tidy and wise. But what are its applications, if any? The cow sings "Jimmy Crack Corn" with a circular mouth that expands and contracts. I think of a poisonous anemone. Not pertinent, not interesting, but habitual. Jumpcuts, static— memories are made of this. I cannot visualize what is invisible above me, the angle of sun at this hour and how it might intersect with an expanse of tinted glass. But I can see words hanging bannerlike in the recirculated air: *subtext cipher indoctrinate*. Not penetrating, not even palliative. An empty, reflexive habit of coloring/covering over, then discovering a secret underneath. I wish Ellen could share some of her insensibility. I wish, I wish.

Fountains of plastic foliage, a fermenting sugar smell from crushed candy and spilled pop. The lounge is quiet. I close my eyes and concentrate on the texture of the upholstery.

Foley skids in, hangs furtively by the vending machines like he's planning to bust them open, then sits next to me and talks with a copy of *Architectural Digest* in front of his face. He says he's being watched. Light beams aimed at his apartment window, probably a transmitter somewhere in his car.

"Come on, why would they bother you? You've got seniority."

"Exactly it."

He mentions stress tests, voice printing. His hand digs at my shoulder.

"You may be next," he says. "I just wanted you to have the information."

I watch him hurry away. I think how good it will be to get out of here and into the barren landscapes, traces of lava long gone cold.

The Dodgers were filling the ballpark in spite of first-stage smog alerts. A Russian defector and paladin of the cello washed up on Seal Beach. *Daily Variety* reported that a certain TVIP had decided on a career change after waking in the middle of the night with bleeding palms. I had been back from Las Vegas six weeks, moving from couch to couch, wearing out the patience of friends, most of whom were Violet's to begin with. Time was heavy. I spent a good deal of it trodding hillside neighborhoods, eating fruit out of the yards. Even pampered housedogs could sense my inner funk, growling and showing their teeth as I passed.

I cataloged my pretensions and deceptions in rigorous, forensic detail. I overlapped and interlocked disparate strands like a weaverbird building its nest. Nothing was too distant in time for my construction, too petty, too confused. In this I began to take a habitual type of pleasure, began to anticipate the warming rush that came with a newly incorporated perfidy. But at the same time I recognized that all my raveling up was pulling me to pieces, and uselessly.

Violet, usually at the high end of the spectrum, advised normalcy. "Not simplistic; simplified. Otherwise, you're boring anyone that comes near you."

"To philosophize is to learn to die," I quoted.

"Why not try something new?"

A little later I drifted into Bullock's, and here, where sedative music played, I saw the effort that went into choosing towels that would coordinate with bathroom decor, the ecstasy of a first bathing suit. I saw newlyweds frightened by the price of sofas, an old woman icily dissatisfied with the gift wrapping of a pen-and-pencil set. This normalcy was so dreamy, so foreign, as to seem almost paradisiacal. All I could do was watch.

In the appliance department I found a bank of televisions all tuned to the same channel, a crystalline arrangement. The show was called *Open Market,* and pitted four contestants against one another in the trading of international commodities. The set looked like a State Department nerve center. The emcee wore a vested suit and a watchchain. His name was Troy.

"Sorry, Gladys, but that spin means a rollback in world soybean prices and disaster for you."

How much normalcy could I buy with their fifty-thousand-dollar grand prize? Enough to keep me from stealing fruit, I thought. At the end of the show they gave an address and phone number which I memorized by repetition on my way to the library, where for the next couple of weeks I would study climatology, currency fluctuations, rates of consumption. I read journals containing the work of speculative econometricians and slept in a moribund Ford belonging to Violet's graduate assistant. I made daily calls to the production office to ask about auditions and kept up my energies with so much coffee it must have stained my bladder brown.

From the American pulpit: The relentless man gains result, if not always reward. So, inevitably, my time arrived, like some tiny glacial shift. Violet drove me out to Studio City for my pre-interview and said I was more boring than ever.

"They don't want scholarly, they want telegenic," she said. "You ought to know that."

"Me Mr. Citizen," I answered, caught up in last-minute cramming.

Violet's good-luck kiss was grudging. "I'll be busy for a while. You're on your own."

The *Open Market* office was somewhere in a reclaimed

manufacturing plant—high windows, lots of exposed brick. Somewhere. I waded through an open call for a diaper commercial, blundered into a photo session involving scuba gear. Everyone seemed irritated. The receptionists, every one an album-cover slut analog, were too preoccupied with health shakes, the trades, furtive phoning, to offer assistance.

"Interviews, right," one finally said, an androgynous redhead browsing through a tropical fish magazine. She pointed down a fern-choked hall. "The brown door with the porthole."

I had expected a younger, less formal man. And I was puzzled by words chalked on the blackboard behind him.

Data Search
Continuity
Diagnosis

Amplitude (testing)
Total Coverage

"You're late. I'm afraid you missed the slide presentation."

In fact, I'd come early, but I wasn't about to argue. Not for fifty grand. The man parted his gray hair down the middle and wore rimless glasses. Was he trying to look like Woodrow Wilson? He sighed.

"All right, you might as well tell me about yourself."

I had a bio all ready, the novel and the ordinary mixed in exact proportions.

He looked hesitant. "And your video experience?"

Telegenic, not scholarly. I couldn't decipher the aim of this question, but determination drowned out unease and I gave a deftly exaggerated account of my stint with CBS News.

My interrogator was visibly pleased. He reviewed his notes, underlining several items.

"And how much do you know about us?"

I enthused over the exciting and imaginative concept, the genuinely educational thrust behind . . .

Eyes of comparable grayness appeared to bubble outward toward the rimless lenses, and, inescapably, our cross-purposes came clear. He was recruiting manpower, I was spinning my wheels. He indicated rather huffily that he had never even heard of *Open Market,* and I said there would now be no need for the personal information I'd given. Our chairs scraped on the linoleum.

So that was it? No, we had begun a ritual, reiterative process and could only see it through, like some form of hormonal imprinting that cancels volition.

"No such prize, but we offer a very generous benefits package." He paused fractionally between words, as if in fear of damaging his remarkably small teeth. "A long-term relationship."

In cajolery and salesmanship we contested, seesawing in our chairs, only slightly less non sequiturious than before. The Wilson man described the new undertaking in terms of utopian splendor.

"Your own satellites," I said thoughtfully.

The Wilson man drew something in the air with his pencil.

"Yeah, I got in on the periphery of some of the microwave research they were doing at RPI a few years ago."

"RPI?"

"Isn't it remarkable that the same thing that roasts your holiday turkey can send a Liza Minnelli concert to Brazil?"

The Wilson man scribbled. "We always have ham."

On and on we went, like men of stature talking over the noise of a bar car, constantly assessing, never really warming to each other. In the end, the deal closed, we couldn't say goodbye fast enough. Aimless at ritual's end. Spent.

"Take care now."

"Thanks."

"Thank you."

I carried away a Ziploc info kit and instructions to phone headquarters in a month. I took away the very latest thing in normalcy, and all at no charge.

Violet took the news rather badly.

"But isn't this what you meant? Something new?"

"What I meant was . . . What I meant was . . ."

Cursing me for a male moron, she hung up.

I thought: This must be how your mom acts when you enlist in the Marines.

The overseers are long on application, short on things to do. Telephone numbers and parking spaces are continually being reassigned. Arriving today, a directive on bulletin boards (no personal messages, solicitations to buy or sell, clippings, or cartoons), and report of heated committee wrangling over which hue of stationery will best set off the new logo. This sort of thing is placed under the heading of Systems Maintenance. Is this what we're learning from the Japanese?

Sometimes it is useful, even imperative, to go below, to reach the shiny, packed, irrefutable innards of this place and rest.

The archives are housed in a core of hexagonal cells running three levels deep, this supremely efficient design tactic plagiarized from the bee. Loose-leaf catalog binders are chained like pens in a bank, and against white styrene walls the black cassettes achieve blunt grandeur, the cold authority of a vault. Form fascinates function.

I clang down one of the narrow iron stairways—curious anachronism—and find Ellen at the bottom.

"Hiding?"

"No. More like hibernating."

Padded shoulders, full skirt, black stockings, noncommittal

mouth. Why do I feel intimidated? Like I've been caught out? Ellen swings a big leather carry-bag at me. In a satiric sort of way, she's been trying to take weight off in the employee gym. I've watched her run in the rubber suit and the ankle weights and it's not flattering. This is the idea, she tells me.

Nothing to sit on but the floor, so we drop down, facing one another.

"Don't look up my skirt," Ellen barks. "You know there's no future in it."

She's annoyed, but doesn't change her posture any.

I'm stung. "Well, I see you're not getting any thinner."

"No, I know. And now I'm reading the worst magazines. 'Bolstering Your Style Awareness.' Recipes with seaweed, ads for panty-liners. What do you suppose is the matter with me?"

"Nothing."

"Oh, use your imagination."

"I don't know. Random jumps? Venus envy?"

For a moment she looks timid, swallowed up in tiers of videotape, a refugee in a ship's dark hold; then her leg shoots out to kick me hard.

"Really, you're okay. Strength to spare."

Ellen rolls her eyes, then looks away. "Have you ever wanted eminence? Ever cast yourself as a star?"

"Once. At sixteen, I was going to solve the Kennedy assassination. I made charts. I did a concordance of the Warren Report."

"And?"

"I got to be seventeen."

"I think it's the biggest thing between us. That we share that ambition deficiency." She stretches, waggles the sole of her shoe against mine. "Come on, why don't you drive me home."

If only this were the invitation it sounds like.

We're zipping right along. No traffic at all. Ellen inspects my car like a detective.

"What's this?" Fingering a brown potsherd glued to the dash.

"Found it out by the Salt River. It could be a relic with some spirit power or it could be nothing."

"Spirit power? That costume doesn't fit on you."

"Why not?"

She tips back against the seat, rolls her head from side to side. "Too calculated."

But I have a spot in mind where the power is hard to dismiss. Half a mile along the frontage road, then left. Castellated sandstone bluffs with a stream running slow underneath, colors enriched and outlines sharpened by the late sun. The air is light and perfumed with minerals. We drape over the warm hood, backs against the windshield.

"I'm learning to love the terrain," Ellen says, teeth clamped on a barrette as she gathers her hair. "It frightened me at first. Merciless. Too raw. But I adjusted."

"Where were you before?"

"Seattle. Lots of water, lots of green. Relaxing to the eye and ear."

"Why leave?"

"I got toxoplasmosis. From our cat."

"That doesn't sound good."

"It's not. Parasitic microbes swimming around in your cells." The way she folds her arms around herself it's as though the story has to be squeezed out. "She really was a sweet little girl. I met her in a ticket line for *La Bohème*. We had a house right by Lake Union with big bay windows and a plum tree in the yard. She played piano, I did some production for the PBS station. What a soft life. But I got a rash across my breasts, fevers of a hundred three, my throat swollen so I could barely swallow. Mono, they said at the hospital, and by the time someone really figured it out, I was in bad shape. The girl got scared and went back to Alaska. I got a permanent infestation of the kidneys. Little fuckers are in there now, latent, ready to activate anytime."

Ellen slides over the fender and walks away, anomalous in her office clothes amid the scrub and rock. I watch her move down to the stream, squat to rub water on her face over and over. Powerful. And so much grief from a cat.

We stop at a place outside the city where the chili verde is supposed to be good. Ellen smokes irritably and leaves her plate full. I drink Tecate and lime and feel my admiration pass through stages, like an insect taking on protective colors, ending in spite. A distasteful image immobile in sepia, then disappearing into the noise of families all around us. The heart, I think, is just a muscle.

We drive in darkness now. Golden oldies are barely audible on the radio, but with spearing headlights and briefly impaled signs they substitute for conversation. "Don't forget who's taking you home and in his arms you're gonna be . . . So, darlin', save the last dance for me." Abruptly, Ellen puts her hand on the wheel. I let go and she steers intently for several miles, her face a prow. But then it's all relinquished. She fidgets with my lighter, thumbing silent butane at herself, loitering somewhere in her mind. I'd like to floor it, but we've reached the limits of the city. Ellen directs me in a flat voice, and on the radio a tractor pull is being promoted. She stares at adjacent drivers, some of whom speed up, some of whom slow down.

The apartment tower is unpleasantly sheer, an ugly spindle behind its landscaping. Some sort of complex tax deal for the company, Foley has intimated. Free rental to the workers and an open road for the accountants.

"Have coffee with me?"

I cannot allow myself to imagine . . . But as we cross the plaza and push through big glass doors, I feel like someone entering a seraglio in disguise. The lobby fountain gurgles. I am emboldened, elated by the odor of acrylic carpet and the glare inside the elevator.

"Home on the range," Ellen says, letting me go in first.

So little in it, but a space that seems cramped. All the colors are pale. There are toast crumbs by the sink, smears of fat. There is a varnished bamboo screen by windows facing north toward the airport, a Max Ernst reproduction, dried berry branches in a blue bottle.

"Not much, is it?" she says, scuffling in the kitchenette. "I think of moving all the time, but that's as far as I get."

While the coffee drips, she shows me photographs, large

color prints of wall murals over on the East Side. In some the artists stand in the foreground, raising their fists to *la raza*. She talks of Siqueiros and Diego Rivera with an excitement that lingers on my skin. But when all you do is watch, things pass by.

She has a little Dutch cigar with her coffee and speaks softly. "Part of the Seattle thing was having something under me. A kind of scaffolding. We were much involved up there. Aid for Guatemalan refugees, the Fremont Women's Health Collective, volunteer time at the food bank. But the biologists say altruism doesn't exist. I realized all that righteous solidarity was a way of comforting myself. Moral obligations were really emotional ones."

She winces at herself, looks to me for a reaction. I am desperate in my obligations, seeing her once again as she squats beside the stream. I yearn for the dizziness of abjection, the smell of her secrecy.

"So how do I replace these things? With a practical attitude? Run your laps, cash your checks. Cut down on sugar and red meats." She surrounds her empty cup for warmth. "Retreat, retreat. Rehearse yourself. There are all sorts of things to give up, but I don't see anything pious in being solitary. Where are the fucking replacements?"

Clearly, she wants words and not my arms.

I say, in the irrelevance of my desire, "This is not a tender age."

"Okay. What do we do about that?"

"We're supposed to 'play hardball' and 'stonewall it.' "

Ellen moves to the window and looks out. "You are a complacent, gutless asshole."

"Yes, but I'm other things too."

She ignores my hand on her back, glaring hard into the distance where runways are long and flat, where tower lights spin tirelessly and never retreat.

It begins to rain as I reach the car. A cold wash. Wipers and defroster on, I head through the strip zone for home, past a chain of mansard roofs, floodlights blaring on wet asphalt and chrome, savannas of plate glass, a fiberglas drumstick rotating atop a pole. The city's population has doubled in the last ten years. In another five it will double again, pouring out hydrocarbons and sucking up the aquifer.

I bless the sterility of the desert.

While many marched smartly, even proudly, through the era of the airline hijacking and the happening, of self-immolations, lettuce boycotts, astrological medallions, and the aluminum can, I straggled. My hands were slack, my eyes unwatchful. I chainsmoked to the monotonous beat of history. Disposable history, as I discovered.

I was a tender of newswire machines, those tireless contraptions which, on white cylinders like massive rolls of toilet paper, recorded and arranged the soot-black dung smears of the day. The richly fertilized sheets which I distributed were inhaled and combed through for special nuggets; they were segmented and scribbled on, spiked on the wall, and soon enough balled up in the Dumpster. Event revealed Trend which grew into Crisis, all of which evaporated as soon as the next movement of tanks, the next celebrity drug arraignment, the next violated child thrown from an apartment rooftop. There really was no keeping up, so I straggled. And sometimes things turned up in the litter at the end of the line.

Also under my care was a wirephoto machine which, by some electronic process I could never grasp, transmitted images simultaneously to subscribers great and small. Unfurling one afternoon from its slowly turning drum was a picture of a former First Lady arriving at or departing from some airport, her glamorously delicate breasts clearly visible behind a gauzy blouse. Its caption was followed by the parenthetical slug "Editors please note: This photo may contain offensive material." What, I pondered, could possibly offend? Those royal breasts, curiously upturned like a pair of Persian slippers, with their intimations of . . . All right then, into the wastebasket, so disposed. On to the next historical square—a ditch full of corpses or a race driver grinning in victory lane.

The wire machines were equipped with a simple menu of alerts: One bell for, say, the World Series final, two bells for a major disaster, natural or manmade, three bells for the assassination of a head of state, and four bells, which could only mean a nuclear exchange, so that every time the system kicked in it brought on a Pavlovian apprehension that this would be The Time, and that fourth bell would go off. What relief to find that it was nothing more than a prime minister fatally slashed.

Yes, many and varied were the mental contortions necessary to the profession. How, for example, to maintain the traditional hardbitten, seen-it-all demeanor alongside reverent gravity for information control and the public trust? How to reconcile instinctive skepticism with the "objective" approach? Much wiser to straggle.

Our newsroom, a large oblong space where bottling operations had taken place in the days of the old milk factory, was irrevocably, if invisibly, divided between the "radio side" and the "TV side." These phrases were often spoken bluntly, challengingly, in the manner of a *Maverick* saloon rat, lacking only the casually accurate jet of tobacco juice. If the resentment of the radio tribe—purveying their drab and archaic product to cabbies, potato farmers, and the bedridden—was intense, so likewise was the scorn in which they were held by the glamour boys and girls on the other side of the line.

I straggled sure enough, barely avoiding classification as a deserter.

"If you're just here to take up space . . ." warned my supervisor.

Where were my ambitions? My dreams of network glory? Right where they belonged, in the Dumpster with yesterday's firsthand combat accounts.

"This is no stand-pat type of game," my supervisor declared, fingering the ivory polar bear at the far edge of his desk.

I said: "Milk but no sugar, right?"

Straggling home from work that night, I came up against Sabra, my moll of high school, in a crowded subway car. She was slender as an asparagus and ripe with patchouli oil. Her eyes glistened. We swayed coyly under an advertisement for breath mints.

"You're looking great," I said.

"Your job really sounds exciting," she returned.

We got off at the next station and found a nearly empty bar. Sabra ordered Kahlúa and milk and I broke the seal on a third pack of cigarettes.

"So I just found a place near Morningside Heights," erasing milky residue from her lips with curled tongue, "and I'm sleeping in one corner, with paint rags and spackle cans all around."

I blew across the rim of my beer glass. "Noxious fumes. You should protect your singing voice."

Behind the words shinily coated with an oozing caution, we reviewed our past, the missteps and misgivings of frightened romance.

"Oh, that's a lost cause more or less. I'd like to get into personal management now."

The unfinished business between us would be completed that night, we were confident of that. And as we concurrently imagined each ideal and tender phase, an occult mental fusion—confirmed by what we could see of ourselves in the other's eyes—flamed inside the forlorn brownness of the nearly empty bar. Sabra's olive face lightened, expanded, and the Formica seemed to heat and move under my hands. Dazing cranial pressure slowly released and our breathing stopped. I squeezed shut my eyes, wanting to prolong this astonishing conjunction, but it was finished the very moment I did.

Sabra had curtained herself behind a tumble of black hair. My knees shimmied as I crossed to the bar to reorder. Someone dropped a quarter in the jukebox and the garish tones of Sergio Franchi invaded the brown room.

What do you say afterwards? Desperate to fill the emptily echoing air, you may blare out the first and worst thing that comes to your mind. I asked Sabra about her sister.

"Rachel lives in France now. She's the organist at the cathedral in Arles."

During the summer between my junior and senior years, Rachel, both tireless and regally calm, had shown me how it was done. By late August ten pounds had drained from me and been soaked up by her designer sheets. Sabra, feigning disinterest, had spent the summer snorting heroin and learning her Sarah Vaughan records by rote.

Now here was a wedge of history to be reckoned with, a site we could spend all night picking through with trowels and sieves and little archaeological brushes. This was history of a kind not so easily disposed of, a deeper stratum. But the reflexes of the newsroom made me incapable of shame.

"A Jewish girl playing liturgical music for the froggies," I said. "Do you have her address?"

"It'd make quite a feature piece for the weekend news," the little sister said hopelessly, jotting on a napkin.

We emptied our glasses and went home, she to her noxious fumes and I to a spiral notebook in which I made a few lugubrious attempts at letter writing before shredding Rachel's address.

It is said that when sparrows in the city of Peking became an infestation, citizens gathered by the thousands in the central square to shout and sing and scream, keeping the terrified birds in the air for many hours until they fell to the pavement twitching with exhaustion and died, also by the thousands.

But we are all individuals here, each in our own precious

compartment, walls smoothly spackled and painted sea foam or egg yolk or terra cotta, but rest assured, a color of our own choosing. Multiplicity, diversity—privileges for which to kneel in gratitude and launch red glaring rockets. Inalienable conflict, indivisible confusion. And in our little compartments we hoard like survival rations our opinions freely arrived at (here, here!), our memories of perfidy and injustice, our strategies for advancement and revenge. One nation, underdog. One rugged individual after another pleading for attention. Looka me, ma! Looka me!

And, when it all becomes too much, you may embark—no questions asked—for a tropical isle where unique coral formations may be seen, or for France, where a cathedral organ awaits your special hands.

Back at my desk assistant's desk next day, I methodically filled the ashtray and beheld the urgent diversities that unrolled from my machines. The governor of Wisconsin revealed that a serious fiscal shortfall was due to his compulsive golf betting, elections in Paraguay were once more postponed, a former middleweight champion appealed for the return of school prayer, black nationalists continued to occupy the lobby of the Dunes Hotel, rivers in the Southwest crested dangerously with more rain expected, preparations were under way for the state visit of Golda Meir, a diabetic Omaha baker was arrested for rape and dismemberment, and angry Sikhs in the state of Punjab had flung a dozen pigs' heads into the courtyard of a mosque.

Noticing my supervisor glaring out of his glassed-in office, I waved energetically, increasing the amount of space I was taking up. Too much, indeed. I considered phoning Arles on the WATS line, but no, what could not be cured had to be endured.

Then Gosden was pressing against the back of my chair. Gosden, hanging on to five weekly minutes of nostalgic pipe slobber on the "radio side," who, after liquid lunches, would corner mailroom boys and replay his exploits in the European theater ("Murrow, Mountbatten . . . I knew them all"), who had no worries about information control and the public trust, had come to wheedle stamps.

"Help yourself," I said.

"Good show, good show."

And plunging toward the open drawer, Gosden somehow tangled with the casters of my chair, causing it to slide backward and me to pitch forward, striking my nose on the console telephone. Pain webbed over my face. Blood poured from my nostrils.

Gosden, trapped in a historical site of his own, must have thought we were under attack. "Down, you fool. Get down," he yelled, bellyflopping to the floor. "We've got too many reasons to live."

"And God bless us," I said, straggling off to the bathroom. "Every one."

It was, unavoidably, a season of vehemence, the already turbid New York air dense with convolutions. To argue became obligatory, the refusal to do so an opinion in itself. Private problems were absorbed into public furor, small shoots amid the infinite jungle of Plot. Meals were hurried and phone calls protracted. A Senate Select Committee was investigating the Watergate affair.

I had quit CBS, was getting along on family handouts taken without apology or gratitude. I spent my time indoors mapping previously unknown tracts of insensibility. Out there, I knew, people were continually affronted, were exhausted by their outrage and in terror of being at a loss. How childish. How unnecessary.

I was systematically testing every recipe in a bartender's guide issued by the old Hotel Luxor and on the initial morning of Maurice Stans's testimony mixed a pitcher of Sazeracs.

"In Republica Dominicana this would never happen," commented Nito, who had the apartment next to mine. "There a leader is permitted to lead."

Nito worked part-time as an animal-control officer, sometimes sat in on timbales with a *conjunto* that played dance halls in the Bronx. He was very seldom surprised by anything. I could appreciate the wisdom of accepting corruption as part of the natural order, but that was off the point.

My position: "It's not about politics." I pointed to the set, where Stans, a member of the CPA Hall of Fame, read his prepared statement in a grain belt monotone. "This is a passion play. A rite."

"High mass?" Nito made the sign of the cross. "I would rather watch the Ursula Andress movie."

"Stay tuned. Study our national culture."

"But where are the breasts?"

I took pride in those days in my total lack of purpose. It seemed to me a mark of real clarity, of harmony with the future. But in this role of disaffection, I'm afraid, there was too much ham. Even Carla, summering with friends on a farm in Pennsylvania, was sending me checks.

Bad Boy—
Am having dire word of you and your life in the slums.
Mom and her inflations, you know. But here anyway
a small contribution toward socket wrenches, or what-
ever you might need. Very muggy here, sleep difficult.
The cukes, tomatoes, etc., seem to thrive on it, though.
Raccoons come out of the woods at night and beg at
the porch for scraps. Did you know they're related to
the panda? Neither did I.
Love and birdwatching,
C

For sure, the heat was on. Gordo suggested I enroll in electronics school. Casually, Alexander Butterfield betrayed the existence of a White House taping system. I slept with all the windows open and listened to sirens. I cracked ice trays into the bathtub and sat there reading about intrigue in the Ottoman Empire.

The Constitution in jeopardy. Our republic foundering. But I found no alarm in my surrounding streets. Nothing new at Katz Laundry, or at Three Bros. Coffee Shop, radio tuned to the Mets game. Elders outside the grocery sipped beer and slapped their dominoes, and of Nixon only amusement—"The fuckin' guy." Still, the indignant shock was out there, in some other part of town, or in green counties to the north, beside ponds and croquet courts, where values hard arrived at seemed to warp. Such blather. Such density of ego.

By the time John Dean began the careful relinquishing of his confidences, I had reached Chapter 7 in my bartender's guide: Punches & Coolers. My cache of lemons attracted canny urban flies and scented the days with a pleasant bitterness. "A cancer in the White House." The analogy anyone could understand. Clever Dean, nothing left to chance. Writers of enterprise flew off to interview his teachers and tennis buddies.

I filled a two-gallon pot with something called Rum Cockade and invited the Roysters. Chip and Dale had the apartment above mine. They were emigrants from northern Ohio, exponents of social change. Their walls were hung with serapes, the floor littered with cat toys. Their flattened vowels and cumbersome honesty charmed me, though I knew they were in for it. The city, having lured them, would no doubt show no mercy.

Dale assessed the President. "It's like he wanted to get caught," she said, swinging her braids. "Like when you're a kid and do things just to test your mother. To see if she's paying attention."

Chip snorted and touched his bald spot. "Special attention for Dickie. He's so misunderstood."

Dale worked in a daycare center.

"Mr. Above-it-all," she said, and drained her third cup. "You should be in a seminary."

It struck me that this was one of those relationships based on the fact of its never working. Yet how tenderly Chip would comfort his wife a few hours later, cradling her as she retched over the sink.

I ladled out more punch. "Think we'll ever get to hear those tapes?" What a host.

"Which tapes?" Chip said. "I mean, how do you ever know or not if what you're listening to is fake?"

"He wants punishment," Dale insisted. Hugging her knees, mouth hidden behind the tin cup, she was beginning to suggest an ad layout for CARE. "He wants to be stripped naked and flogged."

"Yes, a ceremony." I toasted her. "You've got a grip on it now."

"What this country needs," Chip said grandly, "is less humiliation and more humility."

Chip had been with the Peace Corps in Guyana.

I slept heavily that night and dreamed I was a bagman for the Mormon Church. Gordon Liddy took me to lunch. The prime rib was rare. We talked about theocracy and gauchos and how to kill someone with a sharpened pencil. Waking in late afternoon, I told myself: Stop fighting the odds and you'll make a fine apologist.

A few days later I met Dale in front of Katz Laundry. Her little face was pinched and she kept looking over her shoulder. Chip, she confided, was unwell. His vision blurred; he had ringing in his ears. Just that morning, short of breath and twitching uncontrollably, he had been admitted to Roosevelt Hospital for evaluation.

"We wanted to come here so bad. We said, 'It's the nerve center.' "

Now Dale pined for the simplicities of Dayton, molded-salad luncheons and covered-dish suppers. Chip was afraid of having to work the line like his father, but could it be worse than this?

Shortly after Judge Sirica ordered release of the tapes, Nito was stabbed in the arm by a junior high kid who wanted his radio. By the time impeachment proceedings were under way, I had moved back to Lake Success, regained my job with the network, and become a commuter. The democratic system, it was widely announced, was proving its special merit. I was relatively sober, flirting with accommodation. And, unbeknownst to anyone, my mother was preparing to leave the world behind.

Have I mentioned to you the stretch I pulled in San Francisco? Of course, yes, the story of the shoes with the holes cut in them. So. There I was in the city that has always wanted to be somewhere else. The place and the people in it were arch and overindulged and wanted their sophistication to be appreciated. The locale, in short, was all too fitting.

I had a cheap apartment with a view of the Oakland shipyards. Above an Italian restaurant, it was furnished like something out of a thirties detective novel and redolent of singed garlic. My landlady left small packets of anisette cookies in front of my door.

I had a job that brought me into contact with the sort of underworld I needed as an antidote to Lake Success. If I was going to shake loose of that depleting heritage, Le Sex Shoppe was ideal territory. It was undemanding work besides and afforded me nearly limitless reading time—B. Traven and Vargas Llosa were my fascinations at the time. I had barely to glance up from *The Green House* in order to make change for the peep booths.

I had an Olds 88 that enabled me to learn the city like an anatomy chart. I knew a spot in the Mission where tamarind or hibiscus popsicles could be had, and out the avenues toward the sea, a Korean grocery with the cheapest carton of cigarettes that side of the Bay and homemade kimchi that made your eyes water. In a light industrial zone south of Market, I found a record store called Tommy's Soul Shack where I could get a bet down on anything from the sixth race exacta at Longacres to the bottom of a fight card in Stockton. In the apartment directly overhead lived a conceptual artist named Irv who made masks out of hair scrounged from beauty salon Dumpsters. Irv was a lapsed Jew from Baltimore, a fellow fugitive. He supplied me with high-grade black hashish at very reasonable rates.

The fabled city at my fingertips? The life of Riley? Well, not altogether. Ambivalence comes with every territory.

I was having an affair with an Armenian art student who wept while she fucked. "What is it? What is it?" I'd say, but Andrea would only pull her dark hair over her dark face and shudder. The tendons in her neck would stand out wire-tight. I'd stroke them, matching her silence for silence. Her mysteries filled me with loathing as often as with tenderness, but I couldn't say goodbye. Andrea was short, round, not particularly beautiful. Still, I was enormously aroused by her almost complete lack of humor, by the warm morning smell that stayed all day with her and which no perfume could fully mask. Also, I suppose, I was unduly fascinated by my own reactions to the first woman I had known for whom there seemed to be so much at stake.

Evidently, Andrea was very much in love with me, although I had given her no good reason to be so. It unnerved me. Anyway, she was so bloody earnest about it, blew the notes so hard. Combined with some mutant species of Old World submissiveness, this studious approach of Andrea's sometimes tempted me to strangle her.

We had known each other but a few days when she came to see where I worked. The presence of a living woman made the customers fractious and a few regulars grumbled across the street to the bar to sit in the dark. With the same sharp attention she would bring to a gallery full of Mirós or Rosenquists, Andrea looked over the merchandise. After a few minutes she carried an open magazine to the counter.

"Would you like for me to do this?" she asked quietly.

The photograph showed a woman cleaving herself with a black rubber dildo. I began to wish I were in the bar.

"You only have to ask." Her eyes were shiny brown lakes.

The woman in the photograph grimaced; Andrea was expressionless. Her somber zeal bored into my skull like a steel screw.

"I'd ask you out for shots at the Forest Club," I said, barely able to control myself.

But we had our harmonic periods as well. One of Andrea's uncles was a grocery broker with a warehouse at China Basin. We'd head over there on a Saturday and load up with garbanzo beans, macaroni, olives, pomegranates, and marinated artichoke hearts. Then we'd go back to her one-room flat and eat like starved nomads while listening to the Giants game on the radio. Then we would ascend.

A previous tenant had cut a hatchway to the roof and installed a ladder. He wasn't much as a carpenter and when it rained—which in San Francisco could be any minute now—the hatch was a difficulty. But Andrea had a tarpaulin she'd fasten over the top and a spaghetti pot to catch whatever leaked through to the bottom.

"I've got to have open space," she said.

Golden Gate Park was at least three miles away.

Andrea had extra-long wiring on her record machine so that along with cushions and army blankets, we could haul it on up and listen to the atonal composers she liked so much. In each other's arms, in the soot and waning sunlight, we would whisper like children.

Andrea told me stories about her family: the very devout

grandfather with no left arm who several years ago had brought in the largest raisin harvest in the history of Inyo County; the cousin who, at least peripherally, had been involved in the assassination of a Turkish diplomat; and her eldest sister, who'd moved south, changed her name, and could now be seen as a corrupt D.A. on a semipopular daytime serial.

But the point of it all was simply this: We were so young we had no stories about ourselves. Probably that is a large part of what kept us after one another despite the negative signposts—the eagerness, even desperation, for heightened moments we could hoard away.

Must I always present things in such crass relief? Where is the balance? I should say that holding tight on that asphalt roof, I didn't care that her paintings were derivative and cold, her dark mysteries so unnecessary. I felt enveloped and pleasantly stupid and I loved her.

Then in October Andrea was raped. Not by drunken seamen or nonwhite sociopaths, but by two fellow art students who cornered her late one night in the sculpture studio. They threw her over stacked bags of plaster of paris and pummeled her. As the second one burst in her, one flailing arm reached the purse that had fallen behind her. She plunged the nail file into the film major's neck and ran, ran for blocks thinking of water to clean herself. On the apron of an all-night gas station bright as an operating theater, she remembered not to.

"You want a case, we need the semen," said the bland resident.

I saw a 4-H sponsor petting a prize Charolais bull.

We sat on turquoise plastic chairs in the ER. The bruises on Andrea's face were turning four or five different colors, but she was dreadfully calm.

I said: "You should have gone for his eye."

"Blind him, shit, I was trying to kill him," Andrea said. "Missed the jugular, that's all."

And that was the end of her weeping in bed. By instinctive understanding, no words passed between us; we simply resumed. Her silent encouragements were new, and the hardened ridges of her muscle. Even her surface textures seemed different: glassier, more like an altar statue. In her face, which I could watch without pangs now, was something I was certain had not been there before. She seemed distanced in a dream. I realized that I was to her now no more than a bright but finally weightless preoccupation, like a silver boar's-head toothpick holder shipped to a lonely colonial outpost along with the rum and ropes of tobacco. I felt a kind of sick relief.

The trial came up just after New Year's. Both defendants wore J.C. Penney suits and dark ties. Andrea appeared in a navy pleated skirt, and a different Peter Pan blouse each day. The gallery was so packed with her relatives that the usual afficionados—spidery women with liver spots, retired meat cutters—could only whine and cajole in the marble hallway outside.

The "forensic" phase was disastrous: The hospital resident was furtive and snappish, the color enlargements of Andrea's lacerations stuck at the processing lab. Prosecutor Tedesci told us not to worry.

As the sole witness to the crime, Andrea was required to take the stand. She averted her eyes, spoke in the same low, liquid voice no matter what the question. The impression she gave was of sorrowful resignation, her spirit damaged beyond repair. Tedesci was overjoyed.

He said: "You want to work any more of my cases, sweetie, just name a figure."

The jury was out less than an hour. Andrea's relatives applauded the verdict, but grumbled at the ten-year sentences.

Tedesci had more reassurance. "They'll be nothing but dog meat down at Chino, believe me."

"The way I feel, I don't know . . . not vindicated."

Andrea stared at the vertical punch cards of the downtown skyline and I continued to massage her feet. We were up on the roof, under a cafe umbrella shimmed into a vent pipe. It was misting lightly and there was no moon. What we were really talking about, we weren't talking about. And though I sensed the inevitable out there somewhere, I was convincing myself I had to have her, though she had slipped through a cosmic tear.

"Normalcy," she finally said, drawing back.

"What?"

"I don't think I can afford you anymore."

"Yeah, you're right." My jaws were painfully clenched. "I'd ruin you."

"Normalcy," she repeated.

I had no idea what she meant.

Irv was highly excited when I called that night looking for sympathy. He'd torn up the linoleum in his back room and was testing the stress tolerances of the framing timbers.

"I'm going to have an orange grove," he explained. "PVC pipe irrigation with a controlled drip, Gro-Lux fixtures with . . ."

"Irv, Irv. I'm at the bottom of the shaft and no way up."

"Skip the melodrama," he said irritably. "Swing by here in your tank and let's see what we can do about soil medium at this hour."

"Okay, okay."

Irv always was a good influence. We drove out to the Lincoln Park golf course and filled the trunk of the Olds with sod from the sixteenth green.

"Lotsa worms," Irv said.

We laughed like boys in the pitch dark.

On the way back, he told me of an upcoming houseparty across the Bay. There I met the wise man who cut holes in his shoes.

And it was not long after that I fled the city that has always wanted to be somewhere else.

At four this morning, a Violet intrusion. The receiver nestled conveniently into the pillow, and for the first minute or two her voice blended into my dream: On the *He and She* set, measuring Paula Prentiss for a flight harness, and Violet's the script girl calling out sandwich orders. Some catch or quaver pulled me the rest of the way out of sleep with the knowledge that my ex-wife was at the edge. Wouldn't I come to her?

The immediate instinct was evasion. I was a wily lunker bass sheltered in thick weeds. The shiny lure ran past me again and again, and up from the darkness of my fish memory came Sunday afternoons fuzzed with Librium when Violet would invite me into her deepest bowels and I would feel the length of her spine under me like water-polished stones. But I stayed in the weeds.

"I'm here now. Can't go back."

It was a city of ten thousand gas stations, of countless possibilities, and I had been happy there. Why not go back?

Because one of us would in some way have to die, give up our ghost.

Violet always said: "I'm not ready to be casual about you."

If only she were.

There could be no sleep after that call. I smoked and drank root beers and read the last book my anthropologist had sent, a mystery novel by an Indonesian diplomat. I thought about the banana tree under her bathroom window and the senescent cafeteria across the street.

By seven-thirty there was nothing left to do but head for the job. Out by the flagpole I saw Heidi and her mate, he, I supposed, on his way to dispense bed baths and muscle relaxants at Cherry Ames. They jostled and teased like a couple of study hall sweethearts and I watched from the car as long as I could stand. He knew the touch of her mouse teeth, the press of her bones, as well as I did; and the things that kept her up at night far better. If there was no going back for me, there was no going forward, either. I kept my eyes on the gas gauge as I drove past them.

So now I'm pumping up and down in the tube, looking to relax. It's a voice-activated elevator and by calling out numbers like an auctioneer, you can paralyze its soldered brain so it won't go anywhere. The stainless-steel wall is cool against my back, the softly buzzing alarm quite pleasant.

An overriding mechanical voice on the intercom: "Clearing command block. Clearing command block."

So much for relaxation. I step off at LIB CNTRL equipped with a requisition bearing the supervisory signature (forged) which the new procedure guidelines call for. What I'm looking for is the *G.E. College Bowl* segment on which U.C., Santa Clara—and Violet—appeared. The clerk is a pouty little gum-cracker I've never seen before; and if she's going to wear sunglasses and wing-nut earrings, I probably won't see again. She sighs heavily and the characters crawling across the display terminal reverse themselves in her green lenses.

Behind her, the stacks curve massively like ranked waves. One of the top-tier caliphs was touring through here a few years ago and noted brown patches marring the symmetry, even a stripe of white here and there. His decree appeared the following day: All cassette casings, without exception, shall be black.

This great accumulation has a majesty that never fades for me. I'm as engorged as a miser in a room full of gold, with a sense of completion, of value captured. And always I am wrapped in images of the monastery. There is no self-denial in this life. I am a voluptuary overflowing with time, a lotus-eater in my vault of books. In gold leaf and lapis blue, I illuminate the work of Dalmatian poets. I annotate to exhaustion the long-suppressed memoirs of Scrooge McDuck. And in the mornings, after porridge, I walk windy parapets overlooking a landscape empty of men.

Here it is then: Program #121, 4/17/65, B/W, Synchro-track. I am anxious to see Violet at twenty, deadly serious, as she claims to have been, and still unplucked—though I can't imagine her innocence being any more than a technicality. I would have been just fifteen in April of '65, a weedy snot caught in the embracing tentacles of bogus sophistication and no doubt as unattractive to an ambitious fruit heiress like Violet (her self-portrait) as I was to everyone else. We might have done well to have gotten it over with right then and there.

I'm secured in my cell and about to begin the investigation when quashed. Delvino invades my ear with his hearty hellos. Yeah, he takes a personal interest. In espionage cant, he would be called my "operator." No way to pull a cordless phone out of the wall. Clever, clever.

"We always have something to discuss, am I right?"

There are the usual ambiguities to comb through, certain code phrases to exchange. We're attuned, like an old married couple, so it's no strain to pick out the undertones of threat he's feeling. There might even be someone standing over him and making notes.

I improvise. "We should have dinner sometime soon. There's a good Greek place in town. You know, a neutral site."

He reacts as if I've asked him to spend the night.

"No, no . . . I don't think, well . . . Really, uh, not wise."

And to think I'm here because I wanted to escape California by winning fifty thousand dollars on a quiz show.

"I'm sorry. Five-point penalty, and I'll repeat the entire question for Ohio Wesleyan. British novelist Thomas Hardy was the author of a series of novels set in the mythical county of Wessex. . . ."

Violet's round, cream-puff face has tightened with—what is

it? Fear? Shame? This is her third incorrect, and premature, answer in a row. Her "team" is falling far behind.

"Santa Clara, Feilinghaus."

"Would that be Henry the Fourth?" Her voice sails into a harsh upper register.

"No, I'm sorry. . . ."

It could be my imagination, but Violet's prim sweater seems to have darkened with flop sweat. Her hair, though heavily sprayed, has begun to undo itself in response to some magnetic field of humiliation.

Consider the divergences possible inside the same family. A week or so after our return from Las Vegas, Violet's mother and young sisters came from Redlands for a celebratory weekend of shopping and dining out. A surprise weekend. I'd spent most of that Friday pollinating orchids with my friend Marsh, returned, and found strangers at home. They introduced themselves: Rose and Jonquil. I received new-brother-in-law kisses from two girls who were totally, and quite casually, naked.

"We're cleaning your apartment as a wedding present and we don't want to get our clothes dirty," Rose said, brushing cigarette ash off her breasts.

Smiling, Jonquil returned to her vacuuming. Had to get the job done before Sis and Mom got back from Magnin's.

Compare this nonchalance with the urgent insecurities of Violet, a woman who could negotiate Santa Monica Boulevard at 50 mph, but needed half a bottle of Chablis to nerve herself for a freshman lecture and bowed to the opinions of boutique salesgirls.

I freeze the image. Her circled lips nearly touching the microphone, Violet bends far forward, as though shrinking from a whip. The eyes of the bow-tied classmate on her left are caught in mid-roll; he anticipates another blunder. Had they warned her during the brownie mix commercial to keep her mouth shut?

"Mr. Earl, the work is *Growing Up in Samoa* and the author is Margaret Mead."

"That is correct. All right, once again, Santa Clara, the subject is astronomy and your question is in three parts. . . ."

Consider the artificial logic of one thing we name "destiny." My ex-wife recalls her fascination with the migrants who came to harvest the family orchards and supposes it led her to her current work. My friend and co-worker has told me of the secret attentions paid her by a favorite aunt and how they were crucial to her emergence as a lover of women. But I doubt they believe in this sort of continuity any more than I do.

Consider the pure illogic of the realities that pen us in. For Violet, no medication can shorten the hours of insomniac despair which have dogged her all her life. For Ellen, there is no escaping her Seattle cat disease, tiny parasitic bundles that lie in dormant wait on the surface of her kidneys. For both, sharp intelligence is a frequently unwanted gift, a precision tool for the measurement of pain. But I doubt either one of them would trade places with the other.

It's Ohio Wesleyan in a romp, but Violet has regained her poise. Of the four Santa Clarans, she is the only one to rise above defeat, a flat smile hinting at scorn for the whole exercise. So, with some physical discrepancies (vestiges of baby fat, nails long and painted instead of chewed away), I recognize my wife at thirty-five in this girl of twenty. Switching faces, evading judgment: that mercurial essence is here.

Violet made a joke of subtlety. We were together quite a while before I learned not to anticipate. The fretful neurotic would suddenly take on the hauteur of her noble Bavarian forebears. It was best not to grow comfortable with one's conclusions. Violet could be at her most tyrannical while pleading for support. Similarly, when arranging some form of subjugation for herself, she was always in command, the author of the playlet. But don't let such dualities lead you to suspect a simple scheme. Because Violet made all the stops. Her feelings were irresistibly lush and came in tropical profusion.

I've found all I'm going to in this tape; no point sitting through it a second time. Ah, swollen youth, how quickly it deflates. And anyway, who was it filed for the divorce? Shit. Can't go forward, can't go back. Nobody's fault, no one to prosecute on this one. We can't overcome time, separately or together, or clear away the residue it leaves in passing. Still, it should be possible to replicate small pieces of the past. I know how that would be. . . .

Bit by bit, my sleepless fruit heiress cradles into me. Her skin is hot and smooth, like her breath. I decree the smell of orange blossoms. The trees are reaching in the window, I say. And into fine, Aryan hair, I sing the soft, slow tunes that please her. "Mood Indigo" and "Buttermilk Sky" and so on.

Violet, my fragrant bloom, if only you could learn to be casual about things like that.

The sunset, laced with hydrocarbons, was deep purple. Unseen mechanisms turned on lights that beamed cheerlessly on antique shops and design studios along Wilshire Boulevard. Knees against the dashboard, I filled my nose with the smell of good green government ink. I was with my friend Marsh; we had just delivered three crates of psilocybin mushrooms grown from mycelia sent by his stepmother in Olympia, and the money was spilled between us on the seat—fresh, clean bills like chard right out of the garden.

"I've been curious about the Solomon Islands," Marsh said.

I said that was fine, but neither one of us had a passport.

"They grow a variety of banana that can weigh up to—"

He was interrupted by an oncoming skateboarder with phosphorescent tape strips hanging from his chin and a bubble pipe clenched in his teeth.

"Youth," he said, as the kid swerved around our fenders and jumped the curb. "What a dismal job."

We were passing a carton of orange drink back and forth, working away at a sack of jelly doughnuts. Spotted with confectioners' sugar, the steering wheel looked as if it had been incompetently dusted for prints. What a pair of night crawlers we made. I craved a leather banquette in some maudlin piano bar, but Marsh, whose enthusiasms were unpredictable, wanted to play miniature golf.

"Precision, precision," he said. "Like the blossoming of a . . ."

Who cares! Enough of this aimless remembering. One damn thing I don't need is to develop a new bad habit. Stick to the tense present and thrive.

Good advice. Except the immediate issue is a thing thirty years old. Double takes and padded shoulders. *My Little Margie.*

I could be pulling the lobster shift in a machine shop, crumbs of steel flying off my lathe. I could be sitting on a tractor, discing fragrant black ground for sugar beets. But this is my hazardous profession; it turns me backward, pushes me into not just my own past, but everyone else's. It propels me without pause from one memory bit to another, feeding on parallels and associations.

I see the cardboard skyline through the window of Vern Albright's office at Honeywell and Todd, Investment Bankers. I see the spires of the Woolworth Tower and the Chrysler Building paralleled in the fountain pen set on Vern's desk. I remember staying home from a fourth-grade geography test, the images of a marvelously complete Margie world, city styles distant as Rangoon viewed from a terrace of indulgent pillows.

Enhancement mechanism: I close in and in on the trompe l'oeil skyline until the benday dots of the composite photograph are like a galactic cloud of dust and gas within which time stands still, all motion is perpetual. Negro elevator boys flinch and roll their eyes, powerful men spray frustration through thatchlike mustaches, taxicabs lurch and revolving doors revolve.

With the frame advance control I achieve a kind of lurching space travel, hopping from blur to blur until, deactivating gridlock, I retreat and retreat. . . . And here's Margie in an elfin sportswear creation—white shorts and tunic with saucer-size black buttons—practicing her conga moves in preparation for a trip to Havana with Dad, who'll be closing a big deal with Señor Mercado, owner of vast sugar plantations. (I remember eating flan in a Cuban place on Eighth Avenue with a girl who admired Angela Davis.) Margie's boyfriend, the human ashtray, Freddy Wilson, watches disconsolately from the candy-stripe sofa.

"Sure I want you to have a good time, but what about all those shiny-haired caballeros down there?"

"Honestly, Freddy, do you think I'd fall for . . ."

But wait. Here's Vern emerging from the elevator, puffed with pride at having just been named to a seat on the Traffic Commission.

"Oh, no, it's Dad! Freddy, you've got to hide!"

(I remember part of an old dream: On the lam in bayou land, paying for roadhouse tamales with a Calvin Coolidge twenty-five-dollar bill.)

Freddy crouches on the terrace. Tipsy with civic triumph, Vern decides to view the beauties of Manhattan, to fill his lungs with sweet spring air. Wretched craven Freddy, born to lose, would sooner dangle from a chrome railing eleven stories over Park Avenue than jeopardize little Margie's Havana spree.

I look to my manifest for a client name, but the space is blank. Curious. Paperwork, repellently, is a strong point of mine. Up to my elbows in the long gone, but what I can't remember is why I'm here so late, whether there really is a client, if I'm just running myself through a maze again.

Vern grabs the phone like it's a rainbow trout about to get away.

"But, Mr. Honeywell!"

The Mercados are in town and, of course, Honeywell's invited them to stay at the Albright apartment, given them a key, they're on their way now. . . .

"But!"

(I remember thick, loud people who came one summer, and how the man put me on his lap, said, "Little fella, put up those dukes." Later, I poured bacon grease in his bathrobe pockets.)

Margie chirps and gurgles like a drive-time dj.

"Oh, Freddy, you're so wonderfully brave."

She packs him away in the foyer closet, but Vern has the damning evidence of Freddy's straw fedora, and teeters in his righteous advance like he's just fallen out of a hammock.

"We had a bargain, baby, and you've broken it."

"But, Dad!"

"And as of now, I'm taking that Havana trip alone."

(I remember a dozen collisions with El Gordo, more, and all his rigid relish. How he would rise up like a man pushing darkness away; how, in my night mind, I'd have him begging me to pull the trigger.)

"That must be Freddy now. I'll teach him a lesson he won't soon forget," Vern bleats, greeting Señor Mercado with a windmilling uppercut.

Mrs. Mercado, cocooned in wine-red sateen—or what I imagine to be wine-red sateen (Ella Dean, my algebra tutor, and her soapy breath)—faints through the doorway and into Margie's arms.

"Well, Dad, looks like we can cancel your travel plans too."

"You've got to think of something, baby. I'll be ruined."

Vern whines pitifully; the sick undercurrents of this father/daughter bond have become impossible to ignore.

Enter now Roberta, Vern's girlfriend, conveniently situated across the hall in apartment 10B, totally out of place among these overwound toys. She is lithe and cool; her thin smile emerges from out of a fog of Virginia tobacco.

"Looks like fun. Can anyone play?"

"Roberta, this is no time for . . ."

(Betsy from up the street who took me down to the cellar to watch her sit on a pop bottle, smiling thinly as the glass neck disappeared inside her.)

I imagine Roberta growing up in a Boston townhouse, learning High German from her nanny, attending Mount Holyoke and being seduced by a lit. prof. with the highest, blackest heels. Now she writes articles for gardening magazines and takes Vern for all she can.

Margie has that hophead gleam in her eye. (Carla's nostrils pouring smoke like tailpipes and me thinking: Yes, she's older.) "We can say there was a prowler."

"They'll come to any second now."

"Don't worry, I know just who can play the part."

Freddy gropes out of the closet, puckers faithfully when Margie tells him to close his eyes. Throwing mums over her shoulder (wet aromas of the Lexington Avenue florist where I worked, boy chants from the Catholic school next door), Margie crowns him with a vase.

Roberta looks bemused, as though observing a square dance in the West Virginia hills. (A man told me, at a truck stop outside Wheeling, that bears had stolen furniture from his house.) "Why don't you phone the police, Vern. Before we're all unconscious."

Margie kissing the adhesive tape she's plastered over Freddy's mouth, Señor Mercado gesturing ethnically, his hand-painted tie flapping like a second tongue, the perky violins. Produced by Hal Roach, Jr.

I shut down all the machinery I can and sit in almost-silence. It turns me backward, pushes me and pushes me into places everyone has been: up against the picture window that overlooks the lives of Bat Masterson and Huckleberry Hound, among the pages of glossy magazines, along overlit streets and in the vicious parking lots of doughnut shops, outside and inside of uneasy photographs, under a Christmas tree, behind a fixed expression, above the clouds. I remember that the man who played Molly Goldberg's husband was blacklisted and subsequently killed himself; I remember the first appearance of a gourmet entree you could boil in a bag. And, turning backward, I remember that all experiences are equally synthetic.

I sit so very still because it is dangerous to move. I am like a little old man in a hard chair on a decrepit porch, and memory is a tumor pressing against some vital spot. If it were possible, I would close my eyes. But I'm mean with fatigue and sick from remembering. I roll tiny sips of sour mash around in my mouth and aim evil thoughts at anything that passes by my porch.

I've been absent from work three days and nobody has called. That I find this disturbing shows how hard I am to please. Too ego-bound to favor anonymity as I claim? Oh, well. I got to beat Opatowski at chess, and hear from Tubbs, the cook, of his week as a Sonny Liston sparring partner in Miami Beach. I got to play with Heidi all yesterday, letting her put me in makeup, exploring her mouth like a dentist, lollipopping her icy toes. All this easy leisure and I feel like there's a high, rough wall at my back. Too indulgently morbid to accept pleasure? *Que sera.* I can let today flap by with the wings of magpies rioting for beer nuts, or with the pages of *The Charterhouse of Parma*. But I need to cadge a little spirit. Right now, Sonny Boyers seems as kindred as they come.

Coils of wire, buckets of roofing sealant—there's more sal-

vage in the yard than usual. To one side of the garage, where
the boys' swings used to be, is a corral holding goats with red
plastic tabs in their ears. Dawn comes to the door, a bowl of
raisin-flecked dough braced in front of her, to say Sonny is out
testing products, if I feel like hiking after him. She points to a
web of arroyos behind the house and I look at the web of cellu-
lite on her arm. She doesn't invite me in. The more I learn
about her . . .

Her first year as a wife, Dawn held a job in a penitentiary
kitchen supervised by a 280-pound schemer off a Calgary
wheat farm who took enough kickback money from the meat
and produce suppliers to think about opening a restaurant. He
wanted Dawn for his hostess. In the worst way. He reached to
measure her and she pushed his hands into a vat of bubbling
minestrone. The trusties cheered.

My legs are disobedient and stiff as I climb. Under thin dust
the earth is baked hard and I slide back, paddling my hands
in the air. From the ridge Sonny is probably watching my
struggle, thinking: Another unprepared chump.

"Hoss, you got to stalk quieter than that," is what he says
when I finally reach him. "You could be dead more ways than
a cat has lives by now."

He is trollish, kneeling by some shiny rig, a mess-kit pan of
water balanced on top of it. Solar cookstove that won't boil
water, he grunts. His boots are cracked, the black beret slipping forward. Troll in a quandary. Just beyond are straggling
pines, trash mounds along the fire road.

This is not the picture. This is not the man admirable for his
coherent (or just consistent?) ethics. Oh, well. Learn to settle
for less.

"I have to waste my time with crap." Sonny, in annoyance,
pitches the unboiled water against a rock and watches it evap-
orate. "The small businessman is all on his own."

That's more like it—those conversational slogans.

"What did you do before?"

"Different things. Nothing important."

I'm kneeling now too. "For instance."

"Back in Fort Wayne I assembled clock-radios. It was good money for the time. Out here I painted houses, worked some road crews. Then I got into the necktie stuff. Debt collection. Selling hydraulics and office supplies."

"Job variety is good for you," I recite. "Job monotony can be a real serious danger."

"Wasting your time with crap."

A breeze comes up and we turn to it, letting it dry our faces. The resinous scent of the trees is like a drowsy little meal. What's coherent now is saying nothing, scanning the houses below, the flat black roofs. A stillness of anticipation, uncomfortable. The sky bears down and bright cars are mortar targets in the streets.

"If we had a little more breathing room . . ."

Then Sonny speaks proudly of his goats, of the boys learning to make cheese from the milk, veers inevitably into technical details of rennet content and humidity control. I must know that closely as we kneel in the dirt, as close a resemblance as our fixations sometimes bear, I will never trust as does Sonny with all his heart.

We stroll back into the trees where a plywood sheet is propped. The practiced salesman demonstrates an aluminum blowpipe, placing darts in a line on the pale wood. Silent force, the best kind. "Can't you shut up?" Heidi kept repeating yesterday. She should see me now, my darts arcing, falling silently short of the target.

"It's focus," Sonny instructs, "not lung power."

And learning to settle for less means learning to shut up. Okay. That's a new job.

THE URGE TO BUY TERRORIZES YOU. I saw this in spray paint on a viaduct this morning and it turned me right over. A merciless conditioning network and nowhere to hide. Depths of torment and compulsion, a moment's relief at the checkout counter before beginning all over again.

Into this concept, as I drove, everything seemed to fit. Cacti became part of a bar-b-q sauce label; rock formations were objects to be conquered with the latest in climbers' gear. I passed children playing around a woodpile and they seemed like little tools designed to open, like secret agents of color film and popsicles. Anywhere I looked there were nothing but commodities. To feel, even to breathe, was to consume.

Approaching the facility at half speed, window-shopping along, I ran up on new product. Delusions of the marketplace, poisonous beguilements. There was no getting without some giving up. And so nothing felt strange or uncomfortable any-more since artificial flavors, recreations, and synthetics were all over and done with by way of complete acceptance. Safe as milk. Our bulwark was the imitation of life.

One of those days. I was too full of ideas and should have gone home to Golconda, where people know me better. But I went to my minimart of a desk, which was exactly as I had left it: rubber brontosaurus, eyedrops, yellow water pistol, rolling papers, coupons, dog skull, lockknife, cards. The console was dusty with ashes and the swivel chair's indentations were mine and mine alone. Looking things over, I felt likable. I read my last bit of paperwork.

Annotations: JUGGERNAUT (docu-special re: US industrial birth). Still photos, Ellis Island. Proud past, our heritage of strength./Steam power. Railroad, shipping $$$/ Smokestacks & brick kilns (male & female). / Soft-eyed girl in knitting mill. White spools. Narrator: "The pathos of drudging children."

Exactly as I'd left it. Except that some someone had printed below: "Who asked you? History—we used to grow plants, now we work in them."

Who asked me? Who wrote large in red felt pen? I won't fret about it because that is precisely what they want me to do. Devious but not subtle. As stringent as these overseers try to be, one must be lenient in return, slack. Dispassion denies panic and leaves no marks.

"It has your sound, your style," Ellen says. "Maybe you wrote it yourself and forgot."

"Possible but not plausible."

We are picnicking on the floor of a subarchive editing room, her smoked turkey sandwiches and my thermos of margaritas. Lighting is recessed, the air chilly, this bat cave atmosphere just what we're after.

The barometer lately has been on the rise, a high pressure system. Blooming like a dark stain, ire emerged from between the lines of First Tier memoranda. There were spot checks and speedups; there were interviews conducted by a team of "outside consultants," all of whom wore the same indecipherable lapel pin. Rumors cascaded: an investigation by the SEC, a takeover bid from Coca-Cola, top execs on the brink of indictment for peddling high-tech designs to the Soviets. So now oblique looks are everywhere. People comb their offices for bugs, erase tapes, shred paper. They talk of exposure and reprisal. Karen Silkwood's name has come up.

Cage behavior, Ellen has called it, in reference to the aberrations shown by animals long in captivity. But then everyone is entitled to deal with pressure in ways of her own. She, for example, has altered her hair; now garish red and cropped close, it looks filched from the costume trunk of a Peruvian circus.

"Don't you wonder," I ask, "why you've been assigned to do nothing but watch Channel Tomorrow?"

Channel Tomorrow is a pirate cable operation out of Baja California which televises a mix of industrial films, gay pornography, and political harangues from an old man in safari clothes. He bellows and whispers and twirls a leather quirt. Behind him are gilt-edged chromoliths of Qaddafi and Pol Pot.

"I'm like a hick," Ellen says. "Suspicious but not curious."

"One out of two isn't bad."

She bends a crust of pumpernickel into a bridge and walks two fingers over and back.

"Thousands and thousands of hours going nowhere," she says. "Still, I remember my first sight of this place. I'd slept all the way on the plane coming out and this was like more dreamland. Ancient wisdom, a temple in the sun. I promised myself a life all wired up and painless. Some schmaltz, huh?"

Janos, the editor who goes with the room, comes in with his lunch on a tray, potato salad and four milks.

"The good life for five minutes," he says, looking at our white cloth spread on his floor.

Janos bounced paving stones off the oncoming tanks in Budapest in 1956. His loyal father, withstanding purges and Party shakeouts, still maintains himself as a regional minister of state fisheries. After thirty years in America, most of them in Hollywood, Janos should retain his Slavic sense of machination and deceit, a decoding ability lodged in the genes.

His big insight on the recent intrigues? "For worker ant there is only work and ignore the rest."

"Worker ants are female," Ellen says helpfully. "Without exception."

Janos flips a toggle and monitors blink on, burning squares in a crossword. With the logical elegance of bones, across and down, the images are locked together and the puzzle solves itself, saying: Have a stylish face. Drive a shiny car. Working in reverse, it is possible to retrieve the clues. These are the contradictions, the things not shown. They have no shape unless taken one at a time, saying: Where is the prize? What are the rules? Who asked you?

Janos is describing the Navajo pollen paintings that he bought only last week from the artist himself. He praises their sophistication of design. Ellen listens with interest, compressing her lips. For art of this quality, he says, it was a deal.

I slip out without their noticing, the liquor coming and going in my head like surf. Something in common there. Maybe they even like each other. So what to do after the art discussion is over? No sense in it. But who says you have to do anything? Being attractive, just being pleasant—more buying and selling is all. Selfish. I should track back to the Golconda and give all these words a rest, but instead I prowl.

This passageway, curving downward, ramplike, frightens me a little by being empty. Somewhere nearby is the pistol range where Delvino practices; and on weekends he goes out hunting snakes with a Buntline. Delvino, whom I'd run from if I saw him now, or bash his face. These nude gray walls, the rusty smell (steam pipes? but there aren't any), are like this little door here with the red light above—they remind me of school. School in late afternoon when halls lengthen, empty rooms and stairwells whisper, and you sense the gathered madness which noise covers during the day. The red bulb reflected in gray paint is like blood underwater. When I put my ear to the little door, I can hear relays clicking inside; I can envision ceramic insulators and copper switches, strands of wire lashed thickly together into color-coded muscle. Simple schematics that function in darkness, while up above in offices whose tinted windows filter sunlight there are short circuits, a chaos of fear and rumor, a fixation on security.

The passage levels off and angles to the left. I intersect buried waste ducts: soup, suds, the urine of receptionists. I cross the path of coaxial cable. Things converge at this depth, a good spot for sabotage. More echoes of school. Small resentful boy.

But I'm a grownup now, selfish. Prove it? Sitting cross-legged on this cold gray floor, I challenge myself to remember the store credited with supplying George Burns's wardrobe on *The George Burns and Gracie Allen Show*. Rappaport's? Bienstock's? Tavelman's. There you are. With the miraculous adult mind, I can put myself inside there, ca. 1956. Mr. Lou, the tallis-like measuring tape around his neck, offers a hamantasch and weak coffee. He displays bolts of cloth, leads the ritual fingering. "Let us fit you special for a nice herringbone two-button." I feel languid, serene, with no urge to buy. Radio comes softly from the front of the store. *The Polynesian Hour.* As Mr. Lou takes my inseam, I feel I could stand here forever.

He was wearing an agate bolo tie and blue coveralls and he was in my room when I came back from a double shift at the facility.

"Afternoon, brother."

He seemed quite comfortable in my director's chair, feet propped on the round white table. He pointed with his chin at a Conestoga wagon making its way slowly from right to left across the color console screen.

"Clear as a mountain lake, eh?"

"Do we know each other?"

Needlenose pliers snapped back and forth at me. He ventriloquized: "Frank Goodhue, television doctor with the zeal to heal."

I clicked off the set and turned on the air conditioner.

"Mr. O. has me in several times a year and I give everyone a checkup."

I noticed a plastic bag of brownies under the bedside lamp. Heidi. I felt new fatigue.

"You ought to stretch out," Goodhue said, reaching into his tool bag for a stick of gum. "Just disposed of a body, from the look of you."

How the world's wise guys plagued me. I threw the brownies at him. "Have all you want."

He smiled, rolled up his gum like a prayer rug before crushing it in his molars. "Really. Take a load off."

I undid buttons, closed my eyes. The refrigerated air felt nice and heavy. Goodhue's voice was quick and thin and straw-dry as he told the old story no one ever asked to hear. Eleven years in the monastery hard by Lake Huron, dipping candles and making cheese. Dreadful winters, ice in the washbasin and carillon bells cracking the air. The abbot who sang to his cat, who was exposed in a national magazine as a war criminal, an officer in the Iron Guard. And finally surreptitious correspondence courses, a determination to get out and do something useful.

"Learning to make decisions again was no picnic, I'll tell you for sure."

I pictured Heidi smoothing the sheets, thin babydoll hair hiding her face. My limbs buzzed with imminent sleep. This TV doctor was better than a lullaby.

"And after that?" I murmured.

"Hired on with a high-volume appliance store in Grand Rapids. Very first house call I went on, the husband had blown out their picture tube with a deer rifle."

The facts of his life passed over me like gas. Marriage to a grocery checker, disintegration and aimless flight. Drinking bouts and the stink of charred tubes, the sharp intimacies of uncounted dens and rec rooms where anxious clients waited out the restoration of their sets.

"You'd be amazed at the amount of gratitude . . ."

Goodhue was gone when I woke up. Dim, agitated light in

the black room—TV back on—and there was the brownie bag rising and falling on my chest. Heidi would be calling soon, wanting to be teased. I unhooked the phone, wedged open the door so warm night haze could come inside. Cars went by too fast, radios harsh and windshields splattered with moths. I had brownies and root beer, watched a documentary on Islamic architecture, and had to admit the picture was as clear and clean as a picture could be.

He's wearing a nylon workout suit and eating a taco over my desk.

"You weren't expecting me?"

He seems quite comfortable with my signaled annoyance. The frames of his glasses are of thick lime-green plastic; the embossed card he passes to me is creamy and thin.

KEVIN LUIS DUKES
SENIOR RESEARCH FELLOW
THE CENTER FOR POPULAR CULTURE AT BOWLING GREEN

He swivels in my chair as I read and reread, brushes shredded lettuce onto the floor.

"No, I'm not expecting you."

"And I was hoping to start right in."

"Okay. Why don't you start with what *you're* expecting."

His soft, ballroom dancer's face becomes more credible as it pinches down. Strumming a rubber band stretched between thumb and ring finger, he describes in some detail the assistance promised him in certain investigations necessary to the completion of a book. No outsider gets that kind of access, I think. Not without a reason.

"Who is it you know?"

He mentions the operations director of another department, someone with a reputation for malicious mischief.

"I married her only daughter," he says blandly.

"Nice going."

But, of course, he'd rather talk about his book.

"There's an essay on professional wrestling, and another on the evolution of outdoor advertising. I've done a long piece examining the semiotics of Japanese pornography, and a reappraisal of Sammy Davis, Jr., called 'The One-Eyed Man Is King,' and . . ."

We move briskly down a long corridor carpeted with plastic grass. I nod and shift my eyebrows as though listening, while his voice blends with piped music and the sighing ventilators. I'm replaying this morning's phone call to Ellen, who has now exhausted her allotment of emotional leave days.

"I ran out of food over the weekend," she says from the bedroom of her company apartment. "So I drink lots of tea and chew toothpicks."

"But you're all right? I mean . . ."

"Me and my memory." She coughs, moves inside rustling sheets. "Crazy what you file away. Little ordinary things that keep clicking into place, out of my control for certain. Probably I belong in a nursing home. Among my souvenirs."

Never have I heard her voice quite this way. I'm uneasy, wanting her sullen and strong.

"What I can't get through is why you choose the different bits. Can you sense it maybe? Catching one moment from a sideways kind of angle and there's an essence that . . ."

"Unfuckingreal," K. L. Dukes blurts out.

I've taken him into the South Monitor Wing. He seems genuinely impressed by the long wall of screens, the long motionless line of headphoned workers, the galaxy of control buttons.

"Looks like the war room."

"Someday might be." And I direct him to the data belt streaking green overhead, runic as a stock ticker.

He wipes his glasses in slow, diminishing circles, and reads: "BMANILA 20/05 FI MODE."

"There's a political address in five minutes on Philippine state TV."

"How much do they pay for doing this?"

"Not enough."

We tube down to the deepest level of hexagonal stacks and I take him through a few of the basics. How to run different searches, excerpting protocol, like that. He rattles his fingers back and forth across black container spines, looking undecided. The face is pinched again, the eyes suspicious. He grabs a tape at random, the 1978 Rose Bowl Parade, and examines it thoroughly, touching every part as if expecting a secret message in braille. Likably, his rhetorical smile is gone. I smell the salsa cruda on his breath.

"It's insidious," he says. "Like cancer cells proliferating."

"You could look at it that way."

"But you can't, I suppose." His expression is half sour, half amused. "One analogy too many."

"I've been at it so long I'm immune."

Fine and dandy, you'd think, with his beige GUEST badge and his connections-in-law. Whatever's bothering the boy, it's no research topic. Anyway, my nose is clean; I'm cooperating. We ascend two levels and I show him catalogs, decipher some of the categorization codes. He feigns interest incompetently, his eyes tracking the movements of everyone else in the room in apparent expectation of seeing someone he knows. Hoping to see them before they see him?

"Let's head back to your office."

He sags resignedly, but with a hand on my shoulder pushes me toward the glass doors. Whatever's bothering the boy . . .

"There really isn't any book, but I suppose you already knew that."

I shrug, disarrange files on my desk.

"The way it is, I sweat a pint of blood just to finish a two-page letter."

"And you've never been to Bowling Green in your life."

"Oh, no, all that's genuine. Even my stupid name." He shows once more that mixture of fatigue and insistence. "Why I'm here is to get something out of Katy's mother. Think you could get me a key to one of the editing rooms? Just for an hour."

"Settling a score, is that it?"

"I promise, an hour and no more. In the interest of justice."

I'm not the least curious as to the details of this familial extortion. I have no qualms about furnishing the key.

Cornmeal pie with jalapeño sausage, pitchers of beer half off. That's the Wednesday night special at Boot Hill, and I'm taking advantage. Old ladies waltz to Conway Twitty and linemen play poker dice at the bar. Very homey. So what's Opatowski doing here, I wonder. He and the ex-postmistress who owns the place are supposed to be mighty feuders.

"Nobody cares about appearances in a town this small."

He pours off the dregs of my pitcher to go with his double bourbon, looks blank when I thank him for the fixup on my TV, says he didn't hire any Frank Goodhue.

"I didn't dream the guy. Somebody's going around your motel with a bag of tools and . . ."

"So okay. It's the same as why am I in here when I can drink free in my own joint." He aims a patient, paternal smile. "People are funny."

"Not to me."

Had a fight with Heidi in place of breakfast. Floating instinct: I sensed trouble at the scratch of her passkey, knew how she'd attack when I saw the rag twisting in Ajax-white hands. The indictment popped out of her like bread from a toaster. I didn't play anymore, hardly spoke. I was sullen and distant, made her feel exploited.

"You're about as much fun lately as choir practice." An admiring disgust was visible on her face.

I told her she had a husband to absorb her whines and demands, to leave me clear. Heidi flung a toilet brush at me. I caught a lank twist of hair and spun her around. She scratched the back of my hand. I called her a cheap cunt.

Hard to guess which of us took the greater pleasure from it. For me the effect was of a violent morning fuck, raspy but quenching, with a pleasant absence of mind. I smoked a joint on the way to work and took the long way round.

The early sun brought out strips of orange and verdigris green in the terraced slag at the Apex II mine. I curved south through Government Camp, the refurbished ghost town where a squad of retirees clustered around the largest motor home swilling coffee and loading cameras. See America first. Then came the dead farms: rusted tin and crumpled wire, slanting walls. Something had come through here like a plague. Cutting west on blacktop with no center line, I cranked up the radio and downed the windows, loosed Jerry Lee Lewis into the clear, dry air. Ruins normally soothed me, but not today. Everything I saw made me thirsty: sheepskins drying on a fence, even swaybacked ponies snorting water from a halved oil drum. I passed a Papago in a John Deere cap. He wasn't looking for a ride, just squatting on the shoulder like he had a cottonwood for shade and a slow brown river to watch. What he had was nothing but time.

The guard waves me through and I look for a parking space. I put fruit gum in my mouth and sunglasses over my eyes. This day is too sweet to spoil. Then I meet Foley coming up the center aisle of the lot. He looks a little wobbly.

"Got one for you," Foley says, pulling my arm like a bell rope. "These two programming veeps, see, they're on their way to a convention when the plane crashes in the desert. Only survivors. Desolate, pitiless sun. They're crawling on hands and knees, praying for an oasis before they shrivel up and die. And can you beat it, there's a certified miracle on top of the next dune. It's an ice-cold can of peaches and an opener right beside. With trembling hands, they pry the lid up and there's fruit bobbing in chilled syrup. So the one turns to the other and says, 'Let's piss in it.' "

While Foley chuckles harshly at his joke, I notice for the first time a torn segment of a woman's picture emerging from his shirt pocket and the ink splotch in his hair.

"You know where I grew up?"

"Uh, Foley . . ."

"Troy, New York. It snows there. It snows there every year."

Then he brushes past me as if I were a stranger in a hotel lobby. He doesn't stop when I call to him, or even slow his pace when the torn picture flutters to the asphalt. I watch as he slides into a dented Japanese car and rolls slowly out the gate. I won't be seeing him again.

A puff of dark hair, one apparently indifferent eye, the upper slope of a thick nose, a triangle of sweater, and a suggestion of pearls. The photograph has been severed diagonally. From its yellowed border and almost pulpy texture, I judge it to be more than thirty years old.

I'm examining it under a magnifier at my desk when Ellen comes up behind me. I summarize the Foley encounter without turning around. Ellen's fleshy hands appear on the desktop and her head comes to rest on my shoulder. She sighs. She explains that Foley's been canned, how he'd found his office empty this morning, not so much as a paper clip left on the carpet.

"Been here long as anyone," she says with a certain irrelevancy. "I think he'd built up a sad attachment."

"And the picture?"

"A wife or a sister. Maybe something he found in the trash. Who knows?"

She comes around in front of me. Framed by the chrome edges of my central monitor, by the tight chaos of her own hair, her face takes on the stiff and joyless beauty of a German religious painting.

"Anyway," she says, looking past me, "I don't think he cares about women."

"Let's drink." I pull out the tequila.

Ellen dips a finger into her cup, sucks on it. Her eyes are

still on the distance. "My father has an unpleasant view of the world. He suspects everyone. But he has a story he tells after a couple of Manhattans. It's about Hiroshima." She shakes her head, gives me the cup to finish. "He was with Armed Forces Radio and went in with an inspection team right after the blast. They gave him a jeep and a driver and permission to go wherever he wanted. Bouncing through the ruins, describing into a microphone. Mister Reporter doing a job. Then they happen on a couple of survivors, a father and son who are living in a hole in the ground with a tin sheet for a roof. The driver gives them a pack of cigarettes. Great confusion. Custom requires that the gift be reciprocated, but they have nothing to give. An idea hits the son. He jumps into the hole and comes out with a C melody saxophone on which he proceeds to play, quite badly, 'Someone to Watch Over Me' and 'My Blue Heaven.' Sometimes my father can't get to the end of the story because he's crying too hard."

I cannot prevent myself from asking what this has to do with Foley. Her eyes finally engage mine; they are curiously neutral, pupils nearly disappearing into speckled green.

"Lonely men. Resentment. Old pictures."

I'm chastened and take a long enough drink from the bottle to create air bubbles in the glass neck.

Arms folded, elevating her loose breasts, Ellen again shakes her head.

"You drink," she says. "I'm going to go lock my door."

"What for?"

I hold out my hand to her. She looks at it as if it were something from an archaeological dig.

A line of explosions, small puffs of smoke. One woman clawing, another hiding. A man with ink-stained hair and a man nestled in roadside trash. But no straight line, or I'm too wasted to tell. Nothing in my stomach to sponge up the alcohol, proud essence of the cactus. Ambushed. A long warm spike hammered through the top of my head. Okay, no excuses. Still, everything looking soupy right now. There, where

Ellen was standing, is a jagged black outline of her body. Maybe I should lock my door too?

Better. No security leaks now. I put my ear to the intervening wall, listening for Ellen. She might be one of those silent weepers—fear and loathing without relinquishing control. It wouldn't surprise me. Very precise in her choices. Don't I remember her telling me of a museum in the city which insisted its *Mona Lisa* was genuine, the one in Paris a fake, and that she'd applied for a job there? Or is this an invention of mine? A groove worn into the mind during sleeplessness? It wouldn't surprise me.

The shoddy remorse of the boozer, the inflated sentiments, could be plotted on a graph. Does that stop me? I lift the phone and punch out Violet's number. Buzz, buzz, and that's all. Probably off showing slides in a lecture hall. Early back east, but all I get is Carla's answering machine. "I'm unreachable now. . . ." Muddy stride piano backing her up. In character, red lips, black pumps, and bobbed hair. I don't wait for the tone.

"She ain't here," Opatowski says.

"How long ago did she leave?"

"No timeclocks here, my friend. Why not try her at home?"

A truly unctuous quality in his voice. This could be the highlight of his day. I picture him sprawled in front of the office TV, fingering a cheroot. I picture him, in lime-green golf pants, on the cover of a chamber of commerce brochure above the legend "Ask Me About the Good Life."

"Is Mommy home? Can I talk to her, please?"

The child squeals and drops the receiver; a long dead space then, punctuated by barking and the surging audio of a game show. Heidi comes abruptly onto the line.

"Yeah?"

"How's every little thing?"

"You miserable fucking—"

"Can we meet somewhere for lunch?"

"Get bent. I wouldn't meet you on top of a diamond mine."

But I can tell from her seesawing inflection that really she's glad to hear from me. Takes only another ten minutes to talk her into it. She'll stick Tasha next door, says she has to go back to the motel for something.

"We can start from scratch. The whole thing, I mean."

"My mind's open," she says.

No more explosions today. All is defused by right thinking. I picture her working spray polish into the Mediterranean finish of her home entertainment console. I picture her bending over the edge of my bathtub with nothing on but her running shoes.

Hot in here. Feel like lead balls are hanging from arms and shoulders. For now, stretch out alongside baseboard. No harm. I have plenty of time. Be there first. Resting up briefly is all. In control. Eyes shut for a few minutes only. Minutes. No harm.

I'm dozing in front of the box, light but no sound, when I hear it. There is a vibratory tingle in the glass when I step inside the drapes and tip my head against the window. First thought, what a gorgeous piece of rolling stock—a green-and-white ambulance from Cherry Ames. I see Wade jump out and dash into the office. Right then I snap to who they're going to be carrying out. Fuck all. I want to stay inside with the covers over my head, but really, I can't.

The outline under the sheet could be a child's. They retract the stretcher wheels and slide her on in like a safety-deposit box. Opatowski has no shoes on. The bottled-in-bond Pottstown hard guy doesn't answer me, fights when I try to sit him straight on the bench. His sobbing is so violent, I'm afraid he'll throw a seizure.

"Can't you give him something?"

This is as close to Wade as I've ever come. He has the same pitted cheeks as his wife, the same pallor.

"Like what?" he says.

"Like a sedative. Just look at him, for Christ's sake."

"Yeah, I see. The man just lost his wife." He looks to his partner, a burly guy with a cheek distended by tobacco. "We got no liability coverage for that, right?"

Opatowski is choking on grief, tries to get her name out but can't.

"That don't make me crazy about it. Hell, I know these people personal, and anything else . . ." Wade shrugs. "I wouldn't even be here except for two fellas called in sick."

I throw him against the ambulance door, jerk him back again by the belt.

"Take care of him now, you jerkoff. Right now."

He could flatten me in seconds, but I must look rabid enough to alarm them both, convince them to take the easy way. Wade nods, spits, mumbles something about legalities. They hit Opatowski with something from an ampule and take him inside. I ought to stay with him, but really, I can't.

The sun is high and the road is flat and black as a griddle. I walk over to Boot Hill and subside into a brown booth. Two other thirstys in the place, Virg from the gas station, and the owner's crooked boy. We don't say hi. I have a shot and a beer, then two more.

Then come stinging tears, concentrated, as though I've been holding them a long, long time.

It was cherry blossom time in our nation's capital. The Washington correspondents, who were always fighting for air time, searched out bosky spots to film their opens and closes. Ratings for the Evening News had never been better; I thought of asking for a raise.

It was daffodil time in Lake Success, and they were burying my mother in a memorial park spruce as a tournament golf course. The headstone was white marble. The casket was polished copper, a plush capsule that could have been boostered into space.

Three rows of folding wooden chairs had been set out, but it was still SRO. Aunt Rita, who'd been pinned under a horse, arrived in an electric wheelchair, a slit-eyed chauffeur in attendance. Sonia Brooks, whose Christmas cards had been returned unopened, was there without her husband. My mother commanded loyalty, at least that day—her tennis teacher came, her hair stylist, and a housekeeper she'd fired for drinking. And there was the English character actress she'd toured with one summer, who wept and trembled uncontrollably: On her way to the service in an open convertible, she'd crossed the Verrazano Bridge and a rat had dropped from a girder onto the seat beside her.

My father read some Swinburne and a Unitarian minister mused about "interdependence." A circuit court judge, who, as far as I knew, had never met her, described my mother as a bright clear light. Union workers lowered my mother into ground that belonged to white grubs and blind moles. Flowers were tossed in with her. Strangers embraced me. I felt sick to my stomach but my eyes were dry.

Carla was next to me, silent and still, but her eyes overflowed. She had driven down from Maine, from the cabin she'd fled Boston for, three days earlier, and had barely slept since. Her bloodless face was seraphic, frozen white above a mourning costume improvised from closet depths: black velvet minidress, black tights, pointy shoes with functionless buckles. Back at the house, I spent a long time in the shower.

Gordo said we oughtn't to sink too deep in sorrow, how she would have been the first to say so. He wanted to take us to the Princeton Club for drinks and dinner. We had soup and toast instead and took turns answering the phone.

"Anything at all we can do," offered curious townsfolk.

"There are no words," said bar dwellers from the country club, prefacing advice.

We were dazed, wary of each other, and the sentences we found to speak were museum specimens. Gordo roamed between kitchen and living room, knocking things over. He seemed to be regressing, melting into himself. He played with toast crumbs and told us how proud we made him. The longer he held back the more horrific it would be. Carla, whom he'd always frightened the most, turned stricken eyes to me when he tottered over to ruffle her hair like some stickpinned bachelor. ("You seem like nice kids. Here's a dollar for each of you.") But soon he wandered off, decanter in hand, to their room, their bed.

Not that it was any easier for the two of us. Every surface held her imprint, every object was infected with her presence. We sat on the floor and smoked. Carla drank coffee like it was medicine and talked about Maine, the cold clear nights and the piney air.

"Sometimes I forget to eat for a while and I see things." Her voice was hoarse.

"Things?"

Carla did not elaborate. The house had grown suitably cold and she wrapped up in a blanket, teeth clicking on the rim of her cup. I felt angry and protective and uneasy. It was a sleet storm of impulse and recollection through which there was no visibility. I heard my mother laughing, scolding. She pulled me from a pile of dead leaves and swung me toward the sun.

"If you could hold me for a minute."

Carla opened the raveled wings of the blanket and I crawled inside, smelling her exhaustion. She felt hard and shell-like at first as I held her tightly. Then as I loosened, so did she, her face turning into my neck. Each tear was discrete on my skin, an emission squeezed out of her with the pain and effort of birth. That my mother could have caused such misery seemed unforgivable just then. I had no sympathy to spare for her. Carla's mouth opened against me and I disappeared inside the jagged cadence of her breathing. For an immeasurable time then she ceased to be a sister or a woman, became simply a fellow creature, and I glided up and up a sparking wire, ecstatic with purity of feeling.

A momentous crash overhead, deep bellowing. The widower had snapped his tethers. Carla's hands were like suction cups against my ribs.

"Let him alone. Please."

I pulled free, got to my feet. The velvet dress had ridden up past her hips and her eyes were those of a doe under the gun.

"I live here too," I said. "I don't want him tearing the place up."

My sister curled on the floor, palms over her ears. I turned from her and went up the stairs, toward the sound of breaking glass. There was a dreadful awareness of error, as in the elongated second or two before the car hits the stanchion. It was sheer expedience that placed me in the house and I really didn't care if the old man raved until the very roof spun away across identical lawns and into the night.

"Feckless child! Parasite!"

I had reached the open doorway: Gordo in pajama tops amid a swale of destruction. He'd opened his hand on something; blood globs dropped from his fingers like candies.

"She died in shame . . . looking in a broken mirror. Shame!"

I had left a chance below, an opening.

"Worthless worthless world."

It could have been a kiss alone, a few gasped words, or something far more reckless. It would have been a recognition, a barrier irrevocably passed after so long and contorted a wait. But not now.

Gordo advanced, babbling. Blood had dribbled onto his gray penis, which swayed like a toxic undersea plant.

"Bedtime for you," I said.

"How much did you know about, eh, yardbird?"

I heard behind me the slap-slap of Carla's running feet, the thundercrack of her slamming door. Not now. Not ever.

I weighed my fist, rocked back, and drove it into the bulge of my father's jaw. He flipped backward onto a mound of clothing flung from the walk-in closet, and I left him there to come to or not. Either way.

The cigarettes I smoked downstairs tasted like jet exhaust, which was fine with me. I had one of those infected objects, a circular paperweight enclosing milky glass flowers, and I turned it and turned it in my hand until it was warm, remembering the day she'd bought it. A balmy October, mother and son driving out to check the foliage. We stopped in a little model-railroad town for refreshments, lemonade for her and a maple walnut cone for me. The junk store didn't interest me, so I waited in the car. But through the crowded display window I could see her expressions flash, the motion of her arms as she haggled. Bouncing into the car, she sparkled breathlessly like a swimmer fresh from the pool. The glass ball rolled out of tissue paper and into my hand.

"Did I do good?" she asked.

It was misty outside, halfway to dawn. I walked to the end of the street where woods began, flung the paperweight high and far, heard it crash into the safety of some dirty thicket. I walked back as slowly as I could. I wanted to hang myself from an ornamental tree with a pair of black tights, but my eyes were dry.

Fighting the sun, I grope along the sidewall to a patch of shade where I can retch. The hiss of hot grease comes through the screen door near me. I remember that Tubbs is gone; over to Texas to train quarter horses, he said. A Cambodian émigré mans the kitchen now. Ton Wat, a former architect, a designer of schools and custom bureaus, and the only member of his family left alive.

"It hurts him to have been spared," Opatowski said the day he hired this man.

Ignobly, without a word of explanation, I stole away from the Golconda like a cowardly vagrant father, leaving behind only a kachina doll Heidi had given me and, perhaps, a crucial piece of my integrity. Or possibly departure was the only way to save what little of it is left. But no more questions now; I've abandoned them as well.

I drove south, filling the car with cigarette smoke and the sound of my own tired voice as it spoke the injured contempt of everyone else for my flight. And like the vagrant father, I found solace in their accusations, snug proof of my independence. It was well past midnight when I finally stopped, pulling into a small, deserted rest area where a historic marker shaped like the state recalled the capture of Mexican outlaws. Moths careened and the air crackled with ozone. I nestled on the back seat and slept for several hours, or at least was not awake.

The Pronghorn Bungalow Court is east of the reservation, just north of the dry lake where hot-rod boys race and fight. I paid rent in advance to a man for whom ownership of the place seemed to be a thing inflicted on him.

"Got a beef with the state, don't bring it along." He spat into dead yellow stalks by the toolshed. "People expecting me to go to bat for them, I'm only the zookeeper here."

He wore tooled boots, gray whipcord trousers, stiff denim jacket. There was something unpleasantly fastidious in his manner.

"Stay here long and it's going to bring you down. That's a warning and I don't give it to everybody."

I thanked him. He rubbed his jaw expressionlessly, gazing past me at the single line of cabins, muttering about their needing paint. I was going to take this as a cue to cut a little deal, but he was already walking away, sliding into his long white car. He went off slowly, as though part of a parade.

Norbert Padilla. His name appears on my rent receipt in jagged lowercase letters. According to the only neighbor who will speak to me, Padilla's mother was a painter, a tubercular German who came for the dry air and stayed to marry an older man who sold tortillas from a wagon. Believing in cure by climate, the ill swarmed here in those days. Epidemics swept the southern counties every winter, until the hotel people got the idea of boiling their silverware.

Mind you, this informative neighbor is a dipsomaniac who claims to have served as adjutant to General Omar Bradley and to have played first base for the Washington Senators. When his government check arrives, he rides to the liquor store and back in a taxi. He favors white wine over red because then he can tell when he's vomiting blood.

"Right away I tells 'em I got files of my own," he says, bright-eyed and emphatic, with new ears for the limitless epic of Dag and the Veterans Administration. "Which I've lost the combination to the safe, but not to worry."

On he goes and all I hear are the circular sounds, like gamelan music. I sit here patching screen, calmed by the thinness of the wire, by the smallness of the holes, and I think of my father's law office, brimming with files, of the great desk glowing with lemon oil, and the framed motto of a man who never miscalculated a risk-to-benefit ratio: "Be satisfied with yourself and so thus will be others." I think of the entirely measurable distance between here and Lake Success, congratulating myself on all the subtractions I have worked so hard in my life to make.

"And if I told what them big poohbahs took out of the Reichsbank that night? What then?"

Dag releases my arm, satisfied with the weight of this threat. And I have no good reason to doubt casual pillaging by colonels. No further questions, remember? So I walk Dag back to his cabin, last in line, "the caboose," with its unlockable door and cardboard windows. He is reluctant to let me go, extracts a promise to return in the evening for something to drink and "the real story."

Fed by the sewage line, there are cottonwoods near the road and in their shade the Pronghorn's one and only family unit plays. The tiny wife with blonde hair out of a bottle buffs the chopper's chrome pipes and sips orange pop through a straw. Her jeans are embroidered at the knee with mushrooms. The husband lifts their baby high, making her gurgle and kick. He is shirtless, a rippled scar under his navel like he'd once been cut open with a breadknife. The impending gleam on their mean faces stops me in midwave. Never mind.

Over the sink in my cabin a magazine picture has been pasted. A boy sits at a piano, eyes shut, head tilted back. He bites his lip. The effort of playing from memory. Vertically arranged above him on the white wall are three ceramic fish. They are like thoughts bubbling out of his head, distractions from the tempo and the tune. I can feel him struggling, his fingers slippery on the keys, and I have to scrape him off the wall with a razor blade. Whoever put him up must have been harking back, dangling a piece of regret where it couldn't be missed. Something in Padilla's warning? But I feel fresh and clean, free of any urge to review past decisions. Fuck integrity. I know, I know—you've heard it all before. You ask in exasperation: Won't he ever get off the dime? Patience. I'm in a staging area right now. Formulations first.

   A) Initiate!
   B) Experience doesn't count
   C) Recall sexual extremities, then forget
   D) First aid
   E) Resource checking
   F) Catalysts & anodynes
   G) Research: desert botany

H) Body disciplines
I) Quicksand Syndrome (strive hard, fail fast)
J) Don't speculate—sane limits
K) Deductive vs. Reductive
L) Below sea level?
M) Sleeping exercise
N) Carla's black tights
O) Stick to this list and you will be okay

I can set myself a rigorous program. I can do that, sharpening myself on the small grinders of Padilla's toy town, moving beyond slogans. So then do I betray Ellen by way of these ambitions as I have, in other ways, betrayed Heidi, Chris Bruno, so many others? Who cares. Waste motion. I can discount experience. I can let thoughts bubble out of my head and burst harmlessly at the surface.

But no more chores for today. I would rather rub myself against the greasy mattress ticking. I would rather take another *Reader's Digest* from the pile and read of another Most Embarrassing Moment.

"This is a great country," says Norbert Padilla. "So big it can hold anything."

Because I've given up on distinctions, I don't get started on all the things it might want to let go of. Big country, mother country, underdeveloped country, Marlboro country—here or over there, it's all just country. Fine tuning? What for?

Padilla looks into the distance. "Big enough to smile at trouble," he says.

The air is cold and wet. We are standing at the mouth of the driveway where last night wind blew down the big metal sign. It is stippled with mud and more paint has flaked away. P ON HO N BUNG OW C UR is how it reads now. We blow on our hands. Padilla kicks a dent in the earth.

"I could replace it with neon," he says brightly.

"You'd have to run current out here. An investment."

"The only neon for miles."

Great country of appetite, where a lunger's son can dream of inert gas captured in tubes. Out where the sky's a little bit bluer. Out where delusion's a little bit newer.

Walking beside my landlord, I've got the shivers. Maybe it's all too big.

My last conversation with Ellen came after she'd been beaten outside a roadhouse frequented by butch girls from the reservation. She had cracked ribs.

"It only hurts when I breathe."

Other things hurt worse.

"The rest of the world. Everything rubs me the wrong way. I feel sometimes like I could float right off the planet and it really wouldn't matter." Finally she rested her hands, met my eyes through the smoke from her little cigar. "For a while there I thought you might provide me some gravity. Too much to expect."

"From a man," I added piteously.

"From someone who keeps missing the point." She raked fork furrows in the top of her unnibbled coconut pie. "Who couldn't get the point if it ran him through."

Men nearby discussed megabytes and upload key sequences with evident fervor.

"The rest of the world," she resumed. Her thumb went to her face, moved from scab to scab as if defining a constellation. "Could I be allergic?"

The commissary wallpaper featured Hollywood caricatures: Clark Gable, W. C. Fields, like that—something you'd find in an art house of the Minneapolis suburbs. A little bit of showbiz heaven, the faces smiling ferociously, as if at a malignant practical joke.

Ellen coughed, winced. "I find myself looking at children eight, nine years old. Little girls in sunsuits." Her eyes lurked in caves of swollen tissue. "I think, 'Well, they haven't gone wrong yet.'"

"So that's where you're looking for gravity these days."

"I think of myself at nine, sullen already. Up in my room, sleeping all day. From there to here isn't so very far, either. Room to room to room. Isolation wards. I could be all sealed away. I could clock the next fifty years without a moment of pleasure."

Ellen went for more coffee and didn't come back. The last I saw was her brown pullover consumed by a squad of white shirts at the beverage station.

So, in the end, I had nothing to offer. Too much to expect. With a thankless kind of wisdom she had sought refusal while I, pretending not to, had imagined everything. Pearls for the asking, love in a hammock, wind in the palms.

Moments of pleasure? The gift of cruelty? How easy it is to forget, how easy to feign surprise. The years telescope and I cannot resist. Bravo. Hegel observes that what we learn from history is that no one learns from history.

It was August at its thickest. We had been to a pool party at the home of some gay blade who wrote travel guides and Violet had irritated me all day with her easy chatter and eagerness for gin. Then, as I drove home through Sunset Boulevard stop-and-start, she nagged me to stop at a ladies' room. Her voice was a circular saw. I swung into a towaway zone, reached under her and pulled blue panties over her kneecaps. She giggled like someone in an Italian movie.

"Let go of it," I said.

"What?"

I put my palm over her bladder, pressed hard, and the gin came hosing out of her, splattering her thighs and pooling on the upholstery. I said for her to sit still and shut up. She cried without a sound and as I turned north on Fairfax, reached between my legs.

You cringe and recoil? Very well. But here was a compatibility, awesome in its precision, from which she and I could not turn away. An absence of imagined pearls. What cleaved us to each other and ultimately cleaved us in two were these types of closeness, progressive as a disease. More thankless wisdom, but in time, in desperation, wouldn't we have intertwined mortally, choking in unison? Isn't that true?

Distinctions again, goddammit. Habit of a lifetime, whereas rigor truly is not. Sure enough, there's more to this than erasing the old tapes and inserting the new; those work habits— automatic exchange, alternatives on request—worse than useless now.

A reprise of the wind flattens grass outside and rattles the boards. I'm shivering again. The hotplate's taped cord throws off a few sparks while I heat water for soup. I pull the zipper tab, empty the foil pouch of its yellow powder and dehydrated shreds of chicken. Black birds are skirling, angered by the turbulence. I drink hastily from the bowl and burn my tongue. Clouds are knotting and the wind shifts constantly, erratic as a drunken driver. Still not warm, I feel cloaked and cozy in this unlikely place with its rust-stained toilet and splintery pine walls. I am the fox in her den, the beaver in his lodge.

Before me on the floor I start to empty boxes newly brought from the car, arranging items in no system, improvising a collage of books, postcards, cufflinks, matches, a piece of rose quartz. My fingers are cool and smooth. Objects fall smartly into place, Sir Thomas Browne's *Urn Burial* abutting a broken watch, horseshoe magnet perfectly centered in an ashtray from the Beverly Wilshire hotel. The more I unload, the stronger my impulse to give it all away. That biker's little girl could play with my rubber dinosaur, and Dag, the military man, might appreciate Bernal Diaz's memoir of his years with Cortés. Potlatch at the Pronghorn. Too bad, but I can't fool myself. This is a fatuous ruse, like someone cleaning out the closets after a divorce. Rare things, pretty things, favorite things—standing for themselves alone, all are things and no more. Their addition or subtraction does not transform. Okay, one more issue to give up on: shortcuts. Progress. Elimination process.

Extra socks and a sweatshirt with the hood up aren't helping my shivers any. Muscles down my back contract, recalling New York winters, the snow and ice I haven't missed once in all these western years. "No seasons," transplants to L.A. were forever complaining. Sometimes I bought them one of those Citizen Kane paperweights in which you can shake up an artificial blizzard. Usually I just said, "See you at the beach."

I heat more water, drink more soup. The black birds have gone. From here no trees are to be seen, no cliffs. Maybe they'll find some roof eaves for shelter, or a dry culvert. The wind is repetitious now, singing an autistic little song. Salt from the soup feels to be crystallizing in my belly; the pains are sharp and quick. I get into bed and pull the blanket up to my ears. There, far below, it seems, my possessions are scattered on the floor. I feel weak in mind and body. No rigor. No vigor. Maybe I'll never get out of here.

Padilla, what I'm asking is this: If it's such a great country, why is everything so hard?

Time all hashed up. Lying here how many cycles of light and dark? How many sweats and chills? Wondering must mean I'm coming around, emerging. Every ligament and muscle packed tight with exhaustion. Diaphragm a belt of pain from heaving, mouth a compost hole, hair crisp with evaporated sweat. But now at least stilled, floating like a lily pad, no more shakes and spasms. After much spinning, mind becalmed as well, regaining assessment capability.

Idiot's delight. I've seen faces in the window, heard quiet, repetitious music. A menagerie of stains has galloped and bucked, sometimes browsed in the ceiling pasture.

In troughs between deliria, I've contemplated this bungalow as a place for dying, or rather as a place in which to be found all stiff and yellow like a wax icon. There'd be head-shaking and sucking of teeth. Another friendless derelict. Mercy, but they get younger all the time. Tag him and bag him, another one for the county. Then they'd interview Dag:

"You know how they is nowadays, can't figure which sock to put on first. This boy here, he was leastwise handy. I mean he knowed which end of a screwdriver goes where. But for most of it, he was just as green as the grass we ain't got."

I collapse halfway to the sink, too dizzy even to crawl. Expansion of lungs painful. Eyeballs a half-dozen sizes too large. Safest course is to stay put, lie here like a thumbsucker.

Linkage between sickness and childhood: relinquishing power. A sublime gauze curtain descends and your face may go blank behind it, your voice disappear. Incapacity, given in to, means entry to a private realm where you float around, or through, obstacles on a silent barge.

So here in this shabby drifter's cabin I am a little doll. Time all hashed up, let me repeat. And on gusts of fever these streamers have flapped within reach. . . .

I am a gasping little doll with clotted chest and my mother sponges me with alcohol. She is party ready, smoothly powdered, silhouette enlarged by a fur jacket, her glowing orange lips my night light.

I am eating pureed carrots and gray crumbling meat. Have to finish—while I watch *Circus Boy*, the maid Amanda watches me. "They can't have gone far," says the snake charmer. "Go on, it'll put hair on your chest," says Amanda.

I am nested in the back room of a summer rental that smells of creosote, waiting out the same cold as everyone else. The motorboats on the lake, even Gordo's high-pitched sneezing, seem far off to my congested ears. I have baseball magazines, *Green Lantern* and *Andy Panda* comics. I watch ice melt in the ginger ale.

I am lurking in the doorway of my sister's bedroom where she lies in state, in shadow, peppered with measles. She is typically kempt, bundled in white terry cloth, but spews eager germs with every breath. It is forbidden to go in. From my side of the border I whisper bad news, see her rapidly blink, then turn toward deeper shadow. Carla will not be well enough to attend the final performance of the *Ice Capades*.

Reaching the sink is no triumph, the basin scummed with bile like the foam that dries inside a milkshake cup. Should I risk a trip outdoors? A galvanized tin stall, a narrow stream of rusty water. Anything to slough this fetid skin I'm in. But getting into pants takes all my strength, leaves me marooned on the mattress again. I don't want to sink back. Enough indoor mirages. But I haven't the will of a doorknob. Except to bare my teeth at the dented, demented smile hanging in the windowframe.

Glad of the invitation, in walks Dag just as real as the tear in my pants.

"Shitfire, son. Look like a curse been put on you."

"A virus," I find myself saying, "is the simplest life form."

From what I can hear, my voice is of an automated gunslinger in a penny arcade.

"That's right, simple but smart," Dag says, picking through my canned goods.

"What day is it?"

"We need some lunch." He slaps the air decisively. "So where's the damn opener?"

Watching him empty creamed corn into a bowl is all the lunch I need. Cautiously, I sip from the cup of water he brings over, dribbling it down my bruised throat. *Ice Capades.* I see myself facedown, skimming the length of the rink.

"Fill 'er up, huh? You're all dried out, I can see that."

Dag gets another cooling cup into me before I pass out. Quite a bedside manner. His yammering seeps through the wall of my doze, drenches me as I wake.

He stops, frowns into the scraped-clean bowl, and I can see old stitches like a zipper alongside his head. The Beanball Incident he's forever reciting—but Padilla says he got whanged by a horseshoe-pitcher at a church picnic.

"Get you some fresh air," Dag says.

He hoists me, gets me out the door. Daylight overwhelms my eyes. I subside into crunchy dry grass and feel around with my hands.

"Where are my toys?" I say. Stimulus and response.

Not looking up, Dag points to hazy blue sky. "Worry about gettin' some a that, and that's all."

The big gas ball. I can have all I want.

"Who's worried?"

Across the path, motorcycle parts soak in a pan of oil and a young cat claws at tar paper hanging from Padilla's toolshed. A vista. Farther out, the land is careless and uncolored, has been for so long that its present is as invisible as its past.

As words come out of me and pass through Dag like water through a sieve, I come to see how it will be.

"I'll go out where few things are possible. Where most things are inevitable. I'll give it all up to that place and I'll have a new shape."

"You lookin' for work?" Dag is puzzled as only he can be.

Steep hills to the north, a broken-glass profile. No more intimidating than an afterthought. To the east, where scrub thickens in a gray-green crescent, root webs extend no more than an inch below ground. The cat, coming toward us now, carries a limp brown snake in its mouth. Science can be such a comfort. I explain to Dag that we are just coded strands of nucleic acid.

"Brain fever," he says. "You need dousing down."

But one look tells me it's been a long time since any water has passed through that cracked black hose. Grumbling and spitting, Dag kicks fruitlessly at the spigot.

I sink deeper into the grass. Fading again, that sensation of being hollowed out. But soon I can get to an uncolored place. Already on my way.

I don't mind the heat or the dry grass spiking me or the insects traversing my bare back. My memory is as quiet as a dead snake. I must be getting well.

I am here on the desert floor, alone in a silver pod. I have no telephone, no mailbox. I have no heat, no plumbing, no qualms. The land under me was an inland sea until it dried up a few million years ago. Now it is government land leased to a Japanese corporation. From my window, roughly the size of a picture tube, I can see as far as I might want. Quiet, haggard space. The sky is huge. Nothing moves. But I believe in tidal rhythms here among fossil fish long ago powdered and dispersed on the wind. Nothing moves and I contemplate beginnings: the first men to see patterns in the stars, the discovery of coal, the creation of blue glass, the invention of the Nipkow disc.

For this silver Airstream trailer I gave cash and my car to a newly retired Spec/4 who's leaving the base to live with his daughter in Beaufort, South Carolina. Citizen Sonny towed it out here, his face wrinkling like a sandwich bag with what I took to be envy. He showed me the well a mile or more to the west that I share with some shabby shorthorn cattle. He placed in my hand a copy of "Survival for Desert Commandos."

The old man knew confined space at its best—in Beaufort they should let him get jolly on bourbon and sing the grandkids to sleep. I have brackets for a kerosene lamp. I have a Primus stove, niches and shelves, a writing desk that folds out. From a director's chair, with tequila bottle in hand, on a black-and-white powered by an army surplus generator, I am watching Perry Mason ruin a witness with unfounded and argumentative questions.

So at last I have taken steps, made the final subtractions. Citizen Sonny chastises me about planning, but I have confidence in the undesigned campaign. My belief in grace is firm. That is to say, I take things lightly.

There was my first true experience of sand: soft, warm, and easy. I moved on my stomach like a turtle between Long Island dunes and thought of burying myself. My mother appeared in tears and snatched me. That is to say, you are lost only so long as someone is looking for you.

So I don't worry about being found. I don't worry about dehydration or changing my mind. I remember the old man walking in a tight circle as I counted out his money. "What I'm going to miss is the big picture." Would he find Beaufort tight and foolish, the grandkids a nuisance? Would he yearn for the crush of the mess hall and artillery fire echoing among the rocks and the soft flicker of his kerosene lamp? Let Sonny envy that.

"But you returned that night, didn't you?" Mason says. "You went back determined to destroy the lipstick formula."

I turn from the weeping admission and look out my window. The chemistry of industrial espionage is contained in these pale wastes, in layers of the ancient sea. Sonny claims the Japanese are expecting to take uranium out of here, and are being fleeced. Fuck integrity, eh? Elementary. But is this place as lifeless as it looks? There might be secrets here just waiting to be looked for, a primeval rectitude I can't even guess at.

I built a fire my first night, roasting sweet potatoes in the embers, and wondered who the unfamiliar light would attract.

I was expectant, not fearful, peering into watery shadows. But it was something I heard rather than saw that taught me right off to respect this place. Wet wind put out the flames of my fire as though aimed. The slow prefatory scraping was like two algae-covered slabs pulling apart, and then came a sound both mechanical and animal, an admonitory rumble and roar that had me crouching in the illusory safety of the pod, reduced. I stayed awake while the sky shifted from black to blue, without hearing so much as an elf owl, and this gravid silence was worst of all.

Try as I might, I could not keep myself from interpreting the experience, could not in the now ominous daylight hold down the conviction that my choices were to leave and be doomed or to stay and be absorbed. I felt as though I were being closely examined from above like something in a petri dish. When I said before that I took things lightly, I lied. But you must be used to that by now. In cities where I have lived, candor makes licit all sins: Go ahead and fuck me around, just be honest about it. So, in the current style, I could wrap things up by confessing to solipsism. But a swindle is a swindle. This is what I mean by the doom that awaits me everywhere but here.

Inside my pod there are seeds. I fold down the writing desk, align pencil and paper. What am I going to put down? A grocery list? A letter? Do I want to draw heads or play hangman with myself? Outside a thousand absorptive processes are taking place. Leaves suck sun and make sugar. Maggots take nutrition from pus. I am still wary, still uncomfortable. But at last I have something to write.

Q: Are we not men?
A: No, we are animals

All the consoling fabrications must be waived.

The margin for error is thin. Beware of moods. Ignore quick decisions. Balance, proportion. I learn to walk all over again, canting forward on the lead foot for a gradual transfer of weight. I learn to conserve energy. Information shaped like an arc, my eyes sweeping back and forth across the steadiness of the landscape. Caution, deep cover. I learn to recognize danger signs.

A dust devil swirls off to my right, then replicates itself close by. Light has muted, the temperature is dropping, and the smell of ozone is sharp. Storms blow up fast with so few obstacles in their way. Home is a good half mile away, but the spiraling of larger wind doesn't hurry me, nor the first distant lightning, a yellow crack on three branching legs like a music stand. Time is a broad generality. Water is a gift. Seeds long dormant will sprout; brine shrimp will breed in puddles.

Hard and fat, the first raindrops make my skin draw tight. Tiny craters appear in the dust and splattered rocks darken. I've sighted the Airstream now, a hunk of metal in a wide open space, a target. One speedy bolt could leave me crisped in there like a strip of bacon, but I'll take that chance. The elements—everything falling off the periodic table at once. Hunched under a drenching roar, I move toward shelter like a man crossing a battlefield.

Enclosed, I wrap up in a blanket and roll a cigarette. Rain pounds unrhythmically, winds burst, but my silver shell is riveted tight, no rattles or leaks, solid on its blocks. In a few weeks I have become intimate with its every rib and seam. I pass my hand over some irregularity, comforting as the moles on a lover's back, and feel sound. Firing up the stove, throwing black tea in a cup, I remember the gift of water and fly out the door with jars and pans, anything that will catch some. An edict of water, a decree. I spread my fingers and they're like ten little faucets dripping. Stripping useless clothes, I squeeze them into a bucket already half full. I'm blind, as though standing under a waterfall, but not so entranced as to ignore my own advice: Come away from your senses, boy, before you get swallowed.

Strong tea and stale biscuits, a candle on the floor. Slowly, I go through my scavenge bag, the pickings of the day. One bleach jug, with cap. Five more brass rifle shells (soon I'll hang them all for wind chimes). A roach clip dropped by some dirt biker. Baling wire, no rust. Crow feathers. Not all that bad, considering I never reached the road. Simple rules and small tasks keep me on my good behavior.

Still, old habits die hard. It is not enough to follow the progress of a wolf spider as I once did the sequence of postwar Italian cinema. In fact, it is too much. The student is at a remove, his curiosity a kind of heartless filtration. The further he evaluates, the further he lengthens his distance. The miser of knowledge never will merge. I know all about this. I could accept the accidental and the immutable both, but I kept trying to tell the difference. Humbug. Utility? A niche in the system? Learn to think with the blood.

I put out some pinto beans to soak. These legumes contain bacteria that take nitrogen from the air and inject it into their host soil. Today I found more evidence of cactus rustlers in the area. They drive out from the city in pickups and carry off chollas and saguaros sometimes twice their age to decorate the walkways of a condo high-rise, or to make the centerpiece in a florist's window, strung with colored lights at Christmas. I might ask Sonny to lend me one of his guns.

The storm has nearly passed, a few plops on my roof, thunder muffled like a hostage in the cellar. The thinning air is laced with odors sweet and sour that rain has caused to bloom. Guiltily, I look for a rainbow. There is a rim of heavy mist round the horizon, but nothing more. I remember driving with Andrea up the coast to Mendocino, driving into one end of a cloudburst and out the other. There was a double rainbow, its farthest ends disappearing into the sea. I parked the Olds near a steep drop and we got out. Freshly emerged sun made everything glow. I went into the details of diffraction and spectral density.

"You"—Andrea, as usual, let everything show in her eyes—"you are a book-fed pig."

Then she snatched the car keys and pitched them over the side.

No fresh sun here, and the only thing glowing is the candle on the floor. I have emptied as many rain containers as possible into the storage drum and covered the rest to keep out debris, protecting nameless banes leeched out of the sky from careless gnats, the odd crumb of drifting bark. Now I am sitting by the door in my director's chair, empty and alert. Evening seems reluctant to come, but I'm in no great hurry. The storm has passed and all I see is safely illegible.

Roy Rogers' cook had a jeep named Nellybelle. That's all I can think of as this one comes at me across the sand, even after I spot the whip antenna and the painted emblem on the door. The closer it gets, the slower it seems to travel.

I have the sun at my back and a kitchen knife in my hand. He has the tall hat and the silver star. He knows my name.

"You aware you're on private property?"

"That's what I like so much. The privacy."

He turns his head to smile, as if at a sidekick. His lower lip bulges with snuff.

I know my limits. And he knows my name.

The first time I was ever arrested, it was by a man in a Santa Claus suit. He cursed me through his nylon beard, led me past carolers from a "special education" school and back inside Bloomingdale's. I had two jars of marrons glacés in my parka pocket. It had been a reaction rather than an impulse, brought on by four hours of zombie mobs and holiday smarm. Or at least that's what I told them in the security office, itself mobbed with a gamut of boosters, sullen pros to weeping Brearley girls, where I was fingerprinted by a placid fat man named Vito.

"Ask for Sergeant Faedo," he counseled. "A close personal friend."

They took us up to the Sixty-seventh Street precinct station in an unheated lead-gray bus with grates over the windows, and, after an hour or two, let most of us go. Dramaturgy. A Christmas pageant.

It was dark outside. Jolly cops drew on panatelas. They loaded their car trunks with hams and foil-boxed fifths for the trip across to Queens. I walked home, looking for a crèche to kick over.

The second time around was so frightening I'm amazed to remember it. I had been out here only a few months, was still made uneasy by all the empty space, still a serf in the Monitor wing, a sensory receptacle squirting itself with eyedrops, someone invisibly contorted, floating between the same very few points like a quiet whitebread lunatic. I was bound to walk into a wall, and I did.

It was what they have for winter here: wind stirring up dust and straw, a flat chill in the night. I was staying at a place called Motel Chateau, fifty-some yards off a popular north-south truck route. It was about 10 p.m., overcast. Losing at canfield, working my way to the bottom of a bag of malted milk balls, I noticed a girl moving back and forth in front of my window. She was talking to herself. She grinned at me, ran away, came knocking at my door ten minutes later.

"Got any weed?"

No. But she came in anyway. Snarled wet hair, purple bruise on her neck, long, grimy bedspread skirt, a tarry smell. She belonged on Telegraph Avenue in Berkeley, whapping a tambourine.

"We're just a couple doors down there. Transmission seals is leaking. Wayne says he can fix it and I should go sleep in back. I says fuck you, farmboy. Didn't come through all this so we could live like bugs, you know?" She leaned close to the wall mirror and picked at her face. "But I'm not tired. I mean, Wayne, he just don't care . . . for somebody thinks all the time, and how we're called to help these people find where they belong." She lay back on the bed, feet dangling over the end, kicking slowly. "But I let my mind alone so I won't be tired. Got to be a free bird before something happens."

The burn marks on her arm didn't scare me, but something did. And it wasn't Wayne, either.

"Yo, beautiful people."

A six-pack under each arm, a high cartoon voice. He was jokey and round and vague, the fatboy clerk in the waterbed store, whose every sale was a reminder of why he slept alone. He dropped successive pink-and-gray capsules into successive beers, whispering, "Bombs away." The girl kept teasing him about his penguin arms and living on candy bars all the time and he kept sipping, pawing the hair away from his eyes.

"Make it far as the ocean, okay?" he said.

This irritated her—something heard over and over. She looked across at me and slipped her tongue side to side.

"Go on, go on," Wayne said. "Long as we're here."

She bunched the skirt above her grub-white hips and rocked at the end of the bed.

"Reach that water." Wayne snickered and nodded. "Reach the water and that's all."

"You shut up." The girl bent her knees.

"Touch her. She wants you to."

Wayne's eyes were filmy but hard; he nodded some more. Scary enough; plain enough. I was going to get hurt if I didn't follow instructions. The girl held out her hand, but she was staring in anger at the ceiling. I cupped her and she was cool, like a shucked oyster.

And then the door was splintered, the windows, by a blast of frantic men. The room whirled with cutting light and noise, Wayne begging them to shoot, the girl shrieking. A gun barrel struck me in the mouth.

They held me in a cell barely large enough to stand in, where slogans of defiance and revenge had been charcoaled on the walls. An FBI agent interviewed me in the morning. His method was laborious and his suit was shiny. Wayne Lopat and Lori Dee Carman were to be charged with aggravated murder, aggravated assault, rape, arson, armed robbery, and grand theft auto, all multiple counts. The agent had cheeseburgers brought in, but I wasn't hungry. Well into evening, I repeated answers to irrelevant questions, sick with measuring how close I had been to some unspeakable mutilation. I walked around for hours after my release, watched a plain, metallic sunrise from the doorway of a fire-damaged laundromat, understanding there was no such thing as safety. Things went around, like debris in space, and avoidance was a matter of chance.

"You have any idea what my life would be," says the man with the silver star, "if I had to enforce everything gets printed up?"

"Shorter," I suggest.

He doesn't smile for long. "So you let stuff be. You ain't no beef thief. So a bunch of Japs is on the deed and for them I don't give a flying fuck. But this out here is part of my area and I got to know what you're doing in it."

I'm blank, stopped, since at first I want to tell the truth and don't know what it is. Won't do. I need incoherence of an acceptable type. So I talk about renunciation and retreat, how particle physics had estranged me from God. I describe at length the inspiration of St. Simeon Stylites, who spent thirty-five years atop a pillar of the desert, seeking His grace through abnegation in the sun.

The lawman squints, takes off his hat and looks inside as though crib notes are there.

He says, "I'm not inclined to question a man's choice of worship," shooting a gout of brown snuff juice well past me. "You can pray to the wind and the rocks and the creosote bushes, can't nobody tell you no. Just don't come lookin' for me when you get in trouble and I won't come lookin' to give you any."

I point with my knife at the pair of black snakes hanging from the awning pole and ask if he'll stay for lunch. But already he's swung up into the jeep, next to the pump-action twelve-gauge. He stares at me momentarily through the spotless windshield, the process of forgetting already begun, and wheels away in a long arc.

I'm not thinking of Roy Rogers this time, but of the saint on his desert platform. Maybe he tried to make himself a target up there. Maybe he was waiting for something to come from the heavens. Something like a meteor.

"Not that I know what it is," Sonny told me this morning. "But what you're trying out here is bound to lead somewhere new."

Before, where the earth now stands, say the First People, there were only Cyclone, Water, and Darkness.

I reminded Sonny that everything has already been tried. He smiled dismissively, kneeling to ream the generator's feed line. Why disappoint him? He had brought snare wire and tobacco, sliced fruit Dawn had put through their dehydrator. He'd brought green operating scrubs from a uniform shop, billowy tops and pantaloons. No more jeans, no more heat rash. I thought to return his kindness by clearing away a little worry, by telling him I had a plan, a program.

1) To conserve moisture by day
2) To conserve warmth by night

Of course, he took this for mockery. I was looking at simplified life-forms and passing on the message: Accept, adapt. But Sonny wanted more.

"Resources," he kept muttering.

Why the opacity? Why now? Could it be no more than the usual clog of jargon and cross-purposes? I thought not. I pictured Violet field-tripping past, brisk in sandals and shorts. Overwhelming her face would be the heavy, black-framed sunglasses of a Communist film critic; dangling from her white neck like a piece of life-support equipment would be the ubiquitous Pentax; between her toes would be calcareous grit millions of years old. And Violet would be no more out of place than a centipede.

No, this spate of bad reception between Sonny and myself, our mouths moving around static, must emanate from a source both less and more fundamental.

"How you go about this ought to be your own business," he said.

We slackened, sat next to each other, touching at the knee. This was better, wiser. Not talking, we could be as placid as two Kool penguins.

He has promised to return before dark with a pair of tenderloin steaks. A gesture? A stance? I bewilder myself, turning over suspicions of my last link of a friend, pettily resenting his sustenance. I have nothing that needs to be guarded so selfishly. Still and all, this is not a venture and I'm not looking for partners.

Sonny has a new parabolic dish antenna which he wants to bring out here for me. It is enormous in his hard rutted yard, a pulsating ear with the delicate, blossomy contours of something formed by wind. It is a mechanical extrapolation of the omnivorously versatile human, unable to adapt and so bound to subdue, to capture and control even the air. And, Sonny fervently believes, it is a crucial tool for whatever I am trying.

The free life (not what I'm trying) means noise. Countless signals vie for attention—in one ear, out the other, on to the next ear—signals that in this zone fracture and bend, fly blind, fade in and fade out, that shower magically like particles from a child's divinely smiling planet. Tenderness, fury, amazement. Trial by jury, soccer from Oslo, the cross-talk of pilots. I can have all this in a dish, signals needing no answer, muddy music of the spheres. This is the intrusive gift Sonny wants to bring me. I discourage him as firmly as possible, but he's made it a focal point and hangs on. No compromise. His faithful insistence is liable to crowd me toward something drastic. A matter of preservation, and, probably, another row of spines on my penitent's crown.

Through my pitted window I see lowering clouds shot through with evening tans and coppers. Stepping outside, I come instantly against a vibratory wall composed of nothing measurable, no sawtooth waves launched from towers, bounced off orbiting metalware, but rather of inaudible, invisible motion, the chemically dictated formations of the mass.

Evening light curves listlessly away while a breeze wraps me tightly and the silence of the desert transmutes into the silence of our house on Windsong Terrace. Inside an air of desertion are separate traces of the family, burnt coffee, sweet grass, chlorine from a pool. The silence is pressing and it seems dangerous to move, to climb the stairs and pluck the fruits of Carla's laundry basket. So a motionless son squints into the melancholia of summer and wonders about other sons moving from room to room, bludgeoning anyone they find. Is it the cool silence that they want all to themselves? Take command. Be the son of whom nothing more is ever said.

Those darkening hills, hot mud cooled before it could puddle, are closer than they look, but there aren't any illusions in the land they enclose. I recall a man from that era of silence in our house, of misapplication and bland, lonely bike rides, a man, named after a freshwater baitfish, who compared television content to "a vast wasteland." Such a man would be as oblivious to the furious life of the desert as to the explosive collision of disaster film and cat food commercial. He would be the valuable son, the example forever cited, and certain he had so much to lose that fear would rule him.

"Business has never been better," Sonny says, cupping his hands over the fire. "Those nuclear survival maps, where we pinpoint the twenty safest areas of the country? We can't keep the damn things in stock."

His entrepreneurial glow, reinforced by wine, is overbright. With scattered stars and a new moon, darkness beyond the rim of the fire is like a barrier you could crack your face against.

"We're doing an all-new catalog. Fifty pages, offset printing. Pro all the way."

His belt jangles with keys and useless little tools.

"There's pressure out there. People are feeling it and that's good for you."

"Pressure? Population increases geometrically and food supplies increase arithmetically. That's pressure, my friend."

Citizen Sonny has been reading Malthus. I find this disquieting.

"Anyone who's hungry for more than food, they ought to call it a privilege," he says.

He stretches lazily like a lizard scratching its back, a lizard replete with small bugs. And it's thanks to him that I have fresh supplies, a tub of peanut butter, sacks of beans and rice, that I'm picking strands of meat from between my teeth with a peeled, bone-white stick. Yes, Sonny, protein runs the world. Ethics, rights, liberty—these are leisure pursuits.

"When I start to think of the things I'll never see and the stuff I'll never find out . . ." He looks out and down, as if for a caption.

"Just stop talking," I say somewhat recklessly. "Stop filling my head with reruns."

He spits into the coals. "Poor Sonny," Sonny says. But he's quiet after that.

I understand that appeal has been coming from him all along. And I think I understand that he has no more idea than I do of what the appeal is for. More miscellaneous signals, noise from another disappointed son. The best I can do is forgive the intrusion. The most I can do is nudge him toward home, toward the loyal eyes of his children and the resigned arms of his wife.

He grips me like a priest, winces with goodwill. "You gonna be all right."

It is neither a question nor a statement, only a small collection of sounds.

We push cold mist in front of us as we walk, mist we will find condensed on the chrome of Sonny's four-by-four, squeezed down to its heavier essence. We walk in the long shaft of Sonny's flashlight until, chuckling, he snaps it off. Even then I can make out the strip of his bumper, white Gothic letters, one word: BLESSED. Sonny inserts the ignition key slowly, as though apprehensive of a wired bomb. Gold eyes flash and a low shape wheels away when he clicks the headlights on. Exhaust hangs in the air, condensing on my skin.

Hawks ride high on the thermals, drifting in lazy loops. Their wing adjustments are so slight, their head swivels so quick, and they can spot a rodent's eyes from so far. But for now they're only passing time, floating under the sun.

I sip frugally from the canteen, just enough to smooth the burr at the back of my throat. Wouldn't want to run short on a day like this, have to make it through to sunup, when I could lick dew. This air is so thin and dry that it seems to become powder in the lungs. Sweat disappears in an instant, leaving the pores tight. Kalahari bushmen bury water in empty ostrich eggs along their routes of travel. Saharan nomads drink the urine of their camels. Specialization comes easily to a man without choices, and tends to elude those whom choice has covered like the measles. So we consult texts, carry compasses, shield our eyes behind darkened plastic. And we sip frugally.

According to my compass, a northeasterly diagonal will lead me home. This feels wrong, but I must rely on instruments. My head is a heavy melon and my blurring eyes might be etched with dark spirals like the props of a hypnotist. Far too easy to become a subject of this flat land of mirage. Like right now. What I take for a watchful man couldn't be more than a slender branching bush. I'll be seeing Rommel in his command car next.

It must be time for a drink. I swirl water in my mouth, dribble it into my hand, spread it across my face. The pause that refreshes. And yet the bush has moved, is moving, draws closer. Under a felt hat, a hem of white hair, the face is the color of sand. A wary face.

"Hey!"

I wave but he doesn't wave back. His expression is stern and distant both, and it makes me remember.

"Dobbs," I say. "The gentle hangman."

He folds his arms. "I know you, bub?"

"A few months ago at the hot springs." I flip my sunglasses up. "We had some beers."

"Don't fancy the new beer. Tastes like mop water."

"You wanted the cans for scrap."

He grunts, tipping back, as if memory is a well bucket he's pulling up. "Had a weedy little gal along. Wouldn't leave you alone."

"Dobbs."

"Dobbs," he confirms.

After which there's nothing else to say. We could be in line for food stamps or waiting on the platform for a train. Afternoon is well along, but the sun feels perpendicular. The gentle hangman, humming, strikes the pediment of his chin. He declines when I offer the canteen.

"Best way to clean out the system is leave it empty awhile. Don't let your minerals build up."

The bandanna round his neck has faded from red to pink with countless washings, but the felt hat and the checked shirt are improbably crisp, store-fresh. Here he's shaped in my mind as a natural growth on the land when the mirage could easily stretch as far as a nursing home he walks out of all the time.

"I don't just pick things up from the funny books," he says, reading my thoughts. "It's a way of things sticking to me as I go. Like when the Baxter twins was running sheep all through here, eight, maybe nine hundred head, this was before they shot each other about a second term for Senator Mack, but at the same time there was a lady worked at the hotel who wore her own teeth on a bracelet. And I remember all that together.''

All right. Dobbs, in his time and place, is as true as parthenogenesis.

"Gonna take a whole lot of past with me. And soon.''

I can't help wanting to be briefly vivid, another deposit in his alluvial mind. I invite him to come and see my spot and warily, conditionally, he accepts.

"Long as that little gal won't be present. Her and her temper.''

He motions me impatiently ahead, but his pace is slow, wandering, and it's hard not to distance him. He stoops over rocks, examines the roots of some weed he's pulled, not out for scrap today, but reassurance instead. And, of course, he's disappointed when we get there.

"This ain't no layout, bub. Where's your damn corrals?''

But he seems glad of the shade under the awning, settles into my director's chair with a comfortable exhalation. Watching me gobble jerky, all the gentle hangman asks for is a little sugar to lick from his hand. He nods; his tongue is quick as an anteater's.

"Don't got even an outhouse,'' he grumps, surveying from under his brown hat. "What are you, one of them bagpackers?''

"Backpackers.''

"Anyhow, something for nothing.''

I correct him again. "Nothing for nothing.''

He's slack in the canvas chair; I'm stiff on the ground. His face, lined like river mud, is steady on me. It isn't the wary face, nor the stern one, but I have to answer it.

"Things that stuck to me I want to be rid of, see.''

"On the house.''

He fishes out a pack of mentholated filtertips, the gentle hangman preparing a victim. He snaps the match alight on his teeth and holds it for me. I blow a solemn chain of smoke rings.

"A thing I can tell you—and it ain't for me, since to do it I always felt fine—is I never once pulled the trap on somebody wasn't just as glad at the very end to go."

To believe in a man who's known only clean cases all his life is something I couldn't have done before. Today I can let hard facts go soft, become tractable as a bosun's dream of the Mojave.

Dobbs says, "Maybe you could wrap up a little more sugar in a bag?"

I take time with the old man's bundle, folding corners precisely, but he's gone when I bring it outside, gone without telling me there is nothing to find here.

Birds are low and loud in the sky. Their noise bends around me like water. I take heart. I unfold corners precisely. Wind billows up out of its troughs and blows white grains away, leaving the paper clean.

Isolation distorts as it toughens. It shrinks and magnifies, reroutes, subverts the normal controls. I recognize in myself certain disturbances, reactions that are powerfully wrong. Misplaced objects infuriate me. The faint trail of a jackrabbit fills me with wild, hopeless panic.

But now, I think, I have the sort of companionship that will steady me and smooth me out. Three days ago clanking woke me and I tumbled out the Airstream door to face a scrawny goat with a bell around his neck. I gave him water, and called him Rosing, after the inventor of the cathode-ray receiver. I didn't know how to remove the red plastic clip in his ear that marked him as someone's property, but I cut loose the bell. We shared a tin of sardines and slept in the shade of the awning like comrades of a prolonged desert campaign.

Scarred and underfed, a battered range refugee, Rosing is tranquil. He is unperturbed to the point of hospitality by flies that crawl along his snout, so incurious that only repeated yelling will cause him to turn his head. He consumes cactus methodically, with a nearly circular chewing motion that causes him to resemble a fastidious mandarin. I take comfort in his exemplary resignation. Aid and comfort.

Chuff-chuff-chuff: the soundtrack for embassy evacuations. A bulbous black helicopter passes over our heads, carrying, with equal probability, soldiers or hunters or survey geologists. Or eager Japanese in rayon cowboy shirts, satraps of the company that hopes to feed its reactors with what it can extract from this land. I'd like to take them out of the air with my slingshot, then sit and watch black smoke plume, listen to the sounds of melting. Righteous glory, a boy's idea. These two-legs, eh, Rosing? Fucking parvenus. One blink of biologic time and they zip around as if the place were theirs to own, strewing dead certainties like the rest of their garbage. Sunlight glints and blurs on the rotor blades. Chuff-chuff-chuff.

I lift Rosing's damp muzzle from my lap, probe his expressionless gray eyes. Comrade, is there still time to get away? He blinks. He dips his head. He lifts and lowers one little black hoof, a hoof as cleanly split as any dialectic proposition. It's not my fault they picture Satan with a goat's horned head, then talk about the lamb of God. White woolly innocence versus rancid concupiscence? Not my idea. Everything works together—tendon, ligament, and bone—as Rosing subsides into a drowse. Different genotypes, comrade, different protein codes. It's none of my doing.

I brew chili pod broth on the stove, hot vitamins. The generator's low on fuel, not too many viewing hours left. I dial rapidly around and around, a pinwheel of incoherence, maximum heat load. I stop on the prettiest face.

"Call our eight hundred number now and help us feed the world. Call right now."

A nisei flower with hair to her hips in a tank suit with peek-aboo cutouts. Rear projections flash behind her. Bounty of the ocean, kelp farming, krill-based soft drinks. Metal rings hang from her nipples.

"Take an all-important support posture. Please call right away."

Images recycle, coral and spume, begging bowls. I'm right in my place. Her eyes, shiny as bits of ormolu, as piercing as nipple rings, are fixed on me and me alone. Why do you stay away? they ask. We miss you so. Her tongue slides around the roof of her mouth, waiting for me to open up so she can slip me guilt to suck, grit wrapped in mucus. Women always want to haunt. She speaks of the internment camps so far from water, the dusty barracks, the glare, the heavy stink of trucks.

"I wasn't there, but I can feel the pain," words leaking through her heavy lips. "Pain, if only you'll call right this minute."

It isn't really me you miss. Inviting and inflicting pain are insufficient. You want to understand, to pursue every forensic detail.

"Call." She tugs hard on the rings. "Help us feed the world."

Porpoises leap and plankton luminesce. Poor men pull nets by torchlight. I wasn't there, but . . . She tugs. Her eyes insist. She raises and lowers one open hand, a hand as rigidly flat as any technician's rule.

Drinking heat from a tin can, squatting in front of a pretty face, who am I to refute those eyes? I wasn't there, but I want to see her lap up cold rice, rinse shirts in a bucket, weep beside the wire fence. So I give in, match point conceded. All tracks converge; feast and famine, solitude, solicitude, appearance made weightless, expectation pared—all finish up in pain. Then I click her off.

Getting away like a bug down the slot of a toaster, and staying away. All women want to haunt. Every kiss contains a gift. Each joy may be the last.

Oceania. I wake up more hounded than haunted. The taste in my mouth is like jetty sludge. Hard sun thuds away, saying the same to me as to someone stranded on an atoll: Here again, here forever. No breeze, no breakers, ground zero only. I swallow aspirin dry. I say to myself, You really ought to be keeping a diary. In there you could be thorough. You could talk about animal companionship or bitter women or great blind sea depths impenetrable by light. You could write in a forbidden alphabet, with charcoal.

Unfathomable. And just when I thought everything was under control. Law of the desert: Don't turn around. Anyway, I ought to have suited myself enough by now to the waiting game so as not to need an audience to play to, a little book to fill.

Treading water. I move through the hard, comfortless sun with no determination other than to be on the move. My arms hang limp. Green surgical pants hang low on my hips. I start to remember my sister crying on the beach, stung by . . . But I click that off. The atoll man goes crazy from too many swipes at an irretrievable life. Forever here, nowhere else—hold on to that and don't let yourself sink. White clouds hang at the edges of the sky. Shadows hang in abeyance. I press calluses on the soles of my feet, pleased by their thickness. I feel droplets sliding down my neck like seepage from vestigial gills.

Red tide. Drink from the ocean, so it goes, and you thirst

forever. Without thinking, I've veered over onto the path lead-
ing to the well. In a hounded condition, you gravitate to the familiar, and this is a route I can navigate in the dark. How far
could I walk without resting? How long could I rest and still be
able to stand up? Already I can smell the cows who loiter near
the well like cleaner fish around a reef. Scarred and scrawny
like Rosing (part of somebody's write-off herd, I assume),
they approach expectantly, with lolling, pebbly tongues, as I
climb the fence. I read "help us starve the world" in their
eyes; tight gray hide under my hand . . . But now there is an
evil, uncow smell thickening the air, and I'm drawn along like
a cartoon hobo by the fumes of a cooling pie. Corpses swollen
with gas float in the well water, coyotes beheaded and
skinned.

Undertow. My fear is an approximation, the way barnacles
resemble teeth. What would the atoll man do, his one water
source poisoned? Would he shrug and take another backward
swipe? Dusk eddying around the patio, my sister uncorking
Moselle and saying, "Do we really need glasses?" Click. Click
click. This one doesn't want to be turned off. Fine. I'll just
climb back over the fence then. Fine. I'm dry all over. My feet
break through crusts and the earth below is cool. Continue
down and down, immeasurably, unsoundably down, and there
will be the last pit where marine debris once landed, layers of
shell and bone compressed by the vanished ocean, dry all over.

Sandbar. Rosing greets me with a soft, appealing butt. His
waiting ears are angled forward. Under the awning we nibble
at air and I describe for him the sabotage of our well.

"Gangrene soup." I shrug. "Nothing for it now."

Rosing shuts his eyes, picturing the culprits, no doubt. A
couple of sporting boys, welders on a weekend.

"So I asked myself, what would the atoll man do? And I
thought, well, maybe he'd hunt for it scientifically."

Rosing's eyes remain closed. Probably as he works through
variations of goat revenge.

"Dowsing. Hydromagnetism."

Forking my hands, I demonstrate. Rosing stays slumbrous

as a bivalve, but bears study. I note the angle of his horns, their theoretical point of convergence, and plot therefrom at ninety degrees a line to the damp end of his snout. He's the dowsing rod come to life, far more receptive than any stick. Nose to the ground, comrade! We'll open the ocean.

Immersion. Charlie Manson promised his children underground fountains of chocolate soda to nourish them during the prophesied race wars. If you can posit buried rivers and caverns of porous rock, then why not a favorite flavor too? Posit a Cambrian implosion. Posit the sucking action of a whirlpool.

Rosing wambles, lacking aim, failing to keep his nose to the ground. He is not to be urged or coaxed. I keep my distance, whirling through one liquid supposition after another. How agile my brain, light as cork on a fast current. Shrivel me timbres. I'm smiling buoyantly. I'm smiling a challenge to the atoll man, cell for cell. I'm ready to drown him.

Neap tide. The spot Rosing indicated was a depression between two ocotillos. I bent over the entrenching tool with ceremony. As I dug—patiently, pacing myself—I noticed compositional changes in the earth, sandwiching of a kind. Sun poured; it was thick. The hole, while it got wider, wasn't much deeper. Ants bit my legs. Rocks felt numb. I didn't hear echoing. I didn't feel the big suction. Following after Rosing again, I lost my shovel on the way. I thought about pants made of seaweed.

Unless glare deceives, I'm back on the well path again. Missing heads and the smell of cows. My sister wiping Moselle off her chin. Footprints that fit. Surf in, surf out, the comforting repetition we keep trying to regain, as though to be babies again with our sea in a sac. Pull back and push in. Never quite arriving but forever here: floating bodies.

This is the headline I have furrowed deeply in the sand, in letters so huge it can only be read from aircraft passing overhead: MALAYSIA BANS VIDEO GAMES.

Q: Why is this information important?

A: Because the letters are big.

I shrink; I peel myself. I dig up quail eggs and slurp them down. I dream of tomato-flavored icicles and midair neon and wake up with an erection that won't go away. Or I strike poses in the indistinct mirror of silver Airstream skin, imagine my own skin as a page and the tracks of sweat as something to read.

Nothing moderate or tentative allowed. I am clean. I am decisive as a surgeon. Video games banned, outlawed. I have pulled the circuit boards, yanked the wires. All intervening, interfering material removed. Pure signal only. An unbroken arc from source to target.

Discovery: I can control the air.

It is necessary to set myself out of motion, to disremember the automatic commands I have followed for so long, so many years of willfulness and waste. No more deconstruction or synopsis. Only pure unbroken signal. I open wide and it comes in so loud and clear that I twinge all up and down.

Programming notes: There is viscous, circular music layered like currents of the wind. There are different frequencies of sleep, a reptilian buzz filtered through rock or the slow tick-tock of bats. Most of all, there are the elliptical intimacies of the moderator, her ugly whims and many surprise guests. No topic out of bounds. Always a challenging format.

But still I take up tenuous space, like a razor blade floating on water. Balance is lost on days and nights when nothing comes at all, but suspension hones me for the next time. It's like the difference between an insect's chitinous exterior and the liquid essence held within, two discrete forms, each sustaining each. Shadow wrapped around pure signal.

Rediscovery: The air controls me.

"And that's so awfully trite," says the moderator, beginning in the middle, as usual.

The tight skin and the lax mouth, lower lip swollen as if from a blow, hair awry. Her beauty, as usual, opens me like a dagger.

"But we know he can't help it."

Her face dissolves into the dark rippling underside of a pier and applause overcomes the noise of surf. I race up the beach in lawyer's pinstripes, closer and closer until my face fills the screen.

"Just like his father," the moderator says heavily.

Cut to—

Nineteen forties New York. Prim brownstones on the sunny side of the street. Women in cloche hats and men in long overcoats maneuver around one another. They seem on the verge of dancing.

Moderator: "Suspicious as hermits, both of them."

I slide to the edge of the mattress, peeling myself. "Not so." Heat thick as cream inside the pod.

Rain falls now, the stoops shiny with it. A cortege of black sedans and a voice like paint blistering. "Students of swingology, class is now in session. From the Chatterbox Room of the Endicott Hotel, it's Professor Chester and his Horns of Plenty. Turn it loose!"

Camera pulls back to reveal moderator on high stool. A man in hospital whites kneels on the black studio floor to shave her legs with a piece of copper flashing dipped in grease.

"Our topic?" She thoughtfully taps the foam-padded microphone against her chin. "Subterfuge. Machination. Some people," pulling a minstrel's cakewalk face, "well, some people think that's what power means. But really, they never go through with anything. Hermits, varmints, who needs 'em? I say, strike up the band!"

"Adeste Fideles" by muted brass.

Talking heads in extreme close-up—

Violet: "Did you bring me a present? I thought maybe, for a change . . ."

Opatowski: "Wide open spaces could mean like bomb craters."

Sabra: "Quit it! It's late and I've got to get out of here. Stop. My shoes . . ."

Delvino: "A numbers cruncher? A guy in a tie? So fuck you, I read Moravia in bed and listen to Scarlatti tapes in my car."

Andrea: "You can be like a thug if you want, but I know . . ."

Gordo: "I'd give all that I own if I could but atone to that silver-haired daddy of mine."

Tasha: "Did you bring me a present?"

Rain falls big and hard on the surface of a swimming pool, splats on turquoise cement like newts shot from guns. Then rain forming in a cloud, each step textbook-labeled. Then rain melting the streets of a frontier town, falling on black gangster raincoats, ship decks, parade grounds, cathedrals.

Darkness with ugly mob hubbub, industrial grinding.

Fade up on—

A moiré of the beautiful moderator, like unprocessed data from a compound eye.

"We are back," she says, assembling very slowly into one. "And want to thank the Abbey of Captain Video for supplying footage. Because we can't do it alone."

Her head falls forward with exhaustion, bobs up again, and the skin looks so tight it could rip.

"Would you like to know what we think?" She draws on her throat with a finger. "We think ambiguity is so exciting."

I profuse.

"Believe nothing you hear," says my immoderate sister. "And only half of what you see."

Pure signal. Carla's stubborn angel face coruscates behind gray strings of semen on the cold glass screen.

Rosing was good, fibrous but succulent. The cookfire burned all day. I mounded books, clothes, shelving, the writing desk, my director's chair, and sprinkled on my last can of fuel. The flames went high as a house. I skinned Rosing without skill, wasting a lot of meat. The way the sand sponged up blood made me think of snow. Lovingly, as an Eskimo would, I stroked the yellow fat. Birds were circling, getting too excited. While the fire was too hot to get close to, I tipped the Airstream on its side and pulled one of the axles to use as a spit. I ate the heart and liver first, roasting them in foil. I mounted Rosing's head on a stake. His eyes were still soft and resigned. Days have passed without my counting. Someplace far behind me, many miles, ants and blowflies perform the final cleaning of the bones. Rosing's eyes have been pecked out. Wind stirs up from one direction, now another, and the burial of blackened remnants has already begun. Here the wind is hardly noticeable, an afterthought. Or possibly this has everything to do with the unreceptivity of my skin, which feels old on me and makes me think of dry gray boards. Here even the shortest distances blur, or possibly my sense of sight has dulled as well. I experiment, holding two fingers over the flame of my lighter, relieved when the pain doesn't go away. But why don't I feel hunger or thirst? I lie on my stomach, bracing my chin on both fists. Ahead of me are tall sandstone stacks. They're always ahead of me and I can't seem to get any closer. Or possibly with just a few more steps they will be close enough to touch. I lie on my back, looking at colorless sky. Suppose I were not alone. Suppose I had someone along who had known me all my life. I might say something like this: In our allotted time, it's supposed, we do no more than compete in the passing on of our genes. But suppose the competition is actually among genes and we are merely the temporary receptacles in which they find themselves? Part of me is glad there's no one here and that I don't have to say anything. Part of me wishes to say and say and say until I've used up every word. Still another part perceives these other two but dimly, and very vaguely understands the act of saying. I stand up, brushing myself clean. There ought to be plenty of daylight left, travel time to continue on toward the tall stacks, though they might only be abstractions. Travel time, just walk along. The only things I have to carry with me are the canteen, my lighter, and a knife. Walking along, like I was designed to do just the one thing. Keeping my eyes down, away from targets. Here are dry yellow flowers in three U-shaped clusters branching off from a woody stem. Each flower is a sloping tuft, its longest and brightest bristles at the center. Here is flat red stone furred on its underside with some pupal housing. Here are flapping strands of spider silk, thorny seed containers, rabbit droppings, flaked lichen, chewed husks. Here, even here, is a piece of glass, clear, roughly triangular, deeply scratched along its shortest edge, a vestige. In examining it, I seem to have cut open the pad of my right index finger. The little knob of blood swells to its tensile limit and breaks. I catch the drips on my tongue. I taste like metal. With my other hand I scoop a little hole, put the glass in the bottom and cover it over. Walking along, I can't remember if the cut finger is one of those that I burned. No matter. Vestiges are all buried, just that easy. When I lift my eyes to those stacks, they don't make me re-

member or think of anything else. High rocks all by themselves, unconnected. No images and no figures, not one. Solid
uncompromised rock, and still no closer. Possibly they recede
in proportion to my advance. Possibly they echo with remembering while I do not. But I'm going along in my own way, not
pulled by anything, roadless. I drink from the canteen even
with no thirst in me, unable to remember how other liquids
taste even while my mouth can make their names: sweet ver-
mouth, sour mash, bitter tea, salt water. I walk my way, eyes
down. Here are insteps rising and falling, toes and heels firmly
printing themselves. Here are scallops in sand that could be
recognized. No matter, I'm no more pushed than pulled. This
is a trail that someone who's known me all my life can't follow.
They can't catch up now so as to say something like: What if
we're all empty of genes? What if competition's done and the
end designed right in? So I keep trailing along, eyes soft, and
resigned that if someone caught up I'd make them all juicy at
the end of my knife. And that would only seem to be the end.
There'd be juice in the sand beside my fire with its trail of
smoke, and I'd have to make a mark for the grave, something
to remember. Colorless sky, blank. I am somewhere between
close and far. I see the blood dried on my fingers, still no thirst
in me. Inside, possibly, elements hide, pretending to have
been emptied out. Dry heart, stony glands, and refuge in the
crevices and crannies. I can still be fooled, even here. Un-
pulled, unpushed, eyes down, I still find myself asking. Here
are the things I carry with me. What if? Possibly. My arms in
the air, antennae, pick up whispers that die against unrecep-
tive skin. There is so much daylight left to keep going in that I
can stop here. I can lie down, folding slowly. Stacks ahead and
footprints behind, a closure in between. The ground must be
full of heat and that heat must be expanding into me. I must
want to sleep. With no hunger to dream, I have pictures on my
eyes even so. The pictures go by and they are colorless as the
sky. I do not recognize any of them.

A NOTE ON THE TYPE

This book was set in a film version of a face called Primer, designed by Rudolph Ruzicka (1883–1978). Ruzicka was earlier responsible for the design of Fairfield and Fairfield Medium, faces whose virtues have for some time been accorded wide recognition.

The complete range of sizes of Primer was first made available in 1954, although the pilot size of 12-point was ready as early as 1951. The design of the face makes general reference to Century—long a serviceable type, totally lacking in manner or frills of any kind—but brilliantly corrects its characterless quality.

Composed by American–Stratford Graphic Services, Inc., Brattleboro, Vermont

Printed and bound by Fairfield Graphics, Fairfield, Pennsylvania

Typography by Dorothy Schmiderer Binding design by Marysarah Quinn